Last Mango in Texas

LAST MANGO IN TEXAS

A NOVEL

RAY BLACKSTON

New York   Boston   Nashville

FaithWords
Hachette Book Group
237 Park Avenue
New York, NY 10017

Visit our Web site at www.faithwords.com.
FaithWords is a division of Hachette Book Group, Inc.
The FaithWords name and logo are trademarks
of Hachette Book Group, Inc.

Printed in the United States of America

First Edition: March 2009
10   9   8   7   6   5   4   3   2   1

Library of Congress Cataloging-in-Publication Data

Blackston, Ray.
Last Mango in Texas / Ray Blackston. — 1st ed.
p. cm.
ISBN-13: 978-0-446-57961-2
1. College students—Texas—Fiction.   I. Title.
PS3602.L3255L37 2009
813'.6—dc22
2008022344

For favorite uncles everywhere.

ACKNOWLEDGMENTS

Many thanks to the talented editors who guided this book to completion: Holly Halverson, Anne Horch, and April Stier. You're a blessing in triplicate. Hugs also to my agent, Beth Jusino, for her advice and encouragement.

Last Mango
in Texas

PROLOGUE

During that long Texas summer before I entered tenth grade, I rarely thought about marriage, though I wondered often about the season of life that preceded it — *dating*. I was too inexperienced to discuss the issue with friends, and deep down, I craved the input of an authority figure — which is why I so anticipated what my father was about to say to me.

I was fifteen and male and seated at the family dinner table, just after the family dinner hour. Our house smelled of cooked onions, most of which my father devoured with his meat loaf. My brother and sister, both younger, bolted from the kitchen and piled into the family van behind Mom, and with a toot of the horn they headed for the second performance of my sister's third-grade theater production. She would be Tinkerbell. I would be bored. Dad and I had seen the play the previous night. So with the rest of the clan absent, Dad summoned me into the den and decided that tonight was the perfect time for the two of us to have *the talk*.

He initiated this in a dutiful and fatherly manner. "Kyle, I think it's time for you and me to have the talk."

With pursed lips Dad sank into his beige recliner, which seemed to hug him like an old friend. I sat on the sofa, in the middle. It did not so much hug me as hold me down. The room grew tense. The onions lingered. I waited expectantly.

"Son." Dad's single syllable was warning and greeting and question all in one.

"Yeah, Dad?" Even though public school had educated me in all matters of health, including sex, this was my father speaking, so my posture was Triple A: anxious, alert, attentive.

Dad shifted his feet and glanced at the clock. "Son, you know…you know what's right when it comes to dealing with girls, right?"

My nervous gaze crossed the carpet to his feet, then out the window to our forested back yard, and back to the carpet again. "Oh sure, Dad…yeah, I know."

"Good."

I waited for more questions, a few facts, perhaps a bird, a bee. None of it came. Instead he made a phone call to arrange yet another business trip to New Mexico. Then the television flickered, a swarm of Dallas Cowboys ran onto the field, and over a sportscaster's voice I heard Dad sigh in relief, as if our conversation were something he'd feared since my birth.

At halftime he told me it was his opinion that marrying early in life — he mentioned an age range of 22 to 26 — was far better for a man than endless years of singleness. Said it would speed my maturity.

"Thanks for the tip, Pops," I said and rose from the sofa. Dad lacked follow-through in many areas, but somehow, on this night, I expected more depth. So I tried wooing him with food. "Want some popcorn? I'm gonna make a batch."

He nodded and muttered that he needed to pack for the business trip.

During the second half I waited for more dad-talk, but like

the Cowboys' offense, it never showed. I guessed what he'd said earlier — coupled with my public school wisdom — was enough, and soon I grew all tingly inside, knowing that I was now prepared to enter manhood and make wise decisions about the opposite sex.

In the middle of the fourth quarter Mom and my siblings arrived home, and we all ate ice cream at the table. I sat in the chair on the end — always Dad's seat — and between spoonfuls he winked at me because tonight was a big night for us both.

Dad drove us to church like a government escort instead of a father. Our family attended once per month, never twice, never none. Before service the following Sunday, while everyone chatted with neighbors, I pulled Dad aside and lowered my voice. "Dad, I've been thinking about this all night. What did you mean when you said 'You know what's right when it comes to girls?'"

Clearly uncomfortable, Dad looked around to check if anyone could overhear us. Mom and my siblings had gathered with another family, so the coast was clear.

"Kyle," Dad said with something less than authority, "you just gotta figure it out as you go. That's what I did." He paused, looked around again, leaned near me. "That's what my daddy did as well."

I slinked into the pew beside him, wondering how I'd have time to figure out girls as I go if I was already figuring out geometry as I go. The sermon drifted from sins of ignorance to the consequences of ignorance, and then the pastor mentioned "sins of the fathers" and how they resembled a family disease.

I didn't know what that meant and paid little attention. Dad kept sneaking glances at three college girls seated to our left; I found this much more interesting than anything spoken from the pulpit.

On the drive home I sat slump-shouldered in the backseat with my nose pressed against the window. Any amusement I'd felt over Dad's roving eyes faded as we pulled into our driveway. During the course of our once-per-month dose of religion, I had considered all the evidence: the business trips, the roving eyes, the short conversations at dinner. Dad was going to leave our family soon. I knew this. I was only fifteen, not particularly wise, and certainly not clairvoyant, but somehow I just knew.

Dad cut the engine, and three of four car doors opened in unison. I didn't exit with the rest of them. Though Mom tapped on the glass and waved me out, I just sat in the backseat wondering why we only went to church once a month when lots of my friends went every Sunday. I figured if I went every Sunday, I'd have more chances to ask God for help in figuring out girls as I go. But I also wanted to ask God if I was infected with Sins of the Father disease—and if someday I'd infect my own kids.

The night after my sixteenth birthday—it felt good to reach springtime again and be the same age as the rest of my sophomore class—I attended a marching band contest between all the schools in our district. The only reason I went was because the event took place at Texas Stadium, where the Cowboys played football.

A friend from school—a jock whom everyone called Cool Trent—drove us to the show in his cool Ford Mustang. After it was over he told me he'd spotted a girl in the third row and that "someday I'd like to marry a girl like that." I thought this was so profound for a sixteen-year-old. I knew dozens of sixteen-year-olds at my school, and none of them had ever uttered such a profoundarism. It made me wonder what kind of parenting he'd received.

Trent turned onto my street, and in a last minute, desperate quest for facts, I summoned the nerve to compare his father to my own.

"Trent."

He steered one-handed, head cocked to the side like all the Cool Trents of the world. "Yeah, Kyle?"

"Were you seriously talking about marriage earlier...or were you just playing with me?"

He appeared as serious as a sixteen-year-old can appear. "My dad says that the longer a man waits to marry, the more of a wimp he is. So, I'm thinking twenty or twenty-one. Twenty-two at the latest."

Man.

He pulled into my driveway, shifted into park, and left the engine idling. "So, you gonna get out, Kyle, or are ya gonna sleep in my car?"

My hand gripped the door release, but I could not bring myself to lift it. "How old were you when your dad talked to you about the birds and bees?"

"Eleven," he said. "Then again at twelve and thirteen." Cool Trent checked his hair in the rearview mirror. "But I always dreaded those talks—my dad would go on and on explaining things. One time we sat in the living room for *three* hours and missed an entire Cowboys game."

"Man...that's long."

"Why?" he asked and observed me with a combination of curiosity and pity. "How long did your old man talk to you?"

No lights shone from my house, and without even a glance back at Trent I opened the door and muttered, "Not quite that long."

Six weeks later Dad left our family. For *the Bimbo*. Her real name remained a mystery, but Mom and I knew she lived in New Mexico. In Taos, we were quite certain.

"He only abandoned us in physical form," Mom informed us at Saturday breakfast. Mom was resilient and not a bad cook. She flopped small, crispy pancakes onto our plates, one at a time for each of us, until she'd circled the table three times and everyone was equally supplied. She called the meal "silver dollar pancakes." "Your father still pays our bills," she said before finally joining us at the table, trying to look positive. Her eyes were red, though.

After breakfast I helped her clean up, and while doing so she showed me our monthly check for $1,675. Dad was successful in his medical sales job, and Mom assured me that the money would stretch far, especially with the governor's tax cuts providing a boost to families. She seemed to like the governor much more than she liked Dad.

By 5:00 p.m. — after sports and theater and gardening filled the day for what remained of the Mango household — we all grew hungry again. Since I was the oldest male in the house now and could drive, I captained Mom's Chrysler to the Happy China restaurant and ordered takeout.

I accepted a handful of change from the tiny Chinese woman, and suddenly I felt like a provider, even though it was Dad's money passing through my hands. Seemed to me that this daddyhood stuff was simple: just mail in a check once a month. *Perhaps this is part of figuring it out as you go.*

When I arrived home with the takeout, Mom was in her room

crying. Softly at first, then louder. My little sister consoled her for a while, and soon Mom gathered herself and joined us for sweet-and-sour chicken, steamed rice, and fortune cookies.

Mom ate in silence — until she reached out and gathered our fortune cookies, removed each slip of papery prognostication, and tossed them in the trash before anyone could read them. "They're evil," Mom said. "Like astrology."

Convinced that she was substituting her anger at fortune cookies for anger at Dad, I nevertheless let the subject pass and did my best to be supportive.

After I took out the trash, my brother wanted to play Ping-Pong in the garage, so I joined him there. The score stood 14–12 when it dawned on me that he was now thirteen, and perhaps I needed to give *him* the talk. After all, I was now the father figure around here.

"Philip," I said with authority. "Did you ever get 'the talk' from Dad? Before he left, I mean."

Philip spun his paddle in his hands and shook his head no. "Not the man-to-man talk, if that's what you mean."

I motioned for Philip to set his paddle on the table, then I folded my arms and assumed a fatherly stance. "Philip, you know what's right and wrong when it comes to girls and stuff, right?"

Philip stared across the table blank-faced, as if he couldn't figure out if I was joking with him or not. I was as serious as Dad was with me.

Finally Philip said, "Yeah, Kyle, I…I know."

Though I'm sure he lied — just like I did — I said, "Good," picked up my paddle, and told Philip to serve. I barely won the first game 21–19, which was as it should have been: two brothers in a close game, neither allowing the other to win, since we were both men now and could handle disappointment.

My role as father figure lasted less than a week. Friday night my Uncle Benny—Ben Donaldson was his regular name—drove over to visit. Four honks from his pickup announced his imminent arrival. Mom greeted him at the door and hugged him hard.

Ben was her tall and lanky brother, and he always entered our home in a burst of energy, as if his personality ran ahead of his physical body.

"I'm here!" he announced from the foyer. He even faced the stairs and shouted up again to my brother and sister, who came running. "Hugs for Uncle Benny!" he called out to them, arms wide.

Uncle Benny also made his living in sales—he sold pools and Jacuzzis all over Texas and Arkansas. Mom said he once tried to sell a baptismal to some Baptists over in Texarkana, but he used inappropriate adjectives in describing the longevity of his product and thus lost the sale.

After his enthusiastic round of hugs, Uncle Benny remained in our foyer and stared at a family picture still hanging on the far wall—Dad stoic with his arm around Mom. "I told ya, Helen, that husband of yours was acting suspicious. Now he's in Taos with some bimbo."

Mom ushered him into the den, motioned for Benny to sit, and said, "We don't know for certain he's in Taos, Benny, or that she is in fact a bimbo."

My brother ran through the den and stopped only long enough to blurt, "Yes we do, Mom. She's definitely a bimbo."

"A bimbo for sure," said my sister, never looking up from an old doll she'd pulled from her closet. She flipped the six-inch plastic blonde on its head and bounced it across the carpet on its noggin. *Boing. Boing. Boing.* "Look, it's the bimbo dance."

Mom tried to crack a smile, but somehow she couldn't force one.

Uncle Benny sat in the big recliner, ran a hand through his thick salesman hair, and focused his attention on Mom and me. "I got proof of his indiscretion."

Seated on the couch, Mom and I nodded knowingly—whenever Uncle Benny said he had proof, he usually did. Over the years he'd shown us proof of government surveillance in Fort Worth, proof of unknown planets, proof of a raccoon in our attic, and a bottle of 120-proof whiskey that he claimed he was saving up for Doomsday.

I'd never had the courage to ask Uncle Benny his prediction for Doomsday, but I figured if he stayed the night I'd have lots of opportunity.

Uncle Benny stayed the night. He'd done so before—and always stayed in my room on the cot I kept in the corner. I welcomed his presence—just he and I, two men having more man-talk. From my single bed I knew the two of us would have a long chat about *something*. We waited until everyone else had brushed their teeth and shut the doors to their rooms. I stifled a snort when I saw Uncle Benny spread a Daffy Duck blanket over his cot. Then he turned out the lights and crawled onto his flimsy bed.

"Too bad your daddy left," Benny muttered in the dark. He coughed several times; he usually had a bad one. Mom attributed it to his prior years of smoking too much. I was glad he'd quit; no way would a smoker get to stay in my room.

"Yeah, too bad," I muttered back.

"Do ya miss 'im?"

"I don't want to talk about 'im."

For a couple minutes a silence took over, as if Uncle Benny was only waiting the appropriate amount of time before introducing one of his two favorite subjects.

"I found some alien formations, Kyle…carved in the

ground." This was his second favorite subject—vague evidence of aliens snooping around the great state of Texas.

"Big ones?" I asked, doubting him already but wanting to hear him expound on his discovery.

"Huge," he whispered. "Shaped in geometric swirls."

I had no idea how to imagine a geometric swirl, especially while in the dark and getting sleepier by the minute. "Can I go see 'em?"

He yawned loudly and said, "We'll drive out tomorrow if you like."

"How far of a drive?"

"Just a couple hundred miles. Out in the flatlands...desert country."

I agreed and soon fell asleep.

Saturday morning the two of us munched blueberry Pop-Tarts in his pickup truck, downed them with strong coffee, and raced the rising sun toward Abilene. He didn't talk much on the drive out, though I didn't care since this day was already more adventurous than anything my father ever initiated.

After an hour of listening to some of the worst country music ever sung, Uncle Benny turned without signal onto an empty two-lane highway, an even flatter stretch with road signs advertising the community of Buffalo Gap.

Where we exited was not toward Buffalo Gap, although it definitely could have been where the buffalo roamed. He veered north toward Anson, where the land lay barren of all but the hardiest sprigs of grass—and those just dwarfs of their potential. The landscape made me think perhaps rain last fell here back during the Nixon administration, if not during JFK's.

Uncle Benny parked on the wide orange shoulder of the

highway and motioned for me to climb out. He tossed a fat backpack across his shoulders and began walking into a West Texas desert.

Around the hood and following, I wanted to ask him his theory on JFK but knew this would be a mistake — in subject as well as timing. If alien carvings could keep Uncle Benny talking all night, JFK's death might keep us in the desert for weeks on end. So I followed in silence, turning my head left and right to avoid the orange dust rising from Uncle Benny's shoes.

We both sported ball caps to shield us from the sun. In midstride my uncle said he usually avoided ball caps, since "they give a man hat head."

I walked along and gave this heavy thought. "Is hat head even worse if a man has thick, salesman hair?"

"You're very funny, Kyle."

Our walk unfolded for nearly half a mile. The highway behind us faded from view, and the heat felt hellacious for the morning hour. Everything sat so still and baked that I hadn't seen so much as even a grasshopper. It was as if the ground hardened in proportion to our journey — the farther we walked from the highway, the harder the ground.

"We're not there yet, are we?" I asked, smarter now and walking beside my uncle instead of behind him.

"Just ahead," he said, and a hint of excitement filled his voice.

We looked skyward as a buzzard flew past, its shadow angling darkly. The buzzard did not circle us but kept flying east, into the rising sun.

My uncle said, "He won't eat you if you drink this."

He toted with him a small canteen, metal and housed in an army-green sling. The canteen looked old and not particularly clean, but I was thirsty and didn't care. When Uncle Benny handed it to me I gulped twice and handed it back. He gulped once and said, "Ahhh."

I wiped my mouth with the back of my hand and did likewise. *Ahhh.*

From watching Westerns I knew that men nearly always did this kind of thing when outdoors with other men. It's the John Wayne syndrome. Anytime a group of men—whether just two or several dozen—are out in the wilderness, one of them naturally becomes the leader, i.e., John Wayne. And if Big John swigs his water and says "Ahhh," then eventually all the other men do too. It hides our fear and fosters our sense of community. Even if Cool Trent were out walking the desert with us, he'd forget his ego and sense of coolness; he'd take a long swig from the canteen, say "Ahhh," wipe his mouth, and keep on marching behind John Wayne.

We came upon a dry gulley, crusted at the bottom and sporting the carcass of a baked frog, so flat and cooked that not even any flies lit upon it. Up the other side of the gulley I reached flat land again, and suddenly I noticed that Uncle Benny was not walking beside me.

He'd stopped atop the bank of the gulley, his left hand pointing westward.

"Over there," he said. "Just past those cactuses. That's where I saw the formations."

In a hurry, he moved past me. In seconds our hurried strides became a jog, then a flat-out run. Sweat ran down our faces, and we swiped it away as we ran.

I stopped cold when I saw the formations. Huge like he'd said, they were laid out in a rounded, symmetrical pattern, though wind itself may have been the culprit. But perhaps not;

five swirls like random fire flames, some a hundred feet wide, looked mighty strange in all that dry dirt.

Breathing hard, hands on hips, Uncle Benny pointed at the swirls and said, "Together, Kyle, these swirls form a kind of *obtuse helix.*"

I stared hard, cocked my head to the side, and pondered. "What'd you just call 'em?"

"That was another geometric term."

"Oh."

I stared and stared but could not figure out if obtuse helixes formed in the desert were the work of nature, aliens, or a combination of both. Finally I attributed the shapes to a wayward tornado, though I didn't mention the theory to my overconfident kin.

Full of nervous energy, he strode past me, past the tip of the last geometric swirl, and motioned for me to follow. Since he showed no concern for how far we'd journeyed from the truck and the highway, I followed close but didn't ask any questions. Past low cactus and tall cactus and four waist-high boulders, I kept the pace until Uncle Benny stopped, searched out a particular rock, and motioned at the ground beside it.

"I need to dig a bit," he said and pulled a gardening spade from his backpack.

No one said anything about digging. In this heat?

On his knees atop red dirt, he dug at a steady pace, occasionally looking past me to see if anyone had followed us. I doubted anyone had even come within a country mile.

With his long arms working double time, Benny eventually dug more than two feet down—and he sweated buckets.

Eventually I asked if I could help, and he said okay but to be careful, that I might hit something hard. He rested beside the hole, his back to the sun, while I dropped to my knees and took over as chief digger. Minutes later I hit something hard. At the sound of the strike, Uncle Benny took back the spade and motioned me out of the way. A section of burlap lay covered in dirt. My uncle leaned over the hole, so far I thought he might fall in. Then he dug around the burlap until he could reach in and grip what lay beneath. The corner of a wooden box appeared.

By this time I could no longer hold my questions. "You found something, or did you bury that yourself?"

Benny didn't answer, just dug around the box until he could get his fingers in the gaps, then he lifted out the box and the burlap. With a grunt, he brought it all up and set it on the ground near my feet. The box was thick and apparently quite heavy.

He opened the lid of the box—it had no padlock—and pulled out a second burlap bag, this one cleaner and obviously pregnant with something hefty. A metallic clink sounded from its innards.

"What's in the sack?"

He hesitated for a long while. "Silver dollars. Old ones. Real silver, and some bullion bars too."

"No kidding…Silver coins and stuff?"

Precious metals were another of Uncle Benny's favorite subjects, just ahead of aliens but in a tie with oil, although he'd never told me that he owned any of the metals. Ever since I could remember, he just always liked talking about the metals and oil and commodity prices.

"Bullion and old coins, some of both," he said and unwrapped the tie string securing the bag. "Sometimes it's fun to pretend I live in the Wild Wild West."

I figured he was just bored, being fifty-six and living alone.

Still, this was definitely more adventurous than anything my father ever initiated.

"So you just up and buried it all out here on someone else's land?"

He pointed north, then south, as if marking topography. "Nope, *my* land. I own eight hundred and forty-two acres," he stated with great pride. "Bought it for sixty bucks per. Kinda long and odd-shaped, though, which is why it was such a deal."

I rummaged through the coins and the silver bars, amazed at the bars' brilliance, almost blinding in the sunlight. Next I admired the coins and stacked a few in my palm, their combined heft giving them the feel of real money, not that paper stuff that Benny said was backed by nothing but air. "What's all this stuff worth?" I asked and stacked four more silver dollars in my hand.

"The world spot price of silver is currently four dollars and eighty cents an ounce…as of last night."

I knew my next question was nosy, and probably inappropriate, but I needed the information in order to do the math in my head. "And about how many ounces you think you got here?"

Uncle Benny pursed his lips, wiped his brow. "A little over a thousand, I think."

Stunned at what appeared to be adult stupidity, I repeated myself. "You just bury it all out in the middle of Texas and trust that no one will find it?"

Benny laughed, shook his head in amusement. "Kyle, who would look out here, on this very acreage, beside this very rock, dig exactly two feet down, and discover a bag of silver coins?"

"I dunno. I had my mind on creative tornadoes and geometric swirls."

"Exactly," he said and took back the coins. "Now, help me rebury this box."

He carefully placed his silver back in the bag, tucked the bag in the box, wrapped the box in the burlap, and hoisted the entire lump into his arms. Then he knelt and set the package back in the hole. He exhaled from the effort and said, "To be honest, this stuff ain't the true value on my land. It's what's under the rest of this earth."

"You buried gold too?"

He laughed, wiped sweat from his brow. "Nope. But recent tests show oil reserves on this property. Lots of it. This silver is just...fun money."

When he stood again I noticed that he'd kept out a ten-ounce bar and two silver dollars. These he handed to me.

"Keep 'em hidden, Kyle. Someday you'll need 'em. When all paper money is worthless, this stuff will still be valuable, perhaps *very* valuable. It's been a store of value for thousands of years, even since biblical times."

I tried to imagine Jesus and the disciples burying precious metals in Israel, but the image went fuzzy, what with the loaves and fishes story crowding out the silver. So I stuffed the bar and the coins in my jeans pocket and tightened my belt to keep my pants from falling.

The bar felt heavy and audacious all at once. None of my friends ever strutted around with ten-ounce silver bars in their pockets. The closest anyone had come was a boy named Peter, who sometimes carried his grandfather's pocket watch to school because he thought it made him look mature when actually it just made him look ridiculous.

I helped cover the box with dirt, and soon Uncle Benny and I were on our knees again, brushing the soil and covering our tracks.

"How much you think this bar will be worth in a few years?" I asked, toggling between greed and curiosity as we spread dirt with our feet.

Uncle Benny motioned back toward the highway, and in that direction we walked side by side. "Well, right now it's under five bucks per ounce," he said, as if the price did not quite suit him. "By 2005 I'd say ten dollars an ounce. And by 2008, when supply is short and demand high, perhaps forty or fifty dollars an ounce."

I quickly multiplied ten ounces times fifty dollars, and suddenly it felt awesome to have five hundred future dollars of silver in my pocket. There was nothing else to say now. My uncle trusted me with his secret fun money, and I trusted him as my pseudo-Dad.

Dust clouds rolled behind us as we hiked back toward the truck. Minutes later I grew uneasy, as if this new knowledge of my uncle might be more burden than blessing. Every few steps I reminded myself that I was never good at keeping secrets, a feeling that intensified when I glanced skyward. Overhead the sun looked like a giant orange eyeball observing everything we'd dug up, admired, and reburied.

We passed through the dry gulley and on up the embankment to the highway. There Uncle Benny opened the door to his truck, climbed in, and waited for me to scurry around to the passenger side. "You tell no one about this," he cautioned, and his voice was stern. "Including the oil tests."

I slid into the seat and shut the door. "Um...not at all. I won't tell anybody."

"I just figured someone in the family should know...in case anything ever happens to me."

I strapped on my seat belt. "Won't tell a soul."

He started his truck and U-turned off the shoulder onto the empty highway. "Good," he said finally.

I remained silent, afraid to probe further into his eccentricities.

Benny sped along toward Abilene, tight-lipped, as if our conversation had struck a nerve and only rapid acceleration would
heal it. "Kyle?"

"Yeah?"

"If you ever meet a special girl, don't be afraid to sacrifice
that silver bar for her."

I had no idea what he meant. "You mean bribe her with silver bullion? To get her to go out with me? I hope I'm never *that*
desperate."

Benny's serious tone disappeared in a chuckle. "No, I meant
after you've dated a girl for a while, you can take that bar and
have it made into a custom piece of silver jewelry for her."

"Oh...yeah. Good idea."

He tapped his wrist in the place where a bracelet might hang.
"Just something to keep in mind."

It took ten more miles of Texas highway for this to process
in my head—that I had an uncle who, in the span of an hour,
could show me geometric swirls in the desert, dig up precious
metals in a buried box, and converse on custom jewelry for special women.

This was the kind of adventurous stuff I had hoped for
when Dad wanted to have *the talk*, but now Benny had taken
his place. And besides, Dad only invested in boring ol' savings
bonds. He was much too practical to bury stuff in West Texas
and prospect for oil.

Back on the interstate but still fifty miles from Fort Worth, I
pressed my uncle further. "Did you ever give custom silver jewelry to your wife?"

"Yep....Did it on four different occasions, in fact." My Aunt
Cloe had passed in 1988, though I never understood the disease she had. Her death had ruined the great nickname my

mom was reserving for them. If Aunt Cloe and Uncle Benny had kids, Mom wanted them to name the kids after airlines, names like Delta and United, so that she could call the clan "Benny and the Jets." It was our secret, and Mom and I promised to never tell this to Benny, as it would only make him sad.

On the interstate Benny tuned his radio to a country station, and Mister Alan Jackson himself accompanied us into the outskirts of Fort Worth. By now I'd decided that Uncle Benny was not only eccentric, but he also had a certain romantic streak in him. A romantic eccentric seemed like a good thing to be, and I made a mental note to try and become one, by age thirty at the latest.

That night, however, after a shower to wash away the grit and dust of the day, I said good-bye to my uncle and told him I needed to spend Saturday evening writing letters to colleges. My heart was set on enrolling at Texas Tech—farther west in Lubbock. From Lubbock I could still drive back home if Mom should need me, could still meet Uncle Benny on Saturdays if he needed more help digging up secret stuff, and could still meet my brother for our monthly Ping-Pong match. But mostly I figured Texas Tech was where I'd meet a girl, make good grades, and become a romantic scholastic eccentric engineer.

I had already received brochures from several colleges, and though I remained curious about what went on at frat parties, somehow all of that preppy, fashion-conscious frat stuff was not my true path. I could sense this.

A PROBLEM
WITH SAMENESS

I lived on the second floor of the preppy, fashion-conscious frat house.

But just nine days into my freshman year, I already hated it. I hated the conformity, I hated the secret handshake, and I hated the smothering frat clothes, all of us sporting the same three letters day after day. The members—those so-called *brothers*—recruited me. Said they liked my conservative haircut, and that I "fit in physically"—whatever that meant for a blue-eyed, five-foot-ten freshman. My initial interest stemmed from common collegiate reasoning: they seemed friendly, hospitable, and promised all pledges a "home away from home." After they offered me a bid, however, they told me what to wear and said I wasn't a real man unless I dated a Chi-O.

I had to ask a fellow pledge the meaning of Chi-O. He asked if I was from the sticks. Then he muttered, "Chi Omega, dude."

The Sigmas were also big on family legacy and held in high regard the vocational status of a pledge's parents. Since at least two of Uncle Benny's buried coins came from Canada, I told the frats that my family had a long history of trading in the international commodities markets. Affirmative nods told me that I'd given a satisfactory answer, though I kept to myself the fact that I'd taken out student loans to supplement my partial academic scholarship and had only sixty-one dollars to my name.

The brothers didn't tell me, however, that three times a week I'd be awakened from my bed at 3:00 a.m. and taken into the basement. They didn't tell me I'd be yelled at for being a pledge and that twice I would stand against a wall with a handkerchief tied over my eyes while someone threw beer bottles high over my head, bursting them against a brick wall and showering me with glass. I was sworn to secrecy and got little sleep.

"What happens here stays here!" the house president yelled at the pledges.

"Yeah, little pledge!" shouted his senior buddies, "Take it like a man! Tell no one!"

Friday nights we all acted as if we got along, because on Friday nights the men of Sigma house hosted socials. My second weekend the brothers threw an open party, a retro eighties bash open to anyone on the Texas Tech campus—although the Chi-Os were the only sorority who received personal, mailed invitations. By 9:00 p.m., more than two hundred collegians packed into our long, first-floor party room. Streamers hung from the ceiling and over the buffet table, where Chi-Os huddled together, maneuvered for position, and laughed too hard whenever a brother said anything, no matter how corny.

It was like they were all predisposed toward one another. I hung out on the perimeter of their coolness, trying to figure out to what I was predisposed. It certainly wasn't Greekdom. I figured that, like my uncle, my predisposition lay in the area of adventure and risk—and this life felt at odds with that vision. I sipped from my drink and noted the condescending stares of brothers. In obedience to their authority, I let my gaze fall to the floor and sipped a second time. A third.

It felt like relief when a fellow pledge asked me to help set out more cups and napkins. I retreated to the pantry, and just then someone cranked the music. I had only vague familiarity with retro eighties music—was there really a band called *Kajagoogoo?*—but the synthesized vibes rocked the walls, and all the people cheered.

Various independent sorts wandered into the party, grabbed a drink, perhaps some food, then stood against walls and looked around for a friend. Few friends were available, I supposed, mostly frats and sorority girls beholding their own, oblivious to commoners and destined to marry well.

While setting out plastic forks at the buffet table, I once again felt the brothers watching me. One of them, a senior with a beer gut worthy of a fifty-year-old, asked me to fetch him a brew, and I did so with efficiency and haste.

"Thanks, Kyle," he said, and he said it nicely only because two girls stood nearby. "Now go find yourself a Chi-O freshman and ask her to dance."

Two other brothers toasted the instructions with raised mugs.

I probably made them all mad when I began dancing with Gretchen, the bead-wearing girl who lived in a dorm but snuck into frat parties whenever she heard good music and knew there'd be free food. "Better than the cafeteria fare," she'd said when I met her at the previous weekend's party. She seemed oblivious to peer pressure.

That first evening she'd dipped a celery stalk in a saucer of honey mustard, used it to make her points about the quality of Texas Tech food in general, and convinced me to try it. I crunched a stalk, liked it, and in that moment she and I had made some sort of connection. A new friend? More? Who knew?

Tonight, among all the soft-cottoned conformity, Gretchen

had returned in her throwback hippie jeans, her frilly brown shirt draped again with her nonconformist beads, a thick mane of honey-colored hair spilling over both shoulders. Even the way she scanned the room after we'd finished the dance—as if she couldn't decide if the scene was worth her time—made her stand out from the sorority types gliding by in front of her. Something in me triggered—I just had to get to know her better—and so I squeezed past a huddle of brothers and dipped two more celery stalks in honey mustard.

I offered one to Gretchen, and she accepted with a smile. But then she pointed back to the dance floor, I nodded, and we crunched our stalks en route.

"What do you think of these people?" she asked over the music, and just then the dance floor emptied.

The brother playing the role of DJ had taken a request, popped in another ancient CD, and suddenly an undance-able Talking Heads song sent everyone to the sidelines. But Gretchen and I just stood out there in the middle of the floor, crunching our celery amid the retro music, awash in blue and yellow lighting. The lights combined to turn us both a ghostly green, a flirtatious green even, while all around the good citizens of Greekdom watched us like we were both impossibly self-sufficient.

The music grew louder—and the brothers continued to eye me with skepticism. Twice I turned and raised my cup in a toast to them. None of them toasted back.

Gretchen appeared to sense their skepticism—she impressed me as highly observant—and as the song played she leaned near my head and repeated herself. "What do you think of these people, Kyle?"

I scanned frat brothers whom I doubted would ever truly

love me as a brother. Next I scanned the sorority women before speaking my thoughts into Gretchen's hair—which smelled like honeysuckle with a dash of cinnamon. "They're all so much alike that I believe any one of those guys could date any one of those girls, and it wouldn't make any difference."

Gretchen laughed, nodded her head with enthusiasm. "Exactly!"

A spark, high voltage, something, surged through me in that instant, what I would later discern as the early stages of chemistry. "So," I asked, my mind spinning to grasp the right words and to transfer those words efficiently to my vocal chords and out through my lips, "how many frat parties have you wandered into this week?"

She beamed. "Five! But this one is the most fun."

I leaned into her hair for another brief sniff and raised my voice over the singing Talking Heads. "And just why is that?"

With a blue-lit face she leaned toward me. We were lean-flirting. "Because I met you!...You're the only independent guy I've talked with all week."

"I'm flattered, Gretchen, but I'm not truly independent. I pledged this frat, ya know."

She feigned shock. "Maybe so. But are you really going to *stay*?"

Two senior brothers stood against the wall, observing me as if assigned the duty of overseers. I turned my back to them to prevent them from reading my lips. "It's like this, Gretchen: once a pledge moves into the big house, they won't let him leave. If you tell them you don't want to pledge any longer, the brothers physically force you to stay."

Over the music she blurted, "But that's absurd!"

Under the music I continued talking into her ear. "They keep you up all night talking about how important it is not to give the fraternity a bad image, that Sigmas aren't quitters. I'm not supposed to tell anyone this, but the brothers caught a pledge Wednesday morning packing his bags before class, then they kept him in the basement for nine hours until he agreed to stay. They convinced him that his future happiness and success rested upon whether or not he completed his pledge and became a brother."

Gretchen stepped back and stared at me blank-faced, fingering her beads as if she could not fathom such treatment. "But…but you *want* to leave, right? You can't just stay trapped here with the cookie-cutter people."

I'd never heard that expression before, *cookie-cutter people*, and on this night it felt so appropriate that I moved even closer to her and whispered, "I fear I've made a mistake, that I'm really a dorm rat at heart."

That beaming grin again. This killed me. It felt good to make her laugh, even better that she could return the favor with seemingly no effort at all.

For a long moment she gazed past me at the brothers and sisters gathered at the food table, eating, talking, sipping their drinks. There was something huge going on in this massive frat house on this Friday night in September. Something way beyond the usual socializing and dancing at a begin-the-semester party. Here the upper class sorority girls hunted not just for a boyfriend, but appeared on a quest for genuine pedigree. Here they cooed and flirted and sized up the men of Sigma house, and behind their glossy lips and excited eyes an urgency to ensure their futures pressed forth. I saw it in their body language. Heck, I even heard it outside the restrooms.

Gretchen asked to excuse herself a minute because she had to *go*, and of course I said I had to go as well. In the first-floor hallway we split off; she pushed the door marked *W*, and I pushed the one marked *M*.

No brothers in the men's room. I exhaled my relief.

I finished first and waited in the hallway, greeting faux brothers, faux sisters, some wandering strangers, and acting in general like I belonged. Then the *W* door flew open. Instead of Gretchen, however, out came a pair of bejeweled and stylish Chi-Os, a red sundress speaking excitedly to a pink sundress, all of it gushing forth in hurried whispers. "I hear Paul Ford's dad is, like, a major executive with a beverage company!" said red sundress.

With great urgency, pink sundress said, "Maybe Paul already has a job lined up there when he graduates!"

Paul was my so-called big brother, the senior with whom I shared a room, the guy whose job it was to show me the ropes and instruct me in the proper ways of pledgedom. I wondered how many of these girls wanted him, and if they truly knew what they were getting. Both sundresses reentered the party and made a beeline for Paul and his buddies.

I had no idea what I wanted to be when I graduated. Plus I had no precedent; my dad's software sales job never really struck me as a career path. To follow Uncle Benny's lead — selling pools and hot tubs — seemed interesting though. Lots of outdoor hours, warm weather, not to mention time to be eccentric on the side. But I was only eighteen and hadn't given career much thought — and such thoughts disappeared completely when Gretchen bolted out of the restroom and grabbed my hand.

"Kyle?" she asked, and cunning filled her voice.

For a second I could only observe her with a mix of suspicion and infatuation. "Okay," I said as partygoers weaved around us in the hall, "I don't know you all that well, and I'm sure you're not drunk because you haven't even had a drink, but your mind is really spinning."

That grin again. "Yes...yes it is."

We meandered back into the party and propped ourselves against a wall, facing the buffet and a bevy of brothers—who stood too far away to hear us talking.

Gretchen perused their Greekness and spoke from the side of her mouth. "Would you like some help getting out of this place?"

I didn't know what she meant, but the idea sounded good. Dangerous, but good.

Just then three brothers moved closer, picking at food from the buffet, glancing at me between nibbles. I grew more and more uncomfortable. So I grabbed Gretchen's hand, and we strolled out to the dance floor—the safety zone, since out there the music drowned out conversation—and once again we stood alone while the last strains of a long, undanceable song wound down.

I glanced quickly at the brothers, who seemed to always have one eye on the girls, one eye on the pledges. "What are you gonna do, Gretchen—hold 'em all at gunpoint while I scram out the front door?"

She shook her head and stifled a laugh. "No, but I *can* help you escape this place." She said this loudly into my ear, paused a moment, and continued. "That is, if you really *want* out."

For a third time I caught a whiff of honeysuckle. Combined with the cunning in her voice, the sheer boldness of the topic caused my pulse to race. I knew this because I'd let go of Gretchen's hand to feel my pulse, and it wasn't *one thousand one, one thousand two, one thousand three,* but *thousandOneTwoThreeFourFive.*

Caution and logic merged and gave me pause. "They're always watching me!" I blurted. "Plus all my stuff is upstairs."

She raised her left wrist, pointed at her watch, and traced the second hand around the perimeter.

"You mean *tonight*?" I asked, unprepared for such aggression. "Like right *now*?"

She nodded. "Where's your room?"

"Second floor, but I share it with — "

She shushed me. Right there in my house of residence — which did not feel anything like a home — I'd been shushed.

Gretchen motioned at the khaki-clad brothers, all sipping their beers and observing their kingdom. "Which one is your big brother?" she inquired.

Again I leaned close to her. "How'd you know I had a big brother?"

"All you pledges have one." She motioned at them again. "So, which one?"

I whispered in her ear. "The tall one in the light blue button-down."

She gazed past me again, and soon her smallish frown grew into a larger frown. "Kyle, there must be *twenty-eight* tall guys in light blue button-downs."

I motioned with my head. "Dark curly hair, big teeth. His name is Paul."

She looked again. "Okay, I see him. So, Paul is the guy you room with?"

"Yep. And he'd never let me escape. Nor would his buddies. And all but one of them is bigger than me."

She moved around me so that now her back faced the Greek Squad, and I faced the enemy. Suddenly the undanceable song ended, and a fresh dose of retro music burst forth. "Thriller" boomed through the speakers.

A horde of collegians rushed toward us on the dance floor,

heads and knees bobbing, a gaggle of Greeks all trying to mock the song's infamous video — the mummy dance, we called it.

Gretchen tugged me to the center of the crowd beneath an old chandelier, where we found ourselves next to Paul and some inebriated Chi-O. In seconds the floor grew fully packed, Gretchen and I surrounded by the horde, most of them with the same dance style, if you can call feet-planted-firmly-while-swaying a dance style.

Gretchen waited for the second verse before she tapped Paul on the shoulder. Her voice grew loud, a near shout competing with "Thriller'"s chorus. "Paul, would you mind if Kyle and I use the room for a little while?"

She winked at him, an exaggerated wink that caused me to mimic her enthusiasm and offer Paul a hearty thumbs-up. Inside I shook with nerves.

Paul at first looked as if he could not believe what he'd just heard, as if a freshman like me should not be so lucky, never mind that the attractive female before him wasn't a sorority type. Michael Jackson's screaming chorus vibrated the walls. Indeed, it was a "thriller" night.

Paul met my glance, winked once, and gave us both a nod of approval. "Yeah, sure. Just don't trash the room, little freshman."

Gretchen said over her shoulder, "Thanks, Paulie!" and reached for my hand again.

But Paul grabbed my shoulder and said, "You need to pay more attention to a Chi-O, little bro. Hey, that rhymes."

I had no reply — to his demand or his first-grade poetry skills — plus there was no time to reply anyway since Gretchen was pulling me off the dance floor. We simply left Paul to dance with the Chi-O, she in her own little world, eyes shut, mascara thick, head bobbing in the patented sorority-girl bob.

Gretchen and I pushed through dancers and drinkers and some lonely independents, past the celery, the honey mustard, and a platter of chicken wings. Past the beer kegs we went, out into the hallway and up the stairs to the second floor.

We found the hallway empty, just worn floors, graffitied doors, and the throb of "Thriller" reverberating off the walls. The Sigmas' Big House was home to fifty-four men, sixteen of us pledges. The hallway smelled of Pine-Sol. I was sure of the scent since I'd been the one who cleaned the hall two hours before the party—while four brothers took turns spitting on the sections I'd just cleaned, insisting that I rescrub all obvious flaws. They'd even taken turns kicking my mop bucket, shouting over each other that a strong work ethic was central to a successful pledgeship.

"I've rarely seen a fratty's room," Gretchen said in the hallway, and she giggled when she spoke, as if the concept amused her.

"Keep expectations low."

I opened the door to my room, and Gretchen bolted past me. She looked left and right at the two beds. "Which one?"

"On the left."

She wasted no time. She yanked the blanket off my bed, then pulled off my sheet. "Any of this furniture yours?" she asked.

I helped her spread the sheet on the floor, as wide as possible. "No. It's all Paul's."

"Toss all your belongings into the sheet," she ordered. Then she dropped her two corners. "I'll help."

Paul and I shared a four-drawer chest of drawers. The bottom two drawers belonged to me, so I pulled out the fourth as Gretchen handled the third. Two heaves of clothes from me, two overhead tosses from Gretchen, my sheet filling fast. Likewise my level of fear. "If I get caught, Gretchen, they'll haze me for weeks on end. I may not even survive it."

With finger to her lips she shushed me and tapped her watch again. I rushed to the sink and began clearing my vanity. Toothbrush. Combs. Shaving cream—I used shaving cream twice a week.

Gretchen hurried over beside me at the sink. "This your aftershave?" she asked and held up two bottles.

"The blue bottle, yeah."

She removed the cap and sniffed. "You shoulda worn this at last week's party, when we danced to that Blackie song."

"It was *Blondie*, Gretchen. They were an eighties sensation."

"Oh."

She wheeled around, checked the walls. "What about the Tech posters?"

"Both mine. Grab 'em."

She rolled them up, swiped two rubber bands from Paul's top drawer, and tossed the posters onto the sheet.

"What else?" she asked, and just then I noticed the sweat weighting the tips of her hair, then I noticed the glow of her skin, and I paused amid my anarchy and decided that she was beautiful. Gretchen had a face that, if she were hitchhiking, would produce immediate offers of free rides.

"What did you say?"

She frowned, pointed around the room. "What else is *yours*, Kyle?"

"Um…just my books."

We grabbed the stack of six books and laid them one by one around the pile of clothes in the middle of the sheet.

Gretchen grabbed all four ends of the sheet and hoisted the bundle, which by now looked quite heavy. Too heavy for her to tote alone.

"Let me do it," I said, but just then footsteps pounded in the hallway. "Shhh."

The footsteps grew louder, louder still, then stopped outside the room. We knelt on the floor against the back wall of room 212, my right hand on the window latch, Gretchen leaning into the air vent. "Oh no," she whispered. "Please oh please, no."

We heard laughter, more loud steps, as if the party had bubbled upward to the second floor. The door across the hall opened and shut.

"Out the window," Gretchen whispered. "Let's go."

She raised the window, and I shoved my bundle out onto the roof. The frat house roof was not steep; I knew this because the first weekend's party spilled out onto it—where the brothers took turns bowling beer cans off the edge.

Other brothers down below, in the yard, caught the cans, popped the tops, chugged the spray and, when finished, locked arms and sang, "Fun, fun, fun till Daddy takes the keg fund away." *Not very original,* I thought at the time. A rite of passage, perhaps.

Gretchen stooped and stuck one leg through the dorm window, then the other leg, and when she'd made it out onto the roof she turned and reached for my hand and gave me an assist. I ducked through the window, stepped out, and inhaled the cool night air. Beside her on the roof, my sheeted bundle at our feet, I felt liberated, released from bondage.

"I can't believe I'm doing this," I gushed. "My heart's racing."

She pressed an imaginary stethoscope to my chest. "Over me or your escape?"

"Probably both."

The music throbbed through the roof, into our feet and up through our ankles.

We moved down the roof some twenty feet until we stood directly above the party. For a moment we even mocked them and did the mummy dance right there in the moonlight—the way it was intended. Gretchen watched my moves for a second and said, "Not bad for a prison escapee."

Across campus the giant Texas Tech Red Raider mascot snarled from the side of a building, a pair of spotlights illumining its face. I felt like a Red Raider this night, raiding my own room for the cause of freedom.

Time to go.

Gretchen led the way to the side of the roof. I hoisted the bundle and had it balanced over my back when I remembered that I'd forgotten something.

"Wait, Gretch, my Dallas Cowboys lamp."

Back through the window I went—and tumbled headfirst into my former room. I snatched the lamp but forgot to unplug it first. The lamp snatched back and jerked my elbow socket. Regrouped and listening for more footsteps, I proceeded in proper order, unplugged the cord, and turned to see Gretchen kneeling outside the window, her hands reaching back inside, fingers flexing.

"Hand it to me, Kyle," she whispered. "Quick, we need to hurry!"

I passed her the lamp, and she stuffed it into the sheet, whose girth offered a striking resemblance to Santa's sack. I climbed back out the window and shut it behind me. Then I dragged the sheeted bundle farther out onto the roof and over near the edge. Beyond the campus the lights of downtown Lubbock glowed softly, and for a moment I felt like one of the men in *Escape from Alcatraz* as they stood on the shore staring across the water before swimming away.

I snorted from laughter—this seemed so ridiculous, but I simply had to part ways with the brotherhood. Gretchen peeked over the roof's edge and said "Shhh," but then she snorted as well. I was too tickled to shush her back. Escaping a frat house while the Greeks danced to "Thriller" was the wildest thing I'd done since helping Uncle Benny excavate silver.

"Are we having fun yet?" Gretchen asked. At the edge of the roof she lay on her stomach and peered down over the edge.

I scooted beside her, also on my stomach, one hand on the bundled sheet, one gripping the roof's gutter. Together we peered upside down at the dancing Greeks. "Yep," I said in reflection. "No more cleaning spit off floors."

Gretchen made the icky face before pointing below to the dance floor. In the center of the floor, Paul and the Chi-O raised their beer mugs overhead. Up/down up/down went the mugs, the default dance move for those unable to think of anything better. They turned in circles, eyes shut, heads swaying, mugs spilling.

Gretchen had timed our exit well, and I told her so.

"Hush," she said and pulled me to my feet. "Time to begin your new life."

Only the front and back walls of the frat house had windows, so we scurried along the rooftop like squirrels until we reached the far right corner. There I tied off the ends of the sheeted bundle and dropped it ten feet down onto an unsuspecting bush. The bundle lay waiting there, supported by the thick bush and tempting us to jump. But we found no laddered fire escape to ease our descent. Yet another issue to figure out as I went.

All we found on the side of the frat house was a metal downspout bolted into the bricks, its brace offering timid support for a first step down. With my back to the ground, I shimmied over the edge of the roof with one leg, felt for the brace with my foot, and pushed off.

I'm flying.

For all of one second I fell in free fall—until my back landed on my bundled sheet and I bounced off the bush. I'd forgotten about my lamp, however, and pain shot up under my rib cage. I rolled off the sheet, rearranged it for an incoming coed, and looked up to see Gretchen hanging off the roof, her right foot feeling for the downspout brace. Her toe wouldn't quite reach.

"Just jump, Gretchen!" I whispered as loudly as possible. I rubbed my side twice and diluted the sting.

"Thriller" morphed into "Beat It," and again the music rocked the wall, the roof, the downspout.

Gretchen tried again to reach the downspout with her foot. Failing a second time, she hesitated, and I was glad she did because it gave me time to pull the lamp from the sheet. I set it on the ground behind me and patted the remaining bundle atop the bush, as if urging her to jump from a burning building.

Again she extended her leg and felt for the brace, but in the fifteen seconds since her last attempt, her leg had not grown a single inch.

"Just jump, Gretch!"

She jumped backward and somehow rotated in midair, arms held wide, sort of a backward belly flop. She landed on her back atop my padded sheet, compressed the bush, and bounced off onto the grass.

She lay there laughing, gazing up at the sky. "I was a springboard diver in junior high."

"No kidding." I lugged my sheet of possessions off the bush and twisted the ends into a handle.

"Let's do it again!" Gretchen said from the grass and noted the height of her leap. "Or, perhaps not."

She stood and brushed herself off. Then she fluffed the bush like it was a big green pillow, carefully moving branches back into place, tidying up nature.

"You done yet?" I asked and hoisted my bundle.

She peered into the middle of the bush. "Just checking for any bird nests. I'd feel horrible if I damaged one."

In moonlight that threatened to expose us, I questioned her motives. "How can you think about birds at a time like this?"

She shrugged. "I love nature."

Satisfied that nature remained undisturbed, she crept with me against the brick wall of the frat house. One more peek around the corner, into the windows at the dancing Greeks, and we bolted into the night.

Around the neighboring Alpha house, past cars that seemed too expensive for college students, we ran along best we could while hauling my sheet across lawns. Gretchen toted my lamp, swinging it in rhythm to our pace, the cord dragging the ground behind us.

When at last our pace slowed and we were far away from Greek Circle, she told me about her own brief courtship with a sorority. "I went to a couple of meet-n-greets," she said, "and I met some nice girls, but I just don't have the wardrobe for it."

"So now you rescue fellow freshmen who don't know what they're getting into?"

She switched my lamp into her right hand and said, "Just guys. I don't rescue girls very often. In fact, none so far."

We took turns dragging my bundled sheet toward the middle of campus, and soon it occurred to me that here at Texas Tech I had no home. "Gretchen, thanks for the escape idea and all—I really wanted out—but I haven't lined up any other place to live."

In front of me on a cobblestone path, she walked backward, watching me drag the bulk of my worldly possessions. She put a finger to her temple and appeared to think hard on this issue. Finally she said, "You can stay with Chang. In a dorm."

An exposed root tugged at my bundle and nearly jerked it from my hands. "I think my sheet has a tear in it now...and just *who* is this Chang person?"

She shifted the lamp back to her left hand, the cord still following dutifully along the ground. "He's from Korea, and he's nice. Intelligent and nice."

"Doesn't he have a roommate?"

"Nope. His roommate got homesick first week and flew back."

"To Korea?"

"Mongolia."

Then I asked a stupid Texan question. "Does Chang speak much English?"

My possessions grew heavy, and Gretchen seemed to sense not only their heft, but also my own ignorance. "Of course he does. He's brilliant."

We stopped near Flint Avenue to switch duties, and when we did she stuffed the lamp back inside the bundle and tried hoisting the load over her shoulder. For a minute or so she staggered under its weight but managed to tote it past the clock tower and around the side of Murray Hall.

Soon, however, she too became a dragger instead of a toter. Above us the stars winked their own independence as well as their approval, and suddenly all felt right in my tiny corner of the galaxy.

Five minutes later I hauled my stuff into an empty dorm lobby, Gretchen walking ahead, glancing left and right like a spy. She motioned for me to follow her around into the first-floor hallway, and I tugged my sheet and possessions along a tiled floor, unsure if I could trust her choices. My lamp made a scraping noise until we stopped and Gretchen knocked on the fourth door on the right, room 109.

"Chang, it's me, Gretchen…" She knocked again. "Gretchen, from statistics class."

I heard a TV at high volume, then lower volume. Then the door opened and a trim Asian guy, clean-cut and sporting gold-rimmed glasses, greeted us with a hesitant smile. Gretchen shook his hand with great enthusiasm and said, "Chang, this is my friend Kyle. He's an ex-pledge who needs a place to stay tonight."

Chang met my beggar-like gaze and nodded, but then he quickly looked back over his shoulder at his TV, where the Bachelorette was shattering male egos via an absence of roses.

Just as quickly Chang turned back to us. "She just broke the Asian guy's heart," he said and motioned to his TV. "We always get the shaft on that show."

I extended my hand, and Chang shook it warmly. "Come aboard," he said and motioned me inside. "I see you brought your linens."

I liked this guy already, doubly so when he took my bundle from my shoulder and set it on the empty bed across from his own. Then he picked up a phone off his study desk, dialed a number, and from the talk I deduced that he was speaking with the dorm manager about my arrival. Still in the door-way, Gretchen looked worried. She fidgeted with her beads and shrugged a shrug of hope.

Chang hung up and smiled at me. "Okay to stay."

"I'm good here?" I asked, relieved at the news. "Tonight only or full-time?"

Chang nodded. "He said you're the ninth ex-pledge to move into the dorm this week. Stay all semester if you like."

Gretchen bounced on her toes and clapped, a mini-celebration to cap off our well-executed escape. She and Chang both helped me put away my clothes—I got one drawer of three—and I stuffed the rest of my belongings into a tiny closet.

The three of us sat on the floor and played cards until 3:00 a.m., at which time Gretchen declared herself the winner and told us she was heading for her dorm to get some sleep. She hugged Chang, then me—my hug was longer by at least one second; I counted.

Overcome with a rare confidence, I walked her out into the hallway and asked if she could meet me in the cafeteria for breakfast, a happening that I would later proclaim as our first real date.

Gretchen agreed to meet, and after we'd pushed though the glass doors to the dorm and she'd descended the stairs and waved, I called out, "Breakfast doesn't start until noon."

"Scrambled eggs…with independent waffles," she said over her shoulder. She laughed and rounded the corner and disappeared into the night.

I reentered my dorm giving myself imaginary pats on the back. *You did it, Mango. Escaped the frats AND met the girl, all on the same night.*

Chang was watching the last minute of *The Bachelorette*—he had taped the show earlier in the week since he had a night class—and didn't appear to notice my presence until a commercial played.

"So," he said as I tucked my torn sheet around my bed, "interesting night for you, Kyle?"

"Man, it went way beyond interesting."

Soon after the lights went out in Room 109, I felt the need to make more conversation with Chang—especially since he'd been so hospitable. He seemed to roll with life, offering up an air of acceptance rather than an air of entitlement and privilege. From across the room, flat on my back and too excited to sleep yet, I discovered his somewhat transient history: after spending his grade school years in California, then briefly moving back to Korea with his family, Chang had picked Texas Tech by standing over a map of America, closing his eyes, turning around five times, and then placing his finger on the map. He'd touched the edge of Lubbock, Texas, and that was that. Though he had the grades to get accepted most anywhere, here he was at Tech, sharing a room with me, a local by comparison. In the dark I heard him toss in his bed, as if he needed to find just the right position in order to sleep. I had no such issues.

"Chang," I said, hoping I wasn't waking him. "Does your family watch *The Bachelorette* back in Korea?"

He tossed twice more in his bed. "No, they don't like it much in Seoul. And in my e-mails I tell them to watch the manipulating people on the island with just rice, a machete, and no hut."

"That one's called *Survivor*, Chang."

"Yes, of course. But contrary to opinion, Asians do not eat rice every meal. I mean, if I were on that island, I'd want me some grits and bacon…*y'all*."

Yep, I liked this new roommate, although at this wee hour I could not think of any more conversation starters. So I rolled over, faced the wall, closed my eyes, and thought of Gretchen. "G'night, Chang."

"And good night to you, ex-frat boy who voted himself out of his frat hut."

THE VERY NEXT MORNING

My cell phone rang at 8:45 a.m., a cruel hour on a Saturday to call a college student. At the second ring I trembled in bed. *They've tracked me down; the brothers are coming for me.* I knew this even before I checked my watch a second time and turned over to see my phone sitting atop Chang's desk, right where I'd left it.

Chang was down the hall at the restrooms, and my phone just kept ringing and ringing.

Finally I tumbled off my bed and stood barefoot at the desk, fearing the inevitable. *They'll tie me up in the basement of the frat house, douse me with spoiled beer, and call me a quitter.*

Six rings, seven rings, eight...

At the ninth ring I flipped open my phone and faked a deep voice. "Hello?"

"Kyle, that you? Doesn't sound like you."

"Uncle *Benny*?" Relief flooded my senses. "Are you in some kind of trouble?"

"No trouble at all, now that I dialed the right number. First I called the frat house, and some sleepy pledge said he couldn't find you, that your bed was barren and that you were probably out doing your laundry." He paused as if expecting me to reply, but I was too confused and sleepy to think straight. He continued, "You probably don't have time to meet me, now that you're busy pledging the frat and all."

"Um, I might have some free time."

"How can pledges have free time?" he asked with just a hint of sarcasm.

"Well, it's like this, Uncle Benny. I didn't leave to do laundry. I left for good. So did my sheet and my laundry. Actually we all sorta escaped."

He paused to take in the facts. "You *escaped* the frats? Were they hazing you?" He seemed in protectionist mode.

"A few times, yeah. First week it was just some broken beer bottles and glass in my hair. Then they kept me up too late and I couldn't study, and then I was tired every day. But then I met this girl at a party, and she could tell I didn't belong in that frat. So she came up with a plan, and we climbed out on the roof with all my stuff wadded in a sheet during a frat dance. You'd have loved it, Uncle Benny. I escaped during the party, while 'Thriller' was playing and the brothers were dancing like uncoordinated mummies."

He chuckled and said, "Gotta love the college years, Kyle."

I yawned my agreement. "Um, so why'd you call me again? I forget."

"Because your dad has been sending less money to your mama, and so your mama is short on funds. So I thought we'd make her day by selling half of that silver I got buried. The price has risen lately, and I'm tired of playing Wild Wild West with it."

He's gonna ask me to go help him dig in the dirt again? I was so glad that I had scholarship help; otherwise I might be digging for tuition as well. "Are you wanting me to help dig? Today? I had a late night last night, Uncle Benny."

Short pause. "We'll share the digging. And don't tell anyone else in the family about this. Can you meet me after lunch?"

I deflected his questions with my own question. "You're heading to that same place?"

Another pause. "Yep. Wanna meet me there, say, 1:30?"

It had been several years since he'd taken me to his barren land, and I had trouble picturing the route, even more trouble picturing me using up my Saturday to go meet him. But perhaps if I helped out he'd be generous again. Like most students, I was short on money. "How far is Anson from Lubbock?"

"Just a hundred miles or so. The Toyota should make that with no problem."

When I left for Texas Tech, I drove out of Fort Worth in an old Toyota Celica, a 1985 model that had more than one hundred eighty thousand miles on it. The car was a gift from Benny. He said Toyotas are good for three hundred thousand miles and that the car should get me through all the road trips I'd need in order to make college memorable. He'd bought for himself a BMW sedan, though mostly he drove his old pickup.

Since he'd given me my car, I figured I should at least go help him. Maybe for an hour. No more than two. "Okay," I said, my tone lacking excitement. "I can meet you."

"Good."

But just then I remembered my date with Gretchen. "Uncle Benny, hold on. I can't meet right after lunch because I'm supposed to eat breakfast at lunch—with Gretchen. She's the girl I told you about, the one who helps dumb freshmen escape the frats. We're meeting in the cafeteria at noon."

Short pause. "Is she flexible on where you dine?"

"Well, she was flexible when she climbed through the window to help me escape the frats, so I guess so. Why?"

"Ask her to eat in the car with you...go ahead and bring her along."

I couldn't believe he'd allow anyone else to see his buried horde and whatever else he'd hidden on his land. "You mean drive her out to Anson with me? You sure?"

"Yeah...but once you get within twenty miles of my land, ask her to wear a blindfold—and don't take it off her until you've parked on the shoulder and walked out into the desert. I'll meet you past the cactus. You do remember how to get to the cactus, don't you? Just past the four boulders?"

"I'll find it, Uncle Benny, but I don't know how Gretchen is gonna react after I tell her she's got to eat breakfast in my car *and* wear a blindfold. What if she misses her mouth...or spills chocolate milk on herself?

"The Toyota is old, Kyle. Won't make any difference. And as for your female friend, if she can't drink chocolate milk from a carton without spilling it on herself, you probably don't want to date her. So, wanna meet?"

"Um, okay." I checked the time and scheduled another two hours of sleep. "We can be there by two-ish."

We hung up, and I went right back to sleep. Two more hours of hard, I-love-Saturday-morning sleep. Then a shower and a fast walk to the cafeteria—I hated being late.

My push through the swinging doors at noon revealed Gretchen standing beside the third table on the left, smiling as if she'd slept well. She held something red and plaid in her hands. Whatever it was, it was folded nicely, in the way women fold things.

"This is for you," she said as I hurried over to greet her. "I found it on sale at the school store. It's flannel and very soft. Plus it's red because you're now an independent Red Raider."

She bought me a new sheet. A brand new red sheet.

No girl had ever given me anything so practical. Stunned, I reached out to accept the gift, confirmed with my ego that plaid was indeed masculine, and hugged Gretchen with appreciation and attraction. "I...don't know what to say."

She seemed nonchalant about it, her reciprocal gesture being only a shrug, followed by a bolt toward the food line. Halfway there she turned and motioned for me to follow. "Just say 'thank you' and come eat breakfast with me, Kyle Mango!"

I sniffed my gift's newness before setting it on the table next to her worn leather purse.

In line behind her, staring at biscuits and sausage patties, I felt even worse now that I had to ask her to eat in my car *and* wear a blindfold, this right after she'd gifted me a red flannel sheet folded nicely.

Food trays bumped in the cafeteria line, and impatient collegians sighed behind us—Gretchen held up the line while she scanned the fare. Finally she snatched two napkins from a holder, dropped one onto my plate, and moved forward, rejecting a chicken biscuit because she claimed she couldn't bring herself to eat any kind of bird. I considered teasing her about her phobia but figured I hadn't known her long enough.

She reached under the glass for a plain biscuit, and my hand followed hers. Our biscuits collided as we withdrew them from their brethren. "Um, Gretchen, I have an idea, a slight change of plans."

"Oh...what's up?" She said this while gazing skeptically at sausage patties.

Now *I* held up the line. The tray behind me bumped mine, which rammed Gretchen's, which rammed the tray of some huge guy ahead of her. He turned and frowned. We smiled meekly.

Seconds later I forced a brain dump right there in front of the grits, telling Gretchen all about my nutty uncle, about my mom not getting monies from my deadbeat dad, how Uncle Benny and I wanted to surprise Mom with a gift, and this plan required that Gretchen and I leave the cafeteria, drive toward Abilene, and unearth the gift from desert soil.

I expected Gretchen to ask me to be more specific, but instead she focused on logistics. "Kyle, isn't Abilene over a hundred miles from here?"

I motioned for her to move forward in line. "Yes. But we're not quite going to Abilene. I can't tell you exactly where we're going because that would spoil the surprise."

Gretchen smiled a reserved smile, reached back for a second biscuit, and filled it with a fried egg. I didn't bother to ask her why she ate egg but not chicken; it just didn't seem important at the time. Then she poured honey inside her first biscuit and moseyed ahead. She bided time well, as well as anyone I'd ever met. Near the end of the food line she turned to me, her tray a barrier between us.

"So," she said, "I guess I should get my biscuits to go?"

I reached for a sausage patty and set it on my tray. "And your orange juice as well. Do you mind going? Mind at all?"

Gretchen turned ninety degrees and peered out the long windows on the far side of the cafeteria. "It's a pretty day for a drive." She turned to me. "Mind if I eat in your car?"

Now I really, *really* liked this woman. A check of my watch pressed me to hurry, and I asked the cashier for a to-go bag.

While filling it I said to Gretchen, "We have only two hours to get there."

But Gretchen no longer stood beside me; she'd already hustled over to the table to collect her purse and my new flannel sheet, still folded nicely.

In West Texas, covering a hundred fifty miles in two hours is not too difficult. Straight highways and lack of police would make even the most stringent law abider press the pedal. And I pressed it good.

Windows down, Gretchen and I ate our biscuits and chased them with orange juice. Crumbs fell in our laps and in the seats, but we didn't bother to swipe them. Between bites we talked about our professors and speculated if they had ever lived in the real world or if they'd spent their entire adult lives cocooned in academia.

Gretchen told me that one of her art professors seemed well-versed in the real world, simply because "he spent a year lobbying Congress to protect the Texas ecosystem from the life-destroying agenda of Transocean, Inc., the world's largest driller of undersea oil wells."

I had no idea that a big ol' state like Texas had a fragile ecosystem. Fragile and Texas just didn't go together. Before I could comment, however, panic struck as I read a road sign—Anson, 19 miles.

Gretchen had her nose to the window, sniffing the air and gazing across the plains.

"Um, Gretch…by the way, is it okay if sometimes I call you 'Gretch'?"

"No," she said, still admiring the terrain and not bothering to look my way. "It sounds too much like 'Grinch.'"

"Sure…Um, I have a request of you."

She sensed my seriousness, turned toward me, and placed her hands in her lap, a kind of okay-let's-hear-it pose. "Go ahead. Make your request."

"Can you hold your eyes shut for nineteen miles?"

She thought on this for several seconds, then shook her head no. "Can't do it. I'm not disciplined enough."

The blindfold I'd brought along was not a particularly nice one. Before I walked to the cafeteria for breakfast I had used Chang's scissors—he kept every necessity of life in his top drawer—to cut the bottom four inches off a navy T-shirt.

Thus supplied, I steered one-handed toward Anson and pulled the long strip of cloth from my back pocket. Then I extended it, dangling, toward my confused and pretty passenger.

"What is *that* for?" she asked.

"Can you tie this around your head, Gretchen? Please? I would tie it for you but I have to drive the car."

She stared at the cotton strip as if it were a rotted fish.

"Kyle," she said and moved as far away from me as her door would allow, "I've only known you for a week, and now this little road trip is getting kinda weird. You need to know that I'm not a *weird* kind of girl…unless of course it comes to helping frustrated pledges escape their oppressors."

I set the cloth on the console and kept driving. The next sign whirred past—Anson, 16 miles.

I spoke faster. "Gretchen, it's like this. My uncle is very protective of a certain parcel of land that he owns. On this land he has buried some *stuff,* and he simply doesn't want anyone but me to know the whereabouts. But he wants to meet you because I told him you were cool, and I promise after we walk out to the site you can remove the blindfold."

She remained silent, twitching her lips and tapping her fingers on her knees. "You're sure this is nothing weird?"

I raised my right hand. "Scout's honor."

"Were you a Scout?"

"No, but I still have honor."

Without further comment or further question, she reached for the strip of cloth and looped it behind her head. "Okay, but you have to escort me by the arm when we walk. I don't want to trip."

"Consider yourself escorted."

She tied on the blindfold and sat all ladylike, as if she'd behave like the perfect hostage.

Per Uncle Benny's instructions I turned onto the two-lane highway and followed it north for eleven miles. Soon his old pickup came into view, parked on the left shoulder, beyond it the dry soil, a few cactus, Uncle Benny himself nowhere in sight, having already trekked out to his secret spot.

I parked behind his pickup and hustled around the Toyota to help Gretchen out of the passenger seat. She extended her arms like a mummy and waited for me to guide her. "I shall follow thee, Captain Kyle," she said as I led her around the front bumper.

She took my arm in hers, and we half stepped, half slid down a shallow embankment until we reached flat ground. The terrain was nothing but flatland from that point, just random rocks and sprigs of withered grass dotting the landscape.

For the first couple minutes she walked carefully, clutching my arm but remaining silent. Then, at about the time I felt the sun trying to burn the back of my neck, she adjusted her blind-fold. I steered her around a small cactus.

The trek across the plain kept us sweaty and anticipating—me about this budding relationship, Gretchen about discovering the object of our quest.

Twice she stumbled across stones, and twice I caught her, but in so doing I lost track of my target and veered east of our intended path. Soon, however, I spotted the bigger cactus to our left, the tall ones and the wide ones, beyond them a line of four boulders.

"This way," I said and tugged on her arm.

"Are you sure this isn't something weird?"

"I'm sure, Grinch."

Past the boulders I spotted Uncle Benny's derriere, actually his jeans covering his derriere—he'd assumed a digging position and was whistling an old Hank Williams song.

Uncle Benny stepped on the shovel, pressed it into the soil, and deposited the dirt behind him. The pile was already higher than his knees, and he went at his task with a stiff-lipped determination.

In the distance, what looked like four giant iron grasshoppers pecked at the ground, their heads moving slowly up, then slowly down. Land-based oil wells were common in these parts of Texas, though I had no idea if they were on my uncle's property or if they belonged to someone else. I hadn't been out here in more than two years, however, and had never asked him if he'd developed anything on his land. I figured he just used his property to bury things.

Uncle Benny didn't hear us approach, and from some thirty feet behind him I stopped and watched him expand his hole.

He lifted out yet another big shovelful of dirt and strained to sling the contents behind him.

Finally I said, "So you're digging up the same box you showed me when I was in high school?"

Without turning around or pausing from his work he said, "'Bout time you got here, Kyle."

Gretchen squeezed my arm twice, what I took as her signal to introduce her. So I placed a hand on her shoulder and turned her toward my dirt-sprinkled relative. "Um...Uncle Benny, this is Gretchen."

She smiled beneath the blindfold, its top half moist from sweat. "Hi, y'all."

"Pleased to meet you," Benny said and wiped his brow with the back of his hand—which left a dirt streak on his forehead. "You can take that cloth off your eyes now, miss."

I untied the blindfold and Gretchen squinted hard, as much from the sun as her desire to see clearly who stood before her, the man with the salesman hair and big shovel. "Whoa," she said, turning to scan our whereabouts. "This really is the middle of nowhere."

Uncle Benny briefly shook her hand and returned to his digging.

Gretchen, apparently wanting to make conversation, stepped closer to the hole and peered down inside. "Don't they have *machines* to dig holes now? You look awfully hot."

Uncle Benny flipped another shovelful behind him. "Didn't want the attention. This is where I buried some—" He almost didn't say it, but he did anyway. "Where I buried some...some money—silver dollars and stuff."

Undeterred, Gretchen peered down in the hole a third time.

"Why don't you just keep it in a bank like a normal person, like maybe in a vault or a safe deposit box?"

"'Cause if the banks closed due to a terrorist attack, I couldn't get to it."

"Ah."

My uncle went on to explain to us that everyone ought to have a hidden stash or two and that he'd recently thought up a new hiding place he called "the PVC pipe method." According to Uncle Benny, you buy a three-foot section of two-inch wide PVC pipe, plus two end caps. You put one cap on the two-inch pipe, fill the pipe with silver dollars, gold coins, whatever you have, then install the other cap. Then you stick the pipe vertically beneath your bathroom sink, so it looks like a drain pipe. "Now I ask you, Kyle and Gretchen, what terrorist is gonna think to look under a sink, behind some nasty bottles of Comet and Drano to search for hidden money?"

He had a point.

"You got a point, Uncle Benny."

Gretchen nodded. "Clever…but I'd still use a safe deposit box."

Just like the first time he'd brought me here, Uncle Benny grew tired from his rapid shoveling. After two more wipes of his face, he halted progress and held out the shovel to me. "Wanna give it a go, Kyle?"

"Sure." I flexed my below average biceps to Gretchen—who by now looked skeptical of my whole family—and switched places with my uncle.

He let me dig for several minutes, and I dug hard. Twice I lost concentration from glancing up at Gretchen, and in my haste showered Benny's pant leg with dirt. The dirt didn't seem as hard-packed as before, loose even, and after a few more minutes of shoveling, I hit something hard. I set the shovel aside

and together with Uncle Benny reached in and gripped the burlap beneath two exposed corners.

The box felt heavy, just as it had years earlier, and even
Gretchen knelt and helped pull it up out of the hole. "Cool
box," she said as she yanked the outer burlap away. "Like something from a century ago."

"Wanna do the honors, Kyle?" Uncle Benny said to me. He
moved around to where his shadow wouldn't cover the box,
and I kneeled to raise the lid.

Before I raised it, I turned to Gretchen and said, "Get a load
of this stuff!"

Like a game show host revealing a big prize, I lifted the lid
slowly and with great anticipation.

Perhaps my gasp wasn't audible, but it was definitely a gasp.

Uncle Benny's gasp was definitely audible.

Stunned, I peered inside at nothing but ugly rocks, a grape
soda can, and a piece of plain white stationery, scrawled with a
hurried handwriting.

Uncle Benny's face turned red, his widening eyes proclaiming the first signs of shock.

Gretchen stood over us in silence, hands clasped in front of
her. She appeared very, very confused.

"Someone left a note," I said but got no reply. I remained
on my knees, unsure of what to do—and then Uncle Benny's
shadow moved across me.

He stooped to inspect the box more closely, but he only
stooped halfway. He seemed unable to move any farther. He
just stared and blinked and stared and blinked.

There in the dirt, beside his big box of rocks, I felt his pain,
and all I could think to do was hold the note out before him,
allowing him and Gretchen to read along with me:

I'm trading you these rocks and my empty can of Fanta Grape soda for all your silver. Pleasure doing business with ya!

   Sincerely,

   Bullion Betty

For a long time no one said anything. We just kept reading the note over and over.

"This is bad?" Gretchen asked in a voice overflowing with innocence and concern.

I nodded. Uncle Benny said nothing; he just turned to face the sun, then leaned down and picked up three dirt clods.

Gretchen sensed an extreme reaction coming, so she hurried around him and knelt beside me, one hand on my shoulder, the other tucked in her jean pocket. *Maybe she sees me as her protector, though I'm not anticipating violence.*

White-knuckled and seething, Uncle Benny crushed the dirt clods in his hands. He turned south and seethed, he turned west and seethed, then seething turned to squeezing as he lifted the dirt clods to shoulder level and squeezed the life from them, showers of grains falling between his fingers. For long minutes he alternately picked up more clods, stood erect, and crushed them.

Finally he faced the blue sky and let out a yell worthy of a man disemboweled. Nothing intelligible came from his mouth, just the kind of frustrated yell you'd expect from a man whose silver got stolen.

After a long minute to gather himself, Uncle Benny turned to Gretchen and said, "Sorry, miss, I'm usually not the emotional type."

Gretchen still appeared fearful. Her grip tightened on my shoulder. "That's...okay."

Just then I remembered the silver dollars and the ten-ounce silver bar Uncle Benny had given me upon my first visit here. I had not buried them on the Texas Tech campus, nor anywhere else. Those I kept on my nightstand, a kind of reminder to think about my eccentric uncle from time to time and to compare his life strategies with the rest of the world's.

Today, I suppose the world had won.

For a moment I considered offering the gifts back to him, a kind of consolation. But I figured he'd just turn me down and call it a pittance. Finally I decided the thing to do was to sell my small hoard of precious metals and send the money home to Mom. Like most collegians, I had hoped the flow of funds would come *to* me instead of *from* me, but then most of my experiences at Tech were at odds with normalcy.

In an effort to lessen Uncle Benny's pain, Gretchen and I reburied the box of rocks, though we didn't put a whole lot of effort into our labors and failed to cover the box completely. Uncle Benny stomped off some fifty yards away, farther into the middle of nowhere. He faced the distant oil wells, all four of them still pumping up down, up down. After a minute or so, my uncle kicked a small boulder, though not hard enough to injure his foot. Then he strode past us, heading back to his vehicle on the side of the highway. "Time to go, y'all."

He set off across his acreage toward the highway, hands in pockets, pounding his feet as he went, pounding them like a disappointed kid, as if he wanted all of China to feel the vibrations and sympathize with his loss.

"Guess I should put my blindfold back on now," Gretchen said and pulled the cloth from her pocket and looped it around her head.

I tied it for her, though I felt bad about it and immediately untied the knot and stuffed the cloth back in my pocket. "Don't worry about it. He's in such a bad mood now over the thief that—"

"It's okay, Kyle. Just give me your arm and I'll keep my eyes shut."

After letting Uncle Benny get a good head start, Gretchen and I hurried to catch up. She stayed silent, in the way people are when they find themselves amid another family's dysfunction. Soon we fell in beside Uncle Benny, and on the long walk back to the highway he spoke again. "Still got my pool business, Kyle."

Stride for stride between him and Gretchen, I nodded to affirm him. "Yeah…still got that. I just hope you catch this Bullion Betty and—"

He stopped there in the middle of his barren land and pointed a finger at my chest. With random pokes that stopped inches short of my shirt, he said in a slow, deliberate tone, "Do…*not*…mention…her…name…to me again!"

I wasn't entirely sure what to think of my uncle now. It was as if he'd grown a little too cozy with his possessions, like it was family or something. Maybe even religion. If I ever went missing, I hoped my family would miss me as much as Uncle Benny missed his Wild West money.

Gretchen and I dropped back and walked a few steps behind him again, and as we neared the vehicles and the dirt embankment she whispered into my ear, "Maybe he really should get a safe deposit box."

I helped her up the embankment and over to the Toyota, where she leaned against the hood and told me I had an interesting family.

I almost said bye to my uncle right then and drove back to campus. But he did something that kept me there.

On the shoulder of the highway, before we climbed into our respective vehicles and headed opposite directions, Benny walked a good ways in front of his pickup and began searching the ground. I figured he was looking for tire tracks—and I was right.

Head down and scanning the dirt, he motioned for me to hurry over. I took Gretchen by the hand, and when we arrived in front of his truck Uncle Benny stooped and touched fresh tire tracks with his index finger.

"These are wide, sports car tracks," he said to no one in particular.

I gave the dirt a once-over. "Yep, they look like Goodyears to me."

"Definitely Goodyears," said Gretchen, who sounded quite sure of herself and pulled loose strands of hair from her face.

"Goodyears for sure," said Uncle Benny, and with this he stood and looked east and west down the empty highway. "These are the stock tires on a Corvette. How many Corvettes you see in Lubbock every week, Kyle?"

This seemed an odd question, but Benny was still mad and I figured he wanted a quick answer. "Forty or more, I'd say. Maybe fifty."

Hands on hips now, staring over my shoulder, he said, "And what percentage of those Corvettes are driven by men, Gretchen?"

Surprised that he'd asked her, she thought hard on her answer and did the best she could. "Most of 'em, I'd say. Probably eighty or ninety percent."

Still red-faced and drenched in sweat, Uncle Benny nodded like she'd said just what he wanted to hear. "So, there's a good chance that the note in the box was a total lie, that the thief who signed 'Bullion Betty' is really a man, maybe Bullion *Bobby* or, or…Bullion *Bo*."

I wiped the sweat from my eyes and gave him a thumbs-up. "You're on to something, Uncle Benny. Good thinking."

I only said that to massage his ego. I certainly didn't want to rile him up or be disagreeable, have him take back the keys to the Toyota and leave me and Gretchen on the side of the road, trying to hitchhike back to Lubbock in the heat.

He offered no reply as he lumbered back to his pickup and climbed into the driver's seat. But suddenly he started coughing badly into his right fist, then into his left. The window was down, so I went over and gripped the roof, peering in but not too hard.

"You okay, Uncle? Inhaled some dust?"

The coughing ceased, but his face stayed red. He stared out the windshield, and when he coughed again I couldn't think of what else to say to cheer him up. Things got so uncomfortable there at his pickup—I just wanted him to talk, but he wouldn't—that I figured I should be a man and take the lead.

"Bullion *Billy*," I said and watched him for a reaction. Then I realized he didn't hear me at all.

"What?" Benny shot back, like he'd been in another world.

"Bullion *Billy*," I repeated.

Gretchen squeezed in beside me and stuck her head in the open window. A gust of wind blew her hair across her face, and she pulled at the strands. "It's another name possibility," she said to my uncle. "A criminal name…sorta like Billy the Kid."

Uncle Benny shook his head, slowly and with great frustration. "Just hush, y'all," he said to his steering wheel and coughed a third time. "Just hush for now."

When he drove away I wondered why he didn't make the trip in his BMW, but I figured a pickup parked on the shoulder of a remote Texas highway looked more common, that he must not want to draw attention to himself.

I opened the passenger door of my old Celica, and Gretchen sat dutifully in the seat but held the door open. "Your uncle seems really frustrated," she said. "He had a lot of silver in that hole, huh?"

"Yeah, lots. Probably over a hundred pounds of it."

Halfway home — we hadn't talked much, having spent the miles thinking about the thief — Gretchen speculated if Uncle Benny might become a vigilante. "Think he'll track down Bullion Betty and shoot her?"

"Who knows? But at least he meant well. He was going to sell his silver and give the money to my mother."

During our last phone chat, my mother reiterated to me that she was resourceful enough to find work and was not one to sulk — for very long, anyway. I wished I had more to give her; I knew she much preferred to be a stay-at-home mom.

The miles rolled by against a dry and stagnant terrain, and in the renewed silence of my car I figured I'd blown my chance with Gretchen. *What an awful first date.*

She'd been quite the trouper all day, however, and I felt terrible about making her wear the blindfold on the earlier drive.

Minutes later I turned off the highway onto the interstate and headed west toward Lubbock. Gretchen stared out her window, stoic for a while before finally speaking to the flat horizon. "Ya know, Kyle, my own family invests in mutual funds at Charles Schwab."

Chang had spent his entire Saturday studying physics and statistics in our dorm room. After an hour buried in a civil engineering book I suggested that he join Gretchen and me for dinner in the cafeteria. I believe he suspected that I didn't want him around, that he was just a third wheel, but that was not the case; I wanted to get to know my new roommate. And besides, all three of us had to eat, and we all dined daily in the same cafeteria.

In line behind Gretchen but ahead of Chang, I asked how often he put down the books to attend social events. Chang reached for meat loaf and said, "Rarely. So far I've found little correlation between beer kegs and success in the world economy."

He seemed a nice enough guy, just focused on his education. By the time we'd both reached for a strawberry Jell-O, he'd assured me that over the course of the year we'd find some shared fun and adventure, that he would not become the library-only student who missed out on the lighter side of the collegiate experience.

Nevertheless, as soon as he finished his meat loaf and Jell-O, off he went to study for a statistics test. "Numbers upon numbers, swirling in my head," he said over his tray.

Gretchen smiled up at him. "I may need your help next semester."

"Oh...yes, of course."

We carried our trays to the conveyor and sent them off on the slow train to cleanliness.

"Got any plans?" I asked her.

Gretchen shook her head, then pointed to the glass door to our left. A red poster on the door advertised a student-made film, complete with a monstrous duo facing off like Godzilla versus King Kong. Only the names had changed: *Earth Destroyer versus Corporate Crusher.*

"Want to?" Gretchen asked. "It's free."

"I'm all for free."

The film was a collaborative effort between the Drama Club and a group called ECSGE — Environmentally Conscious Students for a Greener Earth. Apparently only two students collaborated — a pair of sophomores dressed up in costumes: Corporate Crusher in green, Earth Destroyer in red, with dollar signs drawn over the costume in black magic marker. All the two did for the whole hour of the film was run up and down the bleachers of the Texas Tech football stadium, thrashing each other with light sabers and yelling insults.

The film was so dumb it was funny. After it ended — the credits thanked everyone from the producer of *Star Wars* to the volunteers at Greenpeace to the band Green Day — Gretchen greeted in the aisle two girls from her art class. The tall one wore a name tag that read Regina; the shorter one wore no name tag. All I knew was that I had never heard three females talk that fast on so many subjects — in the span of one minute they covered their social lives, impressionist art, and the bright red outfit of Earth Destroyer.

Before I knew it, the root word of their chat became *destroy,* and when the conversation switched to large corporations destroying Planet Earth, I just rolled my eyes and told Gretchen I'd call her the next day.

But she pulled me in and introduced me to her friends, who for reasons I could not understand seemed wary of me. I felt uncomfortable around them, and soon Gretchen and I parted with a hug and a wave. "Thanks, Kyle," she said over her shoulder, "for the interesting tour of your family's land today."

I left the drama building alone, which was not how I had envisioned the balance of the evening. The way Gretchen emphasized *interesting* made me wonder if she'd taken offense over the blindfold issue and if today's bad date was simply circumstantial or the sign of a mismatch.

Optimistic, I walked past the humanities building toward the dorm, imagining the two of us crashing another Greek party, eating their buffet food, and dancing to their retro music. We could never go back to the Sigmas, however, as that would surely lead to my death — or at least a maiming.

I returned to an empty but tidy dorm room and figured Chang must still be studying in the library.

Studying held no appeal for me on a Saturday night — and I certainly didn't feel like going to bed yet — so I picked up the phone and called Uncle Benny. He followed the early months of the Iraq war pretty closely, and when he said "Hello?" I asked his opinion on the war and if he thought we'd fire more cruise missiles at Baghdad.

He paused as if preparing a long-winded answer but then said he might join the military himself just to shoot cruise missiles at Bullion Betty, who probably drove a Corvette.

Then that cough again, that awful, deep cough.

"You been to see a doctor yet?" I asked.

"Not yet," he said. "But I will. I promise I will."

Uncle Benny didn't want to talk much, so I told him to take care of that cough, that I hoped his stolen silver would turn up somewhere, and that I'd be on the lookout for Corvettes with Goodyear tires.

Uncle Benny said it had been a long day, that his throat hurt and he just wanted to go to bed.

I still didn't want to go to bed, so after we hung up I called my mom in Fort Worth.

"Did you have a visitor today?" I inquired.

To my surprise, Mom giggled with delight, the first genuine giggle I'd heard from her since Dad left. "Yes," she said, her voice energetic. "Benny came by and…well, he gave me two thousand dollars in cash. Said he wanted to give me a lot more but he'd had a financial setback earlier in the day. I cannot believe his generosity to our family, Kyle."

"I'm glad for you, Mom." Benny told me she'd gotten hired at Dillard's, but she still needed a little boost.

"Thank you. But I'm worried about Benny; he had the worst cough when he stopped by."

"I think he may have inhaled some dust when he dug up the   " *Oops.*

"He what? Your uncle has cash *buried in the ground*?"

"Maybe…I mean he used to. I can't tell you that." I felt the need to change the course of our chat, but Mom did this for me.

"Kyle, do you ever wonder — "

"How Uncle Benny got the money to buy that land? Yeah, sometimes I wonder about that." Though I didn't voice this to Mom, my hunch was that Benny had, at one time, a very good year in pool sales and invested the bulk of his dough in real estate.

Finally my mother thought a similar thought and said, "Maybe he just sells lots of pools and spas."

"Guess so," I concurred. "Gretchen said investing in land is better than investing in mutual funds because you can walk on the land and use it for environmental purposes, like wildlife sanctuaries."

A long, motherly pause. "And just who is this *Gretchen*, Kyle?"

"A friend, Mom. A good friend."

A second motherly pause followed my mention of *good friend*. I expected further questions, but instead she changed the subject. "Benny said you resigned from a fraternity to concentrate on your grades and that you were thrilled with your decision."

"Something like that. Actually the *music* playing when I left was 'Thriller,' and I left because Gretchen helped me escape out a second story window of the frat house. I'll fill you in later."

"Kyle Mango!"

"Sleep well, Mom. And don't spend all your dough in one place. Love you."

"Love you too, Kyle. But I want more details about this Gretchen. She sounds dangerous."

After we hung up I lay back in my bed, atop my new sheet, and wondered if Gretchen was still talking nonstop with her green friends or was she back in her dorm room hoping I'd call. Or perhaps hoping I *wouldn't* call since she'd been humiliated by the blindfold episode and now figured my family was hopelessly odd.

But I didn't see it that way. As my eyelids grew heavy, I saw Gretchen smiling beneath that blindfold, holding my arm in the desert and walking like a mummy, whispering that hanging out with me was just one adventure after another.

I fell asleep but woke up a couple hours later, the dorm light still on. In my groggy state I decided I just had to hear her voice again. So I glanced at my radio and noted the time. 1:12 a.m. *Still early enough to call the girl's dorm.*

She answered on the fourth ring. "Hello?"

"Hey."

"Hey back to you," she said, her voice also a sleepy whisper.

"I had fun today."

"Me too. Sorry about the thief."

"It's okay," I said. "Uncle Benny has lots of surprises."

"Really?"

"I'm not supposed to tell you that."

"Okay. Well, I just hope while he's digging up the earth that he doesn't harm any wildlife habitats."

According to Gretchen, the most heinous crime of the past century was the 1989 Exxon Valdez oil spill. She even told me that she had a poster of an oil-soaked gull on the wall of her dorm room. Even in my groggy state tonight, I knew not to broach that subject.

"Will I see you tomorrow?" I asked.

"Okay. Meet me for breakfast?"

"Sure. Nine-thirty?"

"Yeah. How's your new flannel sheet?"

"Soft, like your hands."

"Hush and go to bed."

THE ASIAN INVESTIGATOR

Chang insisted he could help. Motivated by the two-hundred-dollar reward my uncle had offered to anyone who tracked down Bullion Betty, Chang and I hurried across campus and pulled Gretchen from her dorm room, explaining that the weekend of fall break was a fine time for the three of us to make some easy money.

"Will this in any way involve the use of guns?" Gretchen inquired as she retied her sneakers in the hallway.

"Nope," Chang said, "but the reward is payable *in cash*."

It was after 9:00 p.m. when the three of us piled into my Celica and aimed it for Anson. On the way out of Lubbock we stopped at a Taco Bell drive-through, and for the first few miles after that I endured the warm smells and constant cracking of tacos as Gretchen and Chang ate their meals and told me how good it all tasted.

Minutes later I pulled over on the interstate and switched places with my roommate, so that Chang drove the Celica and Gretchen rode shotgun. I sat in the backseat and devoured my meal like a man deprived.

We'd brought along a pair of shovels from the dorm supply room, shovels that wouldn't fit all the way in the trunk, their handles protruding out the back of the hood, the trunk tied down with wire. I turned and checked on them as Chang pulled onto the interstate, Gretchen informing him that we were headed for a dry and desolate place, a teenage wasteland for an uncle who missed his youth.

Twenty miles short of Anson, Chang drove in strict obedience to posted speed limits. Gretchen slurped her Pepsi and said, "Don't be surprised, Chang, if Kyle asks you to wear a blindfold when we arrive."

Both hands on the wheel, Chang stared ghostlike at the road ahead. "You probably shouldn't date a guy who makes you wear a blindfold."

We parked on the side of the highway at Uncle Benny's land, trekked out to the cactus via flashlight, but found nothing. Despite searching on our knees—Gretchen thought we might find some clothing fibers or even a hairpin—no further evidence arose. Nothing other than the Fanta Grape can that I'd left at the site on my previous visit.

Tonight the only movement was the slow and steady pumping of oil wells far in the distance. Gretchen said the moonlight revealed them as four giant grasshopper heads bobbing in rhythm to a greedy capitalist beat.

"Oh brother," I muttered, toting both shovels over my shoulder and wondering if I were hanging out with a closet liberal. The three of us walked in silence back toward the highway until finally Gretchen decided it was time for some accountability.

"Okay, Kyle," she said in the moonlight, "this makes two trips out here, and two disappointments. I think you should tell your uncle to give it up, rent a safe deposit box, and let you be a normal college student."

"Agreed."

She turned to Chang and said, "Seems to me that two dirt dates means Kyle should take me out for some fine dining. Don't you agree?"

Chang walked along in stride with us and said, "Just don't ask him to cook for you. All Kyle can make is toast. With jam."

Back at the car I set the shovels back into my trunk, Gretchen tying a red rag to their ends while Chang wired the trunk lid to the bumper.

I had just put a last twist in the wire when the headlights of a police cruiser shone over a rise, clicked to bright, and fixated on my Toyota. My initial instinct was to walk around the front of my car, palms out, to show I had nothing to hide.

Gretchen and Chang came around the passenger side and struck similar poses, the three of us side by side at the Celica's front bumper. The officer pulled in just in front of us and got out slowly, eyeing us with typical cop caution.

Gretchen, standing between Chang and myself, held our lone flashlight, its beam pointed at the ground halfway between the officer and ourselves. As the cop approached with his own light, she turned hers off, what I took as an act of submission. I whispered to her. "Good move."

Flashlight waving, the officer perused us one by one with his beam — which was much more powerful than our own. Illumined in cop-light, the three of us remained tight-lipped and attentive, looking as innocent as possible.

The officer stopped some ten feet in front of us and shone his light in Chang's face. "Where're *you* from, son?"

Chang said, "I live in a dorm at Texas Tech University, sir."

The officer frowned. "I mean, where're you *from*?"

I raised my chin and said, "He's from Korea, sir."

"I didn't ask *you*, mister dirty jeans." He turned back to Chang. "Is that right, son? You from Korea?"

"Yes, sir."

"And you're a student?"

Gretchen said, "Straight A's, sir."

Now his light shone in Gretchen's face. "Y'all are quite the interruptive bunch, aren't ya?"

Silence from all.

With his flashlight the officer scanned us twice more—Chang, Gretchen, Kyle, then Kyle, Gretchen, Chang. "Does anyone here ever answer the question directed solely at him or her?"

Three quick nods.

He waved his light across Gretchen's pursed lips. "You're a student too?"

She nodded. "Mostly A's, sir. A few B's."

"I didn't ask about *grades*, people. I wanna know what you're doing out on this barren land at midnight...with shovels?"

More silence.

"Those are shovels sticking out of the back of that Toyota, are they not?"

"Those are shovels, sir," Gretchen said.

"Shovels indeed, sir," I added.

Chang cleared his throat. "Borrowed from the dorm supply room, sir."

The officer shone his flashlight at the rear of the car and the red rags hanging limp from the shovel handles. In unison the three of us turned to look.

Then, in a moment of boldness, I stepped in front of the others and attempted to explain. "Sir, my uncle owns this land, and recently someone dug up and stole something he'd buried out there. They took his valuables and left him with only a box of rocks and an empty soft drink can."

Chang pulled the crushed can from his back pocket and held it up in the officer's flashlight beam. "See, sir. Fanta Grape…just like Kyle said."

Gretchen snorted and put her hand over her mouth.

The cop shook his head and frowned. "So, what you're saying is that you three are playing vigilante for your uncle who got his valuables stolen?"

"Something like that, sir," I said. "Though we're more like amateur investigators."

"Nonviolent investigators, sir," Gretchen added. "I'm not into violence, especially violence against the environment…or birds."

Chang, in an obvious effort to change the subject, raised his hand in the moonlight. "Sir, I am not sure of the meaning of that word, 'vigilante.' Does that mean 'someone who digs with shovels'?"

The cop laughed and turned off his flashlight. Then he walked back to his squad car and said something into his police radio. After a couple minutes he waved us on. "Y'all get back to campus, kids. And *no*, Mr. Korea, 'vigilante' does not mean 'he who digs with shovels.'"

Gretchen whispered the meaning in Chang's ear, and he smiled and waved okay to the officer. Then Chang whispered, "You both know I was just playing dumb, don't you?"

"We were hoping so, Chang, given your grades."

The cop started his engine and peeled out of the dirt and onto the highway. We waved, but he didn't wave back.

Gretchen shouted at the cop car as it sped hastily away.

"That's totally unnecessary! Wasted gas, and another waste of taxpayer money!"

I drove us out of Anson and turned us on the main highway back toward Lubbock, Chang leaning up from the backseat to hand Gretchen a CD. "Can we listen to this one?"

"*George Strait?*" Gretchen asked, feigning shock.

"I want to broaden my taste of Texas."

After a dozen George Strait songs and two drives around campus, it became evident that all good parking places were taken. So I parked in the graveled overflow lot and told Chang I'd see him later, that I was walking Gretchen back to her dorm. He hurried off, saying over his shoulder that since he hadn't solved the crime and earned the cash reward, he had to call home in Seoul and have some funds wired to his account. "My family is not rich," he said as we parted.

"At least they're not weird like Kyle's," Gretchen said to him.

He turned and nodded. "True, dat."

In the lobby of her dorm, Gretchen wiped a speck of dirt from my cheek and replaced it with a small kiss.

"Meet for breakfast tomorrow?" she asked. "At nine?"

I checked my watch and saw 2:15 a.m. "Make it nine thirty."

That next breakfast went fine—I thought the two of us were doing great—but the following Thursday Gretchen broke things off with me, explaining there in the cafeteria that the pressures of college were too much for her to give proper time to our relationship, that she was a bit worried that I came from a Texas mob family, and besides all that, she was rehearsing five days a week with the Drama Club. They were making a sequel to the very dumb movie, and somehow Gretchen had landed the role of Corporate Crusher.

"I'll try to get you and Chang some front row seats," were her last words to me as she hurried out of the cafeteria and across campus to rehearsals.

The hurt lingered for weeks. I lost myself in civil engineering studies, spending long hours in the library with Chang and dozens of other grade-chasers, all of us sacrificing chunks of social life for the bookish joys of nerddom.

I tried meeting other girls. Even on a long road trip to College Station, Texas, in early November to see Texas Tech play Texas A&M in a football showdown, I tried. But it was as if I had Mr. Not-Quite-Right tattooed on my forehead.

I made the long trip with Chang and two other dorm buddies. We parked on the outskirts of campus and walked toward the stadium, knowing we were in enemy territory—although A&M fans were known to be among the most hospitable in the nation. Past tailgaters clad in maroon and white, I spotted a car that had broken down, a Dodge Neon, it too maroon. Out of the car scrambled a Texas A&M coed. She opened the hood and peered inside, her T-shirt boasting the Aggie mascot. I felt sorry for her, there among all those fans and no one yet volunteering to help her. So I told Chang and the other guys to go ahead, that I'd catch up to them in the stadium, and walked over and volunteered to help the young lady.

"Howdy," I said, approaching from the front. "I usually don't assist the enemy."

She shook her head as if her car disappointed her with regularity. "I don't know what happened," she said and checked the oil stick. "It just died."

Suffice it to say that the issue was only a loose battery cable. After I tightened it for her and we discovered that we were both freshmen, I tried my best to get her phone number. I already had her name — Dana — because it was screen-printed on the back of her T-shirt. After that, all I got was a handshake, plus something not entirely unexpected. She shut the hood of her car, turned and thrust her thumb in the air, and said, "Gig 'em, Aggies!"

And that was that. Four hours later those Aggies had smoked our Red Raiders, 33–15, and I was 0 for 3 in trying to meet girls in the bleachers.

But my grades were good, and I felt certain that someday they would translate into a fine job, which would translate into providing a fine life, which would in turn attract a fine woman. Such thoughts, while optimistic on the surface, turned out to be only a pacifier.

Truth was, I missed Gretchen terribly. Already in my head I could see us married with three kids, the oldest a boy, and him at age thirteen sitting on our sofa, listening to me, the loyal father, give him *the talk*.

SENIOR YEAR

"Uncle Benny has tumors."

My mother spoke those words to me on a Friday afternoon, calling me from her job in Dillard's lingerie department as I lay in my dorm room recovering from a week of classes. Her words stunned me into a numbness of thought; I didn't hear what she said thereafter. Something about, "visit as soon as you can" or "as often as you are able." As soon as we ended the call, someone knocked on my door, and for a moment I wondered how sympathy could find me so quickly.

But then a blunt male voice invited "whoever lives in this dorm room" to join an intramural softball league, that they needed outfielders, preferably ones with strong throwing arms. I didn't answer the guy at all, just stayed there on my bed. The guy moved on to the next room and knocked again.

Saturday morning I left campus early for the drive to a hospital in Fort Worth. I drove with the windows down, wondering how many times I'd get to visit my uncle-pseudo-dad. En route I wished the roads out of Lubbock were hillier and held lots of curves, if only to demand more of my attention. Flat Texas highways tend to magnify loss, since all you do is hold the steering wheel straight and think about your loved one.

Mostly what I thought about was his generosity. Uncle Benny had mailed me eighty bucks every month since the beginning of my junior year in college, saying I'd make better grades if I didn't have to work to earn spending money. Apparently he'd sold lots of pools and spas before he got sick. I supposed that the majority of those revenues now went toward his medical bills.

At his bedside I sat on the edge of a chair and leaned close, since he talked in whispers due to his sickness. He asked about my brother and sister, about mom, and I assured him they were fine and that I'd do my best to look out for them.

He nodded slowly, as if even that small gesture brought pain. But then his right hand reached over the rail and found my left. He squeezed my fingers, and in a raspy whisper said, "You may have to track down our silver thief by yourself, Kyle....I don't think I'll have the stamina for it."

My instinct was to avoid discussing anything that dealt with his work or his possessions. I preferred to tell him that I appreciated all he'd done for me, that the old Celica still ran great, and that after graduation, when I landed a good job, I hoped to give the car to my little brother. But if Uncle Benny wanted me to play detective for him, then I reckoned I should oblige. "You want me to call the police if I find out who stole from you?"

He nodded; then he thought further about it and shook his head no. "Whatever happened to that girl you brought out to my land that day?"

"Gretchen? She acts in student theater and stays busy with an animal rights group. I see her around campus sometimes."

He nodded again, this time slowly, with more strain in the effort "But you and her aren't..." He made a swirling motion with his hand.

I kneeled at his bedside and smiled. "Nah, we're not. But she's invited me to a couple of her plays this year."

"But do you…" Again he made the swirling motion.

"Yeah, Uncle Benny.…I still like her."

He closed his eyes for a while and appeared to fight pain. After a time he said, "Don't tell anyone this, Kyle, but I sorta made some bad—"

I patted his hand. "Bad what, Uncle Benny?"

He motioned to his throat, as if it hurt too much to talk. He then pointed at the nightstand, to a scratch pad that lay beside his water cup.

I handed him the scratch pad and a pen. He wrote as slowly as he'd talked. It took him forever to complete his thoughts, but after a good ten minutes of starting and stopping, he finished and I watched him sign the note "Love, Uncle Benny."

> *Kyle,*
>
> *I am now of the opinion that I managed my finances quite poorly. I fell in with the wrong crowd, and some of my behavior no doubt disappointed God. But as I've laid here in this bed that smells like antiseptic, I've made my peace with God and confessed to Jesus all I did, and I believe I'll make it to heaven. We'll talk more tomorrow. I would do it now, but I'm tired tonight.*
>
> *Make me proud. Take care of your mom. Be responsible with whatever is entrusted to you.*
>
> *Love,*
>
> *Uncle Benny*

For long minutes my sympathy for him clouded what he'd written. But as he fell asleep, the pen dropped from his fingertips and clacked against the hospital floor. I picked it up and set it back on the stand, but I didn't leave the room just yet. I stayed and asked questions, which felt very odd, as already it felt like questioning a corpse.

"What did you do, Uncle Benny?"

The sheet over his torso rose and fell with each breath.

"You did something to make God mad?" I asked. "Is that what you're saying?"

I counted six seconds between each rise and fall of the sheet.

"Do you think God is mad because you buried some stuff in the desert instead of sharing with poor people? I don't understand. What did you *do*?" I was sure I had made God mad on many occasions. I looked at God kind of like I looked at the rpm gauge on my Toyota—if I felt I'd pushed God too far into the red zone, I feared the consequences, backed off the accelerator, and made an attempt at apology. Sorry, God. Didn't mean to *do* that. Just having a bad day.

Benny slept hard, a labored, purposeful sleep. I held his hand for long minutes and watched him rest. Sometime around 3:00 p.m. I patted his head and told him I'd be back soon. On the way out I bought an overcooked chicken sandwich from the hospital cafeteria and ate it on the walk to the parking lot.

Halfway home I decided that I'd visit Uncle Benny as many weekends as possible, a decision that at once felt very right, but also cloaked in bitterness. Having my first dad leave the family to start a new one in Taos, then my second dad withering away in a hospital room seemed about as unfair as life could get. I'm sure it got even more unfair for some people, but for me this felt like a lot.

It was Monday when I finally came out of my funk. I just decided to keep moving forward, one foot in front of the other, to go to my classes and, if given the opportunity, to honor Uncle Benny in some small way.

That small opportunity presented itself in my elective class — Economics.

I walked into the Economics room and up to the fourth row and chose my usual seat, one of twenty students bemoaning a late-afternoon class. Halfway through the hour, the young, bearded professor assigned us a paper to write, with instructions to describe and trace a twenty-five-year history of a particular class of investment, including the ups and downs of public sentiment.

He paced the front of the class in the manner of more seasoned professors; perhaps he was trying to appear older. Regardless, I liked the guy.

"Choose either stocks, bonds, or real estate," he said and returned to his podium.

After class I asked him if I could choose a commodity like precious metals or oil instead, and when he asked why, I told him I had experience.

He wiped his glasses with a handkerchief, paused, and said okay but that it had better be good. So before I met Chang for dinner in the cafeteria, I stopped by the library and jotted down lots of notes about annual production and consumption of silver, its industrial usage, and included a question to the professor asking if he knew that silver was used in x-rays and that I hoped there was enough of the stuff left for the hospitals to help everyone because three years ago some of the world's silver supply was pilfered by Bullion Betty, who just might drive a Corvette.

The following Wednesday I got a B+ and an "active imagination" comment from the professor.

After class the temporary relief from earning a decent grade faded, as I felt in a funk socially. This feeling was reinforced as I walked past the fountain and looked up to see three brothers from the frat house coming my way. In the hours and days after my escape, I had walked around in fear of their retaliation. But not anymore. Today I envied their camaraderie and wondered if I had missed out on something.

When I passed them, however, they turned their heads and looked the other way, as if I were an outcast unfit for their company.

Thursday night, after observing me in my funk, Chang asked me to accompany him to see some NCAA wrestling matches. I had nowhere else to go, so I said sure. The matches started with the lightest guys — featherweight — and worked their way up toward heavyweight. The smaller guys were very quick and quite strong for their size. Gretchen was there also, watching excitedly from the second row of the adjacent grandstand. She kept cheering for a bantamweight wrestler and even yelling his name, "Go, Mike!" She yelled his name fourteen times. I counted.

"C'mon, Chang," I said even before the last match began. "Let's get out of here."

He wanted to watch the superheavyweight match, however, so I walked across campus alone, back past the library and along the stone path where freshman year I'd dragged my worldly possessions in my sheet while the independent girl who'd helped me flee the frats toted my Cowboys lamp, its cord dragging behind us.

I still had that lamp. It was the girl who'd gone missing.

THE FOLLOWING SATURDAY

He never woke up.

Uncle Benny died in his sleep during the wee hours. We buried him in Fort Worth on a cool and cloudy afternoon. I rode in a limousine with Mom and my brother and my sister, a quiet ride interrupted by tears, a few funny stories from Benny's past, and a resumption of sniffles.

The graveside service passed quickly; the pastor did his best, although it was evident he had little personal knowledge of the deceased. I stood between my mother and fresh dirt and wondered if God meant this moment as a lesson of sorts — to make my life count, to not waste it. There in the tented silence I promised him I would not waste it.

After the closing prayer I noted the attendees — thirty-seven of us. Smaller than what I imagined for myself, though I had never even thought of my own funeral. Cool Trent even showed up to pay his respects, home from Baylor, where he played catcher for the baseball team. We talked for a few minutes, but it was the awkward chat of two former high school buddies who had lost commonality.

Back at Mom's house, distant relatives brought ham, potato salad, and those squishy soft rolls — the obligatory foods of mourning—which we all washed down with the obligatory beverage, sweet tea. We hugged folks we did not know and whispered nice things about Benny. After the leftovers were tucked snuggly into Tupperware and the relatives had left in their family sedans, Mom summoned her three children into the kitchen and said a prayer for Benny, giving thanks for his life with us.

We all muttered an "amen" and, to our credit, waited almost an appropriate period of time before discussing Uncle Benny's will.

All of us knew we were his only family, and all of us sported sad faces as we placed containers of food solemnly in the fridge and freezer.

Mom was brief and to the point. She stood in front of the refrigerator, one hand clutching a ham sandwich, the other Benny's will. One by one she made us leave the kitchen so that she could meet privately with each of her children. She began with the youngest, our sister, Marla, who sounded less concerned with what she might receive than she was about the fact that she, at age thirteen, did not have a will of her own.

"Who'd get my CD collection?" she asked our mother.

"We'd figure that out, Marla," Mom assured her. "Now shut the door to the living room and let's chat."

She shut the door behind them, and their meeting lasted all of thirty seconds.

Next Mom summoned my brother, Philip, who ran like a panting dog to discover what he'd been gifted. His meeting with Mom lasted a full minute.

Marla had returned to the living room and sat on the sofa, as far from me as possible. Her expression toggled between sadness and surprise, and she crossed her legs and bounced the top leg with nervous energy.

"What?" I asked her. "What did you get?"

"Can't tell you," she said. "Mom said not to tell you."

Then it was my turn. I passed my brother as he walked proudly back into the living room. "What'd you get?" I whispered.

He pulled a pair of keys from his pocket and held them high. "Jingle, jingle," was all he said in reply. He sat beside my sister and they both stared at the keys, as if debating their worth in comparison to a generous uncle whom they'd never see again.

I pushed through the door to the kitchen and tried to read my mother's expression, but her expression was blank, her eyes fixed on a paper plate. She ate the last bite of a sandwich, rested her back against the refrigerator door, and said, "Kyle, your brother got Benny's old pickup truck, your sister got what was left of his savings, about a thousand dollars, and I was given that BMW 540 he bought two years ago."

A congratulatory gesture seemed appropriate, so I reached out and shook Mom's hand. "Wow, Mom, that's a nice car."

"Yes." She shook back, but let go quickly and looked at me with the sympathy of a mother forced to relay unfair news. "I'm sorry, Kyle."

I stepped toward her and invaded her personal space. "Sorry about what, Mom? I'm not even sure we should be discussing his will so soon after his funeral. I don't even care if he left me anything. I just miss him...a lot."

She motioned to a knee-high cardboard box in the corner of the kitchen, topped with a couple pairs of shoes, some papers, a few books. "I'm afraid that what Uncle Benny left you is just some of his belongings in that box. But don't worry, honey, if you ever want to borrow the BMW to take some girl out on a nice date, you just ask." Just then her eyes sparkled, and the smile creasing the edge of her mouth told me she knew something that I didn't.

Not in a mood to search the box, I nevertheless excused

myself and toted my bequeathal back into the living room, granting myself permission to go ahead and sort through it all. On the sofa my brother and sister talked in hushed tones, discussing their prizes but never looking up to ask what kind of old stuff lay in the box.

Craving privacy, I carried the box out to Mom's back porch, plopped myself down in her rocking chair, and set the box at my feet.

Inside I found Uncle Benny's sales logs from his pool and spa business, plus mileage books dated all the way back to 1975. I even found an old journal, with one entry that made me sad, others that made me shake my head with amusement.

On page 27: *I'm still ticked at the U.S. over Vietnam. Three of my buddies got shot, and two of them died.*

Page 32: *Buy the new Carpenters album, 'cause the Bay City Rollers are terrible.*

Page 37: *I can't believe I bought a pair of white bell-bottoms. Now I look as ridiculous as everyone else.*

Page 39: *Bought a bunch of old silver dollars today. Not sure what I'll do with them, they just looked pretty, though not as pretty as my wife, Cloe.*

Pressed against the side of the box I also found a legal envelope—with something legal inside. In red magic marker the outside of the envelope said only, *For Kyle.* I opened it carefully and found inside a deed to 842 acres of West Texas desert, situated just west of Anson.

A note attached to the deed surprised me: *And all improvements made to the parcel up until the day of my passing.*

Further digging into the files revealed the extent of said improvements: invoices paid to a drilling company during the past year, covering the costs of drilling forty exploratory well holes, one-tenth of which were labeled as productive.

I, Kyle Mango, twenty-something college student, had apparently inherited four oil wells.

Over the ensuing minutes I rummaged further through the box and also discovered that Benny had kept meticulous records of the wells' output, recording it all in one of those grid-lined mileage books used by traveling salesmen. Instead of miles-driven-per-week, he had penned in barrels-of-oil-sold-per-week. At the end of each month he had averaged the production and compared it—in a hand-drawn chart—to the previous month. For January, his records indicated:

Well #1: Average weekly production of 11 barrels
Well #2: Average weekly production of 13 barrels
Well #3: Average weekly production of 14 barrels
Well #4: Average weekly production of 5 barrels.

Already my business sense burst forth. *C'mon, Well #4! Get with the program!*

Still, even with Well #4's impotence, it didn't take long to figure out that what Uncle Benny had left me—43 barrels a week—far exceeded what the rest of my family received. That evening I bought a newspaper, checked prices, and discovered that barrels of West Texas Crude Oil were going for $67.02 each.

Times 43 barrels per week.

Four weeks per month.

Interesting.

Next I read Benny's papers about the company that picked up the oil for transport to a refiner. I found that they bought the oil for a ten percent discount, which I figured was their own profit margin. Everybody gets a cut; I could go along with that.

I felt a bit guilty though—there on my mom's porch pushing buttons on a calculator while Uncle Benny lay in his grave, the dirt above him barely settled. And yet I felt that my being a responsible beneficiary was what he would have wanted. So now I had responsibility for deciding what to do with $2,593 in income—*per week*. I had friends who'd just graduated with education and business degrees who didn't bring home that much *per month*.

Late that night Mom came out on the porch and found me asleep in the rocking chair, the calculator in my lap. She nudged me awake and said, "Kyle, I know what Benny left you, and I just wanted you to know that I think you're the one person in this family who can handle it. Your brother would spend it all on video games, and your sister would blow it all on shoes at the mall."

Her confidence in me overwhelmed my confidence in myself. "I'll do my best...and I'll share some revenue...but I sure miss Uncle Benny."

After I told her that I would route one week's revenue to her checking account every month, she leaned down and hugged me. Then she smiled the motherly smile of approval and told me to get to bed, that my room was still mine whenever I needed it, and that sleeping in a wooden rocking chair would wither a twenty-two-year-old into a sixty-two-year-old in less than a month.

Sunday at dusk I arrived back on campus and found a parking spot in the big gravel lot—overflow parking. The lot was built like a shallow bowl cut into the earth, where one had to look up out of the bowl to see the campus and surrounding roadsides.

For long minutes I just sat there in my Celica and tried to retrieve that off-at-college feeling. During the past few days I'd lost that feeling and now felt distanced from college life. Now I managed what was in effect a successful small business—and during the four-hour drive back to Lubbock it dawned on me that I no longer needed to worry about landing a job when I graduated. *I have a job. It feels weird to have a job.*

That's when I saw her, above me some hundred yards away—Gretchen in her throwback jeans and Red Raider T-shirt, descending the concrete stairs to the parking lot and toting a laundry basket. Her hair looked longer, though still wavy on the sides. I watched to see if some guy would appear with her, but no, she was alone.

During junior year, I'd tried again to date her. The best that happened was she invited me to two of her drama team performances. After the second one—she'd played a schoolgirl in *Grease*—I had walked her back to her dorm, hinted strongly at dating again, and received a reply that I could only qualify as being based not in the category of negativity but in patience. "Kyle," she said, "I'm just so consumed with school, drama, and environmental awareness that I think it's best if I not date anyone until after college. I'm just not one of those nab-a-guy-by-senior-year kind of girls."

I'd replied with off-the-cuff honesty. "At the rate you're

going, you might not even be one of those nab-a-guy-by-the-Geritol-years kind of girls."

At least I'd made her laugh.

Now here she came, down the sloping sidewalk and into the gravel parking lot, carrying her laundry basket topped off with books and red towels. I had not seen Gretchen around campus for weeks, and now I wondered if she was heading home to Dallas or if she was simply going out to study at a Laundromat, perhaps washing a load of darks while hanging out with her girlfriends.

One hand on my door handle, I debated how I should approach her, and for a moment I even allowed myself to wonder how things would be different now if she actually *was* a nab-a-guy-by-senior-year kind of girl and I had returned to campus after Uncle Benny's funeral and sought her comfort. *I'd run across the lot and up the hill to her dorm because that would be what I always did, and she'd meet me in her doorway and I'd fall into her hug.*

A Gretchen hug engulfed a person; there was nothing shallow or temporal about it.

It felt silly, though, savoring imaginary hugs from this almost girlfriend from freshman year. So I repressed the thought, remembered that I was now a mature senior, and climbed out of my car.

I spoke over its roof. "Hey there, stranger!"

Three cars away, she stopped so suddenly that one of her sneakers slid slightly on the gravel and she nearly dropped her laundry basket. "Kyle! How are you?"

She came toward me, and we both stopped at the rear bumper of a Texas-sized pickup truck, complete with tires taller than our waists.

"I'm good," I said, not even thinking of how shallow that comment sounded. "Well, actually I'm just so-so. My Uncle

Benny passed away last week, and I just got home from the funeral. You remember him, don't you?"

She smiled and set her basket on the gravel. "How could I forget Benny? He asked you to ask me to wear a blindfold when we drove out to dig up that box of rocks. A bit of an eccentric man, but polite. I'm sorry to hear he passed."

"Yeah, well…he's in a better place." Again, I wasn't even thinking. Everyone in the South always says a relative is "in a better place." In reality, I had no idea where Uncle Benny was. "So, how are you? Ready to graduate?"

"Yes!" she said and brushed her hair from her eyes. "And I bet you have a big engineering job already lined up."

"Well, actually, my family…um, I sorta was given four—"

A car rolled past, and we both turned to avoid a dust cloud. Gretchen then fixed her gaze on me and grinned. "Guess what, Kyle?!"

She's gonna tell me she's getting married. I just know it.

I mumbled a weak, "Tell me."

Once again, dead wrong.

"I'm going to Alaska!" she gushed.

"But…" I stammered, realizing that her going to Alaska was only slightly better news than her getting married. "But what about Mike the bantamweight wrestler?"

"Mike? He's just a guy in my art class. We're not together, Kyle."

"Oh." With my left foot I nudged her laundry basket, a brief stall that allowed me to form my thoughts and press my agenda. "So, why are you going to Alaska?…To visit some guy?"

"No, silly. To clean birds!" She was bouncing up and down on her toes excitedly, like she did the night she helped me escape the frat house. "You didn't hear that there's been another oil spill? A girl from my dorm asked me to go with her."

I stalled with questions. "When does your flight leave?"

"We're driving."

"Oh brother."

"The professors are letting us graduate early."

Let the government clean up Alaska, Gretchen. Stay in Lubbock and give me another chance. Please!

With no appropriate reply orbiting my noggin, I said, "That's... really exciting. I know how you've always, um...loved wildlife."

Her grin affirmed my comment. "Yep, can't wait to scrub greedy corporate oil from those innocent birds. I'm even to the point where I detest having to put gas into my car, since gas comes from oil. So...what were you going to tell me that you were given by your family?"

Nerves, blinks, a panic stifled. "Oh, not much. Just a few old things."

We parted with a leaned-over hug across her laundry basket and promised to e-mail over the summer.

I picked up her laundry basket and handed it to her, and when she gripped its sides she also caught my schoolboy gaze and held it there above her folded towels, our eyes locked in the spillover parking lot, and all I could do was memorize her face and store it away until someday.

"Cleaning birds, eh?"

"Lots of them. I'll be there awhile. But promise to keep in touch this summer?"

"Promise."

I walked with her over to her car—an old Civic with rust spots over the back bumper and bumper stickers over the rust spots—where she handed me her keys and I opened the rear hatch for her. She whispered "thanks" and stuffed her laundry inside. One brief wave, a second brief hug, and she was gone.

FOLLOW THE
MONEY TRAIL

As graduation neared and my business prospered and my grades edged downward, the question I had for deceased Uncle Benny was this: If you had those four oil wells gushing to the tune of $10,000 per month, how come you didn't have more in savings? Where had all those monies gone?

The answer did not boom forth from his casket, though it did come from a box—the same old cardboard box in which I'd found the deed to the 842 acres. His checkbook register lay inside a folder, and my perusal of its history revealed a strange pattern of deposits and withdrawals: $9,500 every month, dating back for three months.

Each withdrawal of that amount was entered in the check register as a "cowboy payment."

At first I wondered what kind of expensive cowboy Uncle Benny had hired for rodeo lessons. But a call to the bank proved tangential: Benny had indeed withdrawn $9,500 per month for those three months, and according to the branch manager each withdrawal came with the same request. "Ninety-five one hundred dollar bills, please."

Uncle Benny was paying off a bookie.

Further investigation of his phone records and his journal

confirmed that he'd bet $30,000 on the Dallas Cowboys winning the Super Bowl. The team hadn't even *made it* to the Super Bowl, having lost in the playoffs to the Seahawks. And now I was about to discover that bookies are actually bird dogs disguised as humans. They possess great sniffers and can track down anyone, anywhere — even to a college dorm room.

Chang came stumbling into the room under a load of books and a laptop. He answered the phone on the second ring and held it out across the desk. "It's for you, Kyle."

My earnest hello was not boomeranged back.

"Hello?" I repeated.

The voice said, "I'm Sal. And your uncle owes me money."

"You mean my Uncle Benny?"

"Your uncle owes me money."

"But he died."

Short pause. "So, your uncle passed. Nothin' changes on my end."

"But aren't all debts forgotten when someone dies?"

"With interest he still owes me three grand. I need my three grand…to help poor kids."

"A bookie who helps poor kids. That's nice." Get real, dude.

He sounded confused when he asked, "Do you mean nice sarcastic or nice for real?" At least I had him off the subject of money.

"Some of both," I said.

"Well, I still need my three grand."

"You're saying three payments of nine thousand five hundred each wasn't enough? That's over twenty-eight thousand bucks, Sal. And you still want three thousand more? From my dead uncle?"

"Need my three grand....Don't make me visit room 109 at Texas Tech."

Sal-the-bookie knows where I live?

I figured my best move now was to confront this head-on; from what I knew about these bookie types, they could be ruthless and persistent, violent even. So in a sudden burst of courage, I invited Sal to visit me at Texas Tech the next day.

He accepted with one condition. "No authorities, Mr. Mango. Just yous and me."

He spoke like that, making "you" plural.

The next day he met me beside the fountain at noon, where lots of students were hanging out and eating their lunches. Safer this way, I figured. When he approached he stood out from the collegians not only in age but in wardrobe. Sal sported dark sunglasses, black polyester pants, and a leather jacket that just didn't seem right in hot and dry Lubbock. Image, I reckoned. He stopped and turned in a circle, looking for me. I went over and tapped him on the shoulder.

"You're Sal-the-bookie?" I asked.

He turned, eyed me up and down. "Shhh, kid. We don't need no one overhearin' us." When he removed his shades, his eyes seemed too close together. He looked at any moment as if he might try to sell me a used car.

"At least you're punctual," I said and pointed behind us to the campus fountain, popular and bricked and an easy place on which to lean. "But I still can't believe you'd pursue monies from my poor, deceased Uncle Benny." I overemphasized "poor" and "deceased."

Sal leaned against the wall of the fountain and stared straight ahead, talking out the side of his mouth like some tough guy. "Bring the money?" he asked.

I assumed a similar posture, reached into my shirt pocket, and produced a check.

I folded it in half and handed it to him—while staring straight ahead, of course.

"What's this?" he said, as if disgusted at what I'd given him. "I can't take checks. No self-respecting bookie takes checks."

"I'm not asking you to be self-respecting, Sal. I'm just asking you to accept one check. One single check." His appearance was so amusing I felt safe imposing my view.

He stared at the payment as if it were toxic. "I ain't believing this."

I folded his hand around the check. "Believe it. You see, Sal, I want to clear myself from anything to do with my uncle's debts and to get on with my life. I'm young and healthy and have much better things to do with my time. So, you either take that check or you get nothing at all."

I feared he might produce a gun or otherwise threaten me, but Sal-the-bookie only rubbed his chin, twitched his lip. "All right then. For you, Mango, just this once, I'll take your check. But it better not bounce." He shook a finger at me in warning.

"It won't bounce."

He folded the check and tucked it deep into his shirt pocket. "I gotta help some poor kids. Better not bounce."

"Won't bounce."

He removed the check, looked it over a second time and a third, and tucked it back into his pocket. For a long minute he just watched the students coming and going, almost as if he wished he were one of us, as if he'd missed out on this phase of life and was now reminiscing. "Your uncle, that guy Benny...he wasn't much of a gambler, but he always made his payments on time. He and I used to talk about things, like oil and investments and stuff. I suppose he was a good guy, and I don't say that 'bout many people. I'm sorry for your loss."

I pushed away from the brick wall and stuck my hands in my pockets. "The Mango family appreciates your sympathy, Mister Sal."

"Just call me Sal."

"Okay."

He turned from the fountain and faced me, a curious look on his face, "Say, you ever think of putting any money on the Cowboys? Now that they got that new offense, they might win alotta games this next—"

"I don't gamble, Sal."

He held up his hands, conciliatory. "Okay, okay, can't blame a guy for tryin'." Then, just as I thought he would leave, he pressed again. "Know anyone else who has money and likes to play?"

My instinct was to dismiss him, but across campus I spied the top floor of the Sigmas' frat house—and couldn't resist giving Sal a tip.

"I know a few guys, yeah."

Sal said, "You know some guys, eh? For real?"

"Yeah. They're young, aggressive, got family money, and spend it freely." I pointed in the distance. "See that frat house over in Greek Circle?"

Sal stood on his toes. "Yeah, yeah, I see it. The one with the big S on it."

"Knock on the door and ask how to contact an alumni named Paul. He's got big family money."

Sal smiled and swatted me on the shoulder, his version of a thank-you. He left with the briefest of waves, and I followed at a safe distance—until I hid behind a holly bush and watched him hustle up the stairs to Sigma House and pound on the door.

The following week I received two letters in the mail. The first one arrived from Alaska and contained a picture of two birds on a rocky shore, one covered in oil, the other freshly cleaned. Gretchen herself was in the picture, smiling behind the clean bird, about to go to work on the dirty black one. A stack of white towels lay beside her on the beach. She looked happy and involved, content even.

I turned the picture over to find a note:

Kyle, it's BEAUTIFUL up here. I hope at some point you'll be able to come visit. Better yet, come help clean greedy corporate oil off some innocent birds!

That photo I stuck on my refrigerator, held in place by an Allstate magnet.

The second letter—from a probate attorney—notified me that I needed to sign some papers before the four wells were officially mine. So I drove over and met the attorney—an older fellow with horn-rimmed glasses, a pleasant manner, and red suspenders—a kind of old-school lawyer, I reckoned. After I signed everything, he asked me if I knew much about the responsibilities of owning Texas oil wells.

"Not a whole lot," I said and admired his mahogany desk. "Just a few pointers from my uncle. Things like pipe mainte-nance and only selling oil to reputable refiners."

Red Suspenders nodded in the way people do when you've

just shown your true ignorance of a subject. "Take these with you," he said and pulled two books off an enormous bookshelf. "They'll educate you good."

I thanked him and promised to return his two paperbacks when I finished taking notes.

Back in my dorm room I sat on my bed and flipped through both. The first book was titled *Maintaining Your Wells* and looked to be a self-published book with little regard for punctuation. The second was more hefty and official: *A Primer of Oilwell Drilling,* by the Petroleum Extension Service at the University of Texas. It even contained a foldout oil diagram in the middle, like a children's book, only with an oil well instead of a smiling chimpanzee.

I read this one for two hours. Many pages were smudged, highlighted, and otherwise marred. But this didn't prevent me from learning vernacular, as well as some interesting oil well strategy: When a well's production begins to deplete, drilling even deeper sometimes yields even more oil. Here I applied my own vernacular: Cool. Awesome.

The inside back cover held a surprise: Apparently every oil person who had read the book over the years had signed it and noted their alma mater. I read names from SMU, the University of Texas, Texas A&M, the University of Houston, Baylor, Rice, even the El Paso Tri-State Cosmetology Institute.

So I penned in Kyle Mango, Texas Tech and decided that my education in oil well ownership would necessitate much study—but not at the expense of graduating. Hungry, I hurried out of the dorm and over to the cafeteria but saw none of my friends there. So I got a hamburger plate to go and decided to eat in my room and study some American history. I dripped ketchup on Stonewall Jackson, though he didn't seem to mind. Very stoic, ol' Stonewall.

A few minutes later Chang burst into the room. He skipped any hint of greeting and got right to the important stuff. He pointed at my plate. "You gonna eat that pickle, Kyle?"

"Help yourself."

He crunched half of it in two big bites, then lifted the stub high and toasted his day.

"To great pickles and to acing a physics test," he said to the ceiling. "Thank youuuuu, God." Chang fell back onto his bed and laughed, his stub of a pickle still held high. The guy had a definite spiritual bent, which I'd grown to admire.

I lifted my sweet tea to celebrate with him, wondered if God intended for me to be a lifelong oilman, and offered a silent toast to that which dominated my thoughts: "To Gretchen, who invited me to Alaska."

A week before graduation, Chang announced that, since we'd been roommates for so long, we should swap graduation gifts—he suggested a Stetson hat to make me at least *look* like an oilman. Not being very creative and under pressure to reciprocate, I told him I'd be happy to buy him a graduation Stetson as well, as it would surely make him stand out whenever he went back to Korea to visit family.

"What color you like?" I asked from my bed.

"A white one," he replied from across the room. "And you?"

"Leathery brown."

That afternoon we bought the hats at a Western store in Lubbock. We even wore them to class the following Monday, nodding like cowboys as we passed friends along the campus sidewalks.

But as was bound to happen, eventually I passed three of my former pledge brothers from the frat house. They still walked alike and looked alike and dressed alike and, I was about to discover, thought alike. They took one look at my hat before the leader of the pack said, "You never did fit in with us, Mango."

His buddies nodded their agreement.

As I passed them I tipped my Stetson and said, "And you guys never did learn to dance."

The smugness I felt over that encounter lasted a good two hours — until my mother called from Fort Worth and said she'd received a bill for funeral costs in the amount of two thousand seven hundred dollars and could I please use some oil revenues to help out with the bill. She then added, "Because I've already used my portion of the oil money this month, and no way am I going to sell the BMW I inherited from Benny. Over my twenty-two years of motherhood I drove my beater station wagon till it had two hundred fifty-seven thousand miles on it. So I deserve a nice car, Kyle. Don't you think I deserve a nice car?"

"I'll mail you a check, Mom."

Three grand to a bookie, nearly that much to the funeral home. And there went the bulk of my first month of oil profits.

Easy come, easy go.

THE BEST LAID PLANS OF SHORTSIGHTED YOUNG MEN ...

After graduating in May, and with the proceeds from my second month in the oil business adding heft to my checking account, I moved out of the dorm and rented a small one-bedroom apartment not far from campus. I also sent five hundred dollars to the ECSGE, the Environmentally Conscious Students for a Greener Earth, the same organization that sponsored Gretchen's group of wildlife rescuers. I attached a note stating that I hoped the money would be used to pay for more summer volunteers, that I figured their current workers—particularly the hardworking girl from Drama Club—could use some relief. This would save me a trip to Alaska.

Five days later, an e-mail from Gretchen popped onto my computer screen.

Hi, Kyle!

I have cool news: Someone sent a generous grant to our cause here on the Alaskan coast, so now I can stay at least a month longer than I'd planned! After being here for five weeks and seeing the damage inflicted by the spill, I now think oil should be a banned substance, like arsenic or cyanide.

So far I've cleaned and released 237 gulls, 64 ducks, and 9 otters. We mix 1% Dawn dishwashing liquid with 99% water, and that does the trick. Cleans 'em up good! I started work as Assistant Rinser, but I'm now up to Chief Scrubber (my friend Regina and I are working on our doctorates in Scrubology).

How is your job search going?

Write me again,

Gretchen

My initial impulse was to compliment her risk taking, her willingness to volunteer so far away from home. This I spelled out in careful language, employing subtlety and trusting that my words might convince her to return to Lubbock—or at least to her hometown of Dallas. Anywhere within a few hours' drive.

Greetings, Gretchen

I'm so glad you're enjoying your very temporary stay in cold, cold Alaska and will soon be finished with your ultra-stressful volunteer duties. I really respect your concern for wildlife, but I also feel that you and I, now that graduation is over and we've both become mature adults, would be wise to spend some more time together. When do you think you'll be back in Texas?

Happy scrubbing,

Kyle

P.S. I have settled into my vocation and am now financially stable.

When two days passed and no reply came back, I didn't fear the worst, just a close approximation of the worst. Many people think it is only the female gender who obsess and grow anxious over the interweave of romantic possibility. Not so. My guess is that six out of ten males do the same; we just don't talk about it and e-mail about it night and day with our buddies.

When discussing relationships with a male friend, my method consisted of a series of what-ifs instead of using a name. This was the case on the day I incorporated my business, decided that I had the cash flow for a real office, and checked out a fourth-story suite in downtown Lubbock. The office was offered to me by my economics professor, whose father had scaled back his real estate business and had a few vacancies to fill. Most of all, the place was cheap. I had also spoken again with the attorney who lent me the books, and he told me that a single man working alone out of his home would face all kinds of temptations and distractions, that a place to go Monday through Friday might hasten my business maturity.

Chang suggested that I pray about the decision and see if God stirred me to act. That evening I managed to mutter a short prayer, and while I didn't exactly feel stirred—the only thing that truly got stirred was the homemade chili I'd cooked—I did sense that I would benefit from having my own cubicle, a place in which to conduct business and watch the oil markets. Bloomberg real-time quotes, drill trucks drilling for more, this stuff excited me.

So for the bargain price of six hundred bucks a month I got a professional environment in which to toil. And I very much intended to toil—from the notes Uncle Benny had left me, his land held possibilities for even more discoveries.

The two small offices and a reception area were all that Mango Enterprises could afford. One window looked out at the business district, the other offered a partial view of the Texas Tech campus. Chang, ever the helpful one, volunteered to assist me in moving furniture. He would graduate in late July—double major of Computer Science and Civil Engineering—after completing a summer school class.

Today, in the lobby of the office tower, he lifted the opposing end of a desk and we manhandled it up three flights of stairs. The weight of the desk pressed into our palms and wrists, and after one collision with a wall, we set it below my office window and stepped back to admire our efforts.

The place looked sparse with just the desk, a chair, and my Igloo cooler in the room, an empty goldfish bowl on the counter in the reception area. Chang turned in a slow circle, as if about to give advice on décor. "No ambience in this place," he said to himself.

I opened the cooler and handed him a bottled water. "Chang," I said, knowing he would give me a straight answer, "what if a certain girl moved far away, and you weren't sure exactly how she felt about you, but you knew there was a certain chemistry between the two of you?"

Chang unscrewed the top from his water bottle and said, "I would get in my car, drive to Alaska, and talk to Gretchen in person."

I sat on the cooler and considered his idea. "But…but what if a certain girl had not formally expressed interest but had sorta invited you to visit, and she worked far away. Like somewhere up north?"

Chang drank from his bottle and replaced the top. "Kyle, I would get in my car, drive to Alaska, and talk to Gretchen in person."

He left to tend to some duties at the dorm, and I was left with the fact that Lubbock, Texas, lay 3,800 miles from the western coast of Alaska.

Frustrated by my inability to shrink geography—I was not God, though I often wanted to be—I instead lost myself in work. By 3:30 p.m. I had both of my computers hooked up, networked, and wireless. By 3:40, Mango Enterprises had received its first nonwork-related e-mail. And it wasn't spam either:

Hello, Kyle

Many, many more birds to clean here. That nasty oil just seems to glue their soft little feathers together. I may never buy a gallon of gas again!

Not sure when I'll be back in Texas, though you are still welcome to visit me here, hint hint. I'm very "into" my work now, and after viewing this damaged wilderness for the past few weeks, I am for the first time realizing that oil is truly evil.

Write me again.

Gretchen

P.S. I'm glad to hear that you are financially stable. What kind of great engineering job did you land that made that possible?

To lie, or not to lie, *that* was the question. Or perhaps I could employ more vagueness, some small obfuscation. I let those thoughts linger while I shuffled papers on my desk and prepared to interview the first candidate for my recently advertised summer intern position. Mango Enterprises—with plans for expansion—needed a second employee, one that could lead exploratory efforts on the land. A temp position, most likely, plus I really wanted some company during the workweek. My goals for the summer—besides pursuing Gretchen—were to hire a compatible worker, learn as much as possible about the oil biz, and be prudent with the resources my uncle had left me.

The candidate I selected for the first interview arrived five minutes early, greeted me with an overeager handshake, and sat in the guest chair across from my desk. On a Post-it note I scribbled *Candidate A*.

The guy did not dress well—for the interview he wore sandals, knee-length khakis, a red T-shirt, and sunglasses resting atop his head.

Determined to give the guy a chance, I peered into a file like big shots do and rubbed my chin for a moment. "So, Candidate A, why are you interviewing for this position?"

The young interviewee sat up straight. "Because my current position does not pay enough."

"Okay, and why do you think you should gain this exciting new position with Mango Enterprises?"

He thought hard on this before responding, so hard that he removed his sunglasses from atop his head and used them to bolster his point. "Because Candidate A is your former roommate who knows you did not build this business but instead got lucky and inherited it. And besides all that, Candidate A has excellent analytical skills, plus he gives outstanding relational advice, plus he helps you move furniture. So if you do not hire Candidate A, then Candidate A will likely reach across your desk and punch you in the nose."

I set the candidate's file on the desk, leaned back in my chair, and interlocked my fingers. "Okay, Chang, you're hired. Now let's go find a desk for your office."

"That's the *entire* interview?" He appeared stunned.

"Yeah, that's it. I suppose I could make it tougher, but with you threatening me and all, why bother?"

Chang led me down into the lobby where he already had a desk sitting near the stairwell—an impressive sign of confidence for a summer intern.

We hauled the desk up the stairs, and after we'd lugged it through the reception area and into his matching office, he left and returned with an office chair. He rolled it behind his desk and sat, as if to test its comfort level.

"Okay, boss," he said in midspin. "What am I going to do this summer?"

I went to his window and motioned out across West Texas. "I'm thinking you should be in charge of new oil discoveries."

Chang came over to the window, stood beside me, and stared out across the city and the plains. "You think there's more out there? Really?"

I shrugged. "Just a hunch. The land is over eight hundred acres, but the four wells only take up about fifty of those acres. I found notes about further exploration in Uncle Benny's journals."

Chang wiped a smudge off the window and nodded. "What exactly does a Vice President of New Oil Discovery do? I mean, what are my day-to-day responsibilities?"

"*VP* of New Oil Discovery? Is that your title? I was thinking more like Low-Ranking Summer Intern."

"I like my idea better." He then reached into his back pocket and drew out a thick stack of business cards. "See, Kyle, I already have my title printed on my cards."

I took one and admired its quality, the deep red ink and the bold font. "But *I* don't even have business cards yet. And I'm *president*."

He nodded with great sympathy. "Then besides being VP of New Oil Discovery, I'll also be Chief Business Card Printer-Outer. I'll multitask."

"No overtime pay for that," I countered as I hoisted a printer and moved it into my office.

I was under my desk, tying a bread wrapper around computer wires and tucking them against the wall, when Chang coughed behind me. "Boss, you didn't tell me yet about my day-to-day duties."

From beneath the desk I said, "You look for new oil...or you hire someone to help you do it, like a drilling company. Then you drive them out to the site and show them where to drill."

"But how do I know *where* to drill, if there's over eight hundred acres to explore?"

I poked my head out from beneath the desk. "Just do your best, Chang. Close your eyes and put your finger on a map like you did when you chose Texas Tech. Experiment. Pray. Take risks. Wander around the land like Moses with a drill bit."

He nodded slowly and without conviction. "You mean just poke holes in the ground with a long stick and hope the tip comes up black and gooey?"

"I was kidding. We'll use professional drillers, and you can escort them around and do what my uncle did: go to the most productive well, walk a hundred yards north, and try drilling there." I climbed out from under the desk, stood, and stretched my back. "If your first try doesn't yield anything, then go a hundred yards *east* of the well, and drill again. If you fail again, go south, then west. I've heard that only one in every five hundred wells strikes oil. But who knows, we might get lucky."

"Okay. But what about—" And he pointed to his shorts and sandals. "What about a dress code for Mango Enterprises?"

I scanned his shorts, T-shirt, and sandals. "You too have to look like an oil man, Chang. You can't look like some collegiate slacker strolling on the beach."

Chang looked over his outfit and checked his wallet, which held very little cash. "How about a small signing bonus to cover work clothes?"

"How about 'no chance'?" Then, feeling like a meanie, I reconsidered. "Okay, you get eighty bucks for work clothes."

After helping me rearrange our meager office furniture, he left but returned two hours later with his white Stetson, blue jeans, and a slightly used pair of alligator-skin boots. He lifted one leg, showing off his boots like they were his first pair ever—which they were. "Better, boss?"

"Much," I said and stepped across the hall into my office.

I returned to his desk and unrolled a large topographical map of the acreage. We spread it out over his desktop and held down the corners.

On the map we stuck sticky notes containing the names of three exploratory companies whose expertise lay in finding oil and performing land drilling services. Chang traced an index finger across the map, back and forth from Lubbock to Anson. Then he checked his wallet again, which I noted held only a five and a one.

"Do I get a mileage allowance?" he asked, letting go of the map and allowing it to furl toward the middle.

I pointed to the empty goldfish bowl that sat on the counter in the reception area. "I'll keep at least a hundred bucks cash in that bowl. Just dip into it whenever you need some gas or a burger or something."

He scratched the back of his head. "You don't need to formally track expenses for the business?"

"I was kidding again, Chang. That's something I want us to research together—which software is best for handling payroll, expenses, and taxes on our little enterprise here. After we decide, I can handle the day-to-day finances. Oh, and I need to budget for a long trip soon. Up north."

Chang went to the bowl, grabbed some air, and stuffed it into his pocket. "Today I'll buy imaginary gas."

He and I retreated to our offices to personalize our work spaces. Already I sensed the excitement of becoming an entrepreneur. Across the top of my computer screen, the real-time price for crude oil scrolled with regularity, courtesy of Bloomberg. It is an interesting psychology to watch the price of a commodity: if you happen to own some of it, you invariably hope its price will rise; and if you do not own some but wish to, you invariably hope the price will fall, allow you to enter the market at a bargain, then reverse course at that very instant and allow you to profit as price resumes its upward thrust in strict obedience to your greed.

Today, price was, at best, a sideways thrust; the price hovered within a few cents of $71.80 all day. I needed to call transportation companies and compare rates for pumping and transporting the oil, but I put this off until tomorrow as Gretchen thoughts overwhelmed business thoughts. Doubly so when at four thirty I remembered it was my turn to e-mail. I wasn't ready to confess yet—and e-mail felt like the wrong medium—so I merely hinted at my new vocation.

Busy day here, Gretchen. Hope your scrubbing duties are going well. You asked about my own job, and, well, it is quite complex. It involves a combination of geology, financial management, transportation scheduling, and the training of a summer intern.

Any updates on when you might be back in Texas? I'm sure those cold, cold, frigid, frosty, lonely nights in Alaska have you yearning for home.

Scrub 'em well!

Kyle

Work days passed without my hearing from her. Then a weekend. More days.

From somewhere deep in my cranium a tidbit emerged—that a surplus of *men* lived in Alaska. Surely by now a dozen or more of these roughnecks had spotted Gretchen and were doing their bearded best to woo her.

Thursday afternoon—a hot one in Lubbock—I spent the last couple hours of the workday painting my office scarlet red. Chang came in from a day trip to Anson, a sunburn on his neck, and said my choice of paint was the color of passion.

"No, Chang," I corrected and dipped my brush into the can. "It's simply the color of my alma mater. Yours too."

"Could be a passionate alma mater," he said, hands on hips and inspecting the paint below the window, which was not quite dry. "But the color could be psychological as well."

My coworker had baited me, and like a dumb largemouth bass I took his bait deep in my jowls. "How, Mister VP, is the color red psychological?"

He pointed at the wall behind me. "You're imagining red as fire, a very hot fire that spreads north and melts the Alaskan glaciers into a river. Then you imagine the river as south-flowing, one in which Gretchen will be swept up and transported all the way through the states of Washington and Idaho and Colorado, then down into Texas, where you'll be waiting on the bank with a rose in your hand." He then folded his arms and nodded, as if totally confident in his explanation.

I held up a finger to argue, but could not summon an appropriate response. I had hired a nutcase for my VP of New Oil Discovery. Chang just stood there, smiling.

"Chang," I said in my best you-don't-understand tone.

"Yes, boss?"

"What is the shortest period of employment you've ever experienced?"

He scratched his head, scrunched his nose, and in general looked to give deep thought to the question. "Is the right answer 'Mango Enterprises if I don't drop this subject'?"

"Congratulations, you've just earned the right to show up here for work again tomorrow."

During the next few days, Chang became the model employee, studying the local oil industry, consulting with financial software specialists, making contacts with drillers, and staying late to design our company Web page.

Thursday afternoon I let him off early to go study for a test. That evening, for whatever reason—boredom or curiosity or both—I walked into downtown Lubbock and inside a pizzeria that I knew was an after-work gathering spot for alumni.

The place looked barren except for one long table with six guys in suits, all of them fortyish, all sporting wedding bands.

I sat in a booth nearby, fiddling with a packet of Splenda and waiting for a waiter.

The six suits looked so successful and mature, though their conversation seemed surprisingly dour. A bearded guy, who looked like some kind of economist type, told the others in a deep, authoritative voice that the way America amassed its wealth — by having access to cheap energy that fueled the production and transportation of our goods and services — was no longer an option. He said energy costs would drive our country into "the Greatest Depression." I certainly felt depressed listening to him. He even suggested that the suburbs would one day be ghost towns because no one would be able to afford to commute back and forth to cities and that people would migrate more and more toward tropical climates — where heating oil wasn't necessary in winter and crops could be grown in more months of the year.

Is this really the future of the good ol' USA?

Having heard enough, I was about to move to another table when four students — two girls and two guys, all of them looking like fresh-faced freshmen — burst in and sat down at the very table I'd considered. In seconds one had his laptop open, and a minute later the four of them laughed in hysterics over a YouTube video. I only caught a brief glimpse of the video, what looked like a lanky guy trying to snowboard on a cafeteria tray, then wiping out in spectacular fashion. The freshmen kept playing the video over and over, their laughter never diminishing.

Suddenly I felt strangely out of place. Too young to fit in with married suits, too old for giggly freshmen. *Where is the waiter?*

I spelled Splenda backward and tried to distill as many words as possible from its seven letters: *Lend. Den. Pen. Spade. Sap. Lead. Deal. Span. Pan. Nap. Nape. Gretchen.*

I glanced left at the suits and the wedding bands, then right at the youngsters. Freshman year to graduation passed so quickly. Already those four years seemed a blink of fun and youth and tests, followed by a lifetime of fading memories.

I returned Splenda to its fellow Splendites and rose from the booth to leave.

"Maybe our best move would be to buy ourselves a remote island and move our families there," one suit said to his group. "An island with lots of fruit in the trees and lots of fish in the sea."

Heads nodded. I shook my head in disbelief. The freshmen laughed a sixth time at the video.

The person who first made it to a remote island was not one of the suits, but Gretchen. Her postcard arrived in Lubbock the following Tuesday, and the words were big and brief:

> *Hi, Kyle! I'm now on a small island, part of Unalaska! Probably for a month. It is sad to see the birds dying here, but at least the rugged coastline makes me think about creation, how vast God's creative mind must be to form so many different species. Oh, and it also makes me think about the benefits of solar energy and what I can do to eliminate my dependence on oil.*
>
> *Hope all is well in Texas!*
> *—G*

For all of my teenage imaginings of soul mate specifics, the solar-seeking, bird-cleaning-in-Alaska-type had never made it onto the list. And yet, across three time zones and a severe drop in temperature, Unalaska became a kind of beacon.

As for the creation thing, I gave God credit for forming the world; I just didn't always see his day-to-day relevance. For instance, I wondered if he knew much about the oil business. Or, for that matter, how to bid for cheap airfare on Priceline.com.

At noon on Friday—we worked half days on Fridays at Mango Enterprises—I finally did it. I presold my next month's oil production to a refinery, told Chang I was leaving him in charge, and booked a flight to Anchorage for July 5.

On my way out I stopped by his office to tell him good-bye, that I had no idea how long I'd be gone, and to make sure we checked in occasionally by phone. He wrote something on his map before wishing me well.

I stood in the doorway, not quite ready to leave. "By the way, Chang, have you heard the term 'peak oil'?"

He stopped writing on his map and looked at me. "Nope, but I've heard of 'peak romance.' That's when the boss gets smitten with a girl and leaves his VP in charge so that he can fly north to pursue the girl—who may or may not want to date him."

He had a point, and as I locked up my office and departed to the elevator, I dismissed his words as a lack of confidence. Yet by the time the elevator had descended the four floors, my own confidence waned.

Gretchen toiled in a place where men outnumbered women by a huge margin, and once again I pictured them trying to woo her, roughnecks using every corny Alaskan come-on line ever invented. Then I pictured myself arriving at that rocky coast, anticipating a romantic walk with her, but discovering instead that a queue had formed.

NORTH BY NORTHWEST (AIRLINES)

Inside the terminal at DFW, I held my boarding pass in my lap, watching the clock and waiting for an official voice to boom through a loudspeaker and tell me to board.

What boomed instead was my cell phone. I had switched my ring tone to Green Day's "American Idiot," which, now that I thought about it, didn't quite seem the mature ring of an oil-man. I mean, not wanting to be an American idiot, an entire nation controlled by media, was probably too radical of a lyric for a guy who rarely watched the news. But at least my ring wasn't yet another twangy Texan song wailing about losing a trailer-park chick and stepping in cow patties.

"Hello...*Mom*?"

"Where are you, Kyle? I called your office, and you weren't there."

"I'm at DFW airport wondering if we're really a nation controlled by the media."

"Don't be vague, Kyle Mango."

"CNN or FOX News, Mom? Which one controls you?"

"Be serious."

"Okay, I'm headed to Alaska. To visit Gretchen."

"Is she expecting you?"

"Um, sorta maybe."

She paused, as if a change of subject blossomed. "I'll make this blunt, honey. I may need some more of your oil revenue."

"Estate taxes? Didn't we decide we didn't owe the government anything?"

"No, not that," she said. Her voice sounded despondent. "Some men visited me today. They were undercover officers and a bank investigator, and they asked questions about Uncle Benny!"

I did my best to put her at ease. "He's passed, Mom. They can't do anything to him now, but I suppose we should cooperate with 'em."

"The investigator was trying to track down why Benny had three cash withdrawals of nine thousand five hundred dollars each. They say banks are required to report cash withdrawals of ten thousand or more, and so three consistent withdrawals of just less than ten thousand raises red flags. In this case, *three* red flags."

I figured a real man protects his mother from undue stress. "Mom, that's all part of a little debt Benny owed. It was taken care of when I had a business meeting with Sal-the-Bookie. Benny's debt is paid in full."

"Was your uncle gambling?"

"Maybe."

"Kyle Mango."

"Okay, he bet thousands on the Cowboys…but he lost. Or rather, *they* lost. The bookie guy, Sal, was the man he owed. And I'm figuring Benny was on the losing end of several bets in the past. I'm warming to the possibility that Sal could be the real 'Bullion Betty' who dug up and stole Uncle Benny's silver four years ago. Probably to collect on another lost bet."

A long silence ensued. Rare, since Helen Mango was rarely silent. Then, finally, "Kyle, Kyle, Kyle."

My name in triplicate, the voice of motherly conviction.

"What is it, Mom?" I had not endured a Triple Kyle since junior high.

"I have a confession," she said, her voice taking on a reserved tone.

"About the deeper meaning of 'Kyle, Kyle, Kyle'?"

"No...about, well, this isn't easy for me. But I know that there was once a load of silver bars and silver dollars buried on Benny's land."

"You do? How'd you know *that*?"

"Because...because I'm—"

"You're what?"

"*I'm* Bullion Betty."

Confusion, confusion, confusion. Brain gone numb. "But... but you can't be."

"I'm her, Kyle. And I can prove it."

Denial, denial, denial. "No you can't."

"Can too. Did you find an empty Fanta Grape can in the box on the day you discovered the silver was missing?"

For all the crude oil in Arabia. "My own mother is Bullion Betty?"

"In the flesh."

"But how did you know where to look?"

Another pause, a sigh, a second sigh. "I didn't at first, but I knew Benny was up to something when I found my gardening spade missing the morning you two drove out there to see the 'alien carvings.' So, sometime later I took a friend with me, while you kids were in school."

"Did you have a date with *another man*? To steal your own brother's silver?"

terrain below did not inspire confidence; every snowcapped peak reminded me of a rival suitor. I saw those mountains as representative of the men of Alaska — huge, tough men competing for Gretchen's affections, men who towered over me, bent on sending me back to Lubbock stuffed into my luggage.

The long flight offered ample opportunity to further second-guess myself, to stare blankly into an airline magazine and never turn the page. But that was not the way of it. All the high-tech gadgetry for sale lent a welcome distraction. Page four's digital voice recorder caused me to consider my upcoming conversation with Gretchen — how I wish I could practice into the recorder, edit myself, and smoothly woo her back to Texas. Then I wondered if wooing should be necessary in a good relationship. Seemed to me that in the best ones, the two people draw together like magnets, and all efforts to woo become a mute point. The couple becomes natural cowooers.

The plane shook twice, then a third time. A groan emerged from 32A.

Please don't vomit, lady.

With an assist from altitude, the rough ride eventually smoothed, and we touched down in Anchorage without incident. Then, inside the Anchorage terminal, I discovered my allotted time to change planes amounted to a generous twenty-six minutes.

Beneath a flight board a customer service rep — the guy was dressed like a smiling grizzly bear and smelled as much — pointed me to the far end of the corridor.

After a stop in the men's room I hustled north and successfully switched airlines — to a much smaller plane. Seating for twenty.

Stooped in the aisle of that little twin prop, I located seat

7B, stuffed my carry-on bag under the seat as instructed, and noted that I was one of only three passengers on board.

The lone attendant came by and said, "Sir, this ride is usually a bit bumpy. Sorry for the inconvenience." She then repeated the apology to the passengers seated two rows behind me.

She was right about the ride, though: twin props vibrated upon takeoff, and they vibrated in midflight. It felt like an invisible hand held a back massager to the fuselage — right outside my window.

Then the pilot's voice filled the plane and apologized for the noise level. "Thank you for flying Hop Skip 'N Bump Airlines," he said in closing. I imagined his words repeating themselves on each flight to and from Unalaska, my destination island among the long, curving chain of the Aleutians.

That's where I knew Gretchen to be, somewhere on Unalaska. Exactly where — on which mile of shoreline — was a mystery to be solved in real time.

And I loved a good mystery.

THE PART WHEN I ARRIVED ON THE ROCKY ALASKAN SHORE, PARKED MY RENTAL CAR ON THE SHOULDER OF A COASTAL HIGHWAY, AND WENT LOOKING FOR GRETCHEN

Until you've breathed Alaskan air, you do not realize that you've been cheated, that life in the lower forty-eight has duped your lungs into believing that they've sampled the best the Western Hemisphere has to offer. Your lungs have been conned.

I stood beside my rental car—eyes shut, head tilted skyward—and gulped all I could, holding the air for a count of ten before beginning anew. Alaskan air is addictive.

Soon I'd had my fix, and my attention veered to the coastline. No lines of men dotted that rugged shore. No queue had formed. If I had competition for Gretchen, they were out working the fishing boats or the oil fields of Prudhoe Bay—which meant lots of them shared my vocational negative.

I locked the car door, checked to see if its tires were off the highway, and made my way down to the beach. Before leaving the airport I'd called the organization that coordinated the volunteers. After many rings a woman answered and directed me to this section of coastline, with the warning that "the teams sometimes move good distances over the course of their day, so you may have to walk a bit to find them."

Already the afternoon looked gray and brittle. Perhaps the

lack of humidity caused the effect, but so fragile did that sky appear that I felt at any moment it might crumble like a celestial saltine.

I walked for a half hour over small rocks, climbed over and around much larger specimens, but saw no one. The ocean, idle as it was, lapped and swooshed every few seconds. Unlike Texas beaches, Alaska's shore did not accumulate foam; today it held a topcoat of petroleum. To my right a lone bush, skinny and weak and drooping, bowed toward the spill as if resigned to its fate. *Just a matter of time.*

I pressed on, awed by Alaska but stunned by the mess man had made. At least my own oil was transported in small quantities, mere trucks instead of colossal ships with the potential to ruin entire ecosystems. Still, I wondered if any Mango oil tainted this shore.

Ahead a pair of seabirds gathered side by side near the water, trying to peck and scratch an oily sheen from their feathers. They appeared frustrated. Twice I stopped and looked the opposite way, wondering if I were proceeding in the wrong direction, getting farther away from Gretchen rather than closer.

Soon the shoreline turned darker, a charcoal color. Hopes of discovery filled me — the spill was more apparent here. This all-consuming taint of the sand led me farther west until the grayness curved around a mound of boulders. I could not see past them; they stood at least ten feet tall. But perhaps a gathering of wildlife lovers lay beyond those rocks.

That's when the fog rolled in. From off the water it tumbled, at first transparent, then thicker. I thought I could outrun it, but no, this fog was not only damp but fast. It hugged the surface and boiled ahead of me, anticipatory, as if bent on quashing my search. I stepped up between two of the boulders and braced myself for balance. In the gray mist my left hand recoiled from a sprout of barnacles. To my left, three dead birds floated in the surf, dashed repeatedly against the rocks. I stopped and waited for the worst of the fog to pass — and in minutes it did so. Ahead I could make out a shallow lagoon, its shore a carpet of fist-sized stones. Onward.

When the last drift of low clouds passed and the sea sloshed once again, I spotted a fellow human. Near the center of that lagoon sat an old man in a lawn chair, perched some twenty feet back from the water. He held a small gull in his hands and appeared hard at work. The man wore no shoes. His trousers hung soaked from the thigh down, his rolled pant legs exposing pale feet. Beyond him the fog rolled over the island, favoring land and faking out the sea.

I wondered if I too had been faked. For a moment I even considered if the old man, like Paul Revere, had somehow warned Gretchen of my approach:

One if by land, two if by sea
Three if by plane in seat 7B
Four if by YouTube, five if by cell
Six if by chopper, seven by smell
Eight if by text, nine if by sub
Ten ways to Gretchen, ah here's the rub:

It may not matter when she finds out you're an oil baron.

With touristy enthusiasm I approached the old man, though I didn't offer to shake hands. I just stopped in front of him and waved until it was obvious he was preoccupied.

"Howdy, sir. I'm volunteering for a week and was wondering

if you knew anything about the ECS group? College students helping to clean birds? I'm looking for a friend."

He seemed serious about his work and spoke without a glance my way. "Never heard of 'em," he said to the bird. "But then, I work alone. Try to clean at least one per day. Sometimes half a dozen."

His shirt, dampened like my own from the passing mist, clung to his body. He reached for an unmarked spray bottle beneath his chair and sprayed something onto a hand towel. Then he used the towel to wipe the underside of the gull. I could not decide what to ask next and was relieved when he spoke first.

"Son," he said and kept his attention on his patient.

I stooped before him, gaining a closer look at his work. "Sir?"

With his head he motioned west. "Down the coast, couple miles...that's where the worst of the spill came ashore. There's some folks down there, I think. At least they were last week. Saw 'em on the news."

I pointed down the rock-strewn beach, which looked empty except for a few more dark and frustrated gulls. "That way?"

He nodded, resprayed his towel with cleaning concoction, and went back to work on his bird. I waved good-bye, but he never saw me.

In my haste I tried to run, but the stones wobbled beneath my feet and threw me off balance. Seconds later I kneeled to retie my sneakers. Ahead, under gray skies and a threat of drizzle, three tiny figures moved along the shore. *People!* In even more of a hurry, I pulled the knot out of my laces and tied my left shoe a third time. The rocks smelled like warm oil.

I glanced back up the beach, debated for a moment driving versus walking, and decided it was better to proceed on foot.

Up on the coastal highway a news van rumbled past. I imagined Gretchen being interviewed, and wondered if she missed Texas. If she'd someday miss me.

But what if she's no longer even on this island? Lots of other islands in the Aleutian chain. And, to my knowledge, oil slicks held no geographic allegiance. Wherever the tide pushed, that's where a slick spread its slickness.

I spotted a path of smooth sand near the water's edge, lit into a jog, and made for the tiny figures ahead. A half mile of beach later I met three more independent bird cleaners: a pair of junior high kids from a local school and their grandmother. All three paused on the shore to wipe a solitary bird, and all three pointed me farther west.

"Worst of the spill is thataway," said the grandmother. She donned rubber boots with the tops turned down. She also wore a yellow scarf—even in July the temperature here was just upper fifties—and went about her work with great concentration, as if knitting a gift.

More fog rolled in ahead. I even wondered about finding my way back.

I thanked Grandma and trekked across acre after acre of wet rock. Ahead the beach looked barren and dark gray, mostly barren. A foul smell rose incessantly, like steam mixed with motor oil.

Onward.

I spotted her across the next cove, a pixel on a bleak and desolate shore. Though a good ways away, I made out familiar features—her posture, her flexibility as she leaned down to work; she even looked to be wearing the same bell-bottom jeans she'd worn the last time I saw her in Lubbock. Gretchen sat on the second of three boulders, her hair blowing in the wind, her hands cradling a blackened seabird.

From perhaps a hundred yards, I could tell she had yet to recognize me. And somehow it felt wrong to just walk up and say "Hi." Farther down the beach, three other volunteers toiled in a similar fashion. They spaced themselves at wide intervals, like surf fishermen.

Needing a moment to think through my approach, I noted a basketball-sized rock to my left, sat upon it, and tugged my cap low on my head so that she couldn't note my features. Then I turned and faced the sea and weighed various strategies.

Just go running up and shout, "What a shocker to see you here?!"

Stroll casually past, glance her way, and act flabbergasted that she toiled on this very beach?

No, the right way was to immerse myself in her world—and suddenly her world seemed to welcome my plan.

An oil-stained bird, half-grown and wholly confused, waddled nearby on the shore. I went over and tried to catch it, but it hopped away, not quite able to fly. So I circled it until it was forced up against the breakers. With whispered words—"just stay calm, dude, I'm here to help"—I tried to reassure it. When I stepped closer the gull tried to hop past me, but I was faster and scooped it up with both hands. After enduring a couple pecks to the wrist, I adjusted my grip and walked back up the wet sand and sat on my rock. The bird struggled before submitting. Perhaps it could tell I meant no harm.

I glanced again down the beach at Gretchen. Still debating the perfect approach, I held the gull in my lap and kept my head down. Minutes passed. The gull pecked my thumb.

"You here to help?!" a female voice shouted from the west. I didn't have to look up to know it was Gretchen. The girl could shout with volume.

I nodded, tugged my cap even lower, and pointed at yet another feathered victim waddling near the water. Perhaps I scored unimagined points when I cradled my handicapped bird and went to work using the only wiping cloth I had—an airline napkin that I'd stuffed into my shirt pocket somewhere over Idaho.

The napkin disintegrated on the third wipe. Then the gull pecked my fingers, as if it didn't like my methodology. So I set the bird at my feet, removed my left shoe and white athletic sock, put my shoe back on my bare foot, and used the sock to work on the bird. It seemed to appreciate my efforts now that I'd employed real cloth, although I lacked the cleaning liquid the real volunteers used and was thus mediocre in effectiveness. At my next wipe two feathers fell to the sand. I apologized to the gull and promised to be gentler.

A few minutes later Gretchen looked down the beach in my direction and waved—what I took as a simple wave of appreciation for a fellow rescuer. Over my shoulder I waved back, wondering how long I should sit there and prolong surprise. Beneath that brittle sky, alone with nature in need, I figured one moment was as ideal as the next.

I stayed put, even took the time to clean the feet and legs of the seabird. Minutes later I snuck one more glance to the west, across that damp acreage of rocks, and saw Gretchen rise from her spot. She carried her bird-in-progress over to a yellow plastic cage and set the bird inside.

I rewiped my bird's left leg and continued to sneak peeks down the beach. Upon my umpteenth glance, Gretchen lifted the plastic cage with both hands and began walking my way.

Here she came, stepping across rocks and toting her plastic cage. Fifty yards away, then forty, then thirty. Her slow, meandering pace confirmed that she looked on this new volunteer as just another helper. I turned back toward the water and hunched over my bird, acting busy and hiding my profile.

Soon small rocks unsettled to my right and clacked under foot. Louder. Louder still. She was steps away.

"Hi," came her voice from behind me, and I heard her set the cage upon the rocks. "You finished with that gull yet? You've been cleaning it for quite a while."

Without turning my head I said, "Yep, almost done. But I have a question."

"Sure. And by the way, my name's Gretchen. I'm from Texas."

I stared at the sand between my feet. "Okay, Gretchen-from-Texas, I was just wondering if you preferred rescuing lost birds from Alaskan beaches or lost pledges from Texas Tech frat houses?" Only then did I turn around and grin.

Only then did she scream so loud that my partially cleaned bird bolted from my grasp and hopped across the shore and plunged right back into the oily water.

Gretchen's eyes flashed recognition and her jaw dropped to Honolulu. "Ky—?"

She didn't even finish my name—and it was just one syllable. I'd never before bore witness to a hyperventilating bird rescuer.

She didn't finish my name because in that nanosecond of surprise, allegiance overwhelmed her, and she bolted toward the surf and scooped up the reoiled seabird.

"We have to clean this one more thoroughly, Kyle," she said and tucked it under her arm. Then, as if experiencing a second bout of shock, "What are you doing here?!"

I joined her at the water's edge and patted first the bird's head, then Gretchen's. "Nice to see you too, Gretch. I was just passing through the barren Alaskan coast on my lunch hour and thought I'd say hello."

Gretchen held that bird as if it were a lonely orphan. "Thought it might drown, Kyle. Sorry to delay my greeting."

She set the startled bird between her feet and secured it there. Only then did she give me a thorough hug of greeting and surprise. The girl had her priorities. It felt good to hold her again, if even for just a moment. Then her arms slid from around my neck, and she took one step back as if to take stock of her unannounced visitor.

"Okay," she said, her gaze locked on mine. "Tell me again—what are you doing here?"

"I'm starting the Great White North branch of the Texas Tech alumni association. You're my first recruit."

She smiled and started to say something—I thought she was overcome again by surprise—but then she looked past me to the coastal highway and pointed. A pickup truck honked. The driver waved.

"That's the bird transport guy," she said and waved to the driver. "I'm due back in a few. Wanna come along?"

If immersing myself in her world meant a pickup truck ride to the bird center, I was game, and I told her so. Together we cleaned the bird again, dried it best we could, and set it inside the plastic cage with its brethren.

We toted the cage over rocks and up the beach and loaded it in the pickup bed. Then we climbed in after it, sharing glances of surprise while sitting on the wheel wells.

"I can't believe you're here, Kyle."

"I'm here."

The truck's destination was, according to our driver, a place called the More Thorough Cleaning Center, or the MTCC as Gretchen referred to it. From opposing sides of the bird cage we held it steady and spoke to its occupants.

"There there, little gull," Gretchen said into the side of the cage. "We'll get all that profit-obsessed, feather-ruining oil off you, and soon you'll be good as new."

She glanced across the top of the cage at me, as if to urge me to say something to the birds. I tapped the top of the cage. "Hello, um…birdies, we'll clean you up good, although I doubt every single human employed in the oil industry is out to ruin you."

A frown, a headshake, but at least Gretchen didn't question my motives. We just sat in silence for a couple miles and allowed cool Aleutian winds to whip our hair around, the coastline turning murky gray then lighter gray as we rode out of range of the spill.

"Is your day over after we deliver these birds?" I asked, hoping for a quiet dinner date to ensue.

She shook her head no. "The volunteer half is over. I work a real job three hours every afternoon. Gotta make a few dollars, ya know."

"Doing what?"

Again she stared at me in disbelief. "I just can't believe you're in Alaska."

"You said that already. But what do you do in the afternoons here?"

"You'll see," she said and turned to whisper something soft to the birds. Then she caught my overinterested gaze. "I'm glad you're here, Kyle. It's good to see you."

I nodded. "Same."

Her three-hour afternoon job was not what I expected. Gretchen and her cohorts—I had yet to meet any of them—wove hammocks. Not the item one conjures first when thinking of Alaska, but according to Gretchen the summer months bring about a demand for good hammocks, her reasoning being that it stays dark here so much of the year that the natives want to soak up all the sights they can while the sighting is good.

A plain metal building served as the manufacturing center, and when she pressed a button and raised the automatic door, all I saw were bundles of rope in the corners, completed hammocks strung across the ceiling, and pallets of wooden separator bars, predrilled for the ropes to angle through their centers. These were not your regular white-rope hammocks either. Instead they utilized colored rope and produced red hammocks, blue hammocks, yellow ones, orange ones, even a few weaved in a strange shade of purple.

"You weren't kidding," I muttered and scanned the inventory to see if their shade of red matched that of Texas Tech.

After a trip to the restroom to change into a clean shirt, Gretchen went to a stack of boxes, lifted a bundle of electric blue rope, and hauled it over to a workstation. There she let the rope slide from her hands and puddle on the cement floor. "For a small fee," she said and pointed to the finished hammocks on the far wall, "you can have any color you like." Then she added, "But not today."

I stooped beside her and fingered the rope. "Doesn't the dye come out and ruin people's clothes?"

She threaded an end of blue rope through a predrilled separator bar and commenced to weaving. "There isn't any dye in this rope. It's high-tech stuff and fade resistant, unlike that touristy cap you bought." She smiled when she said it, though she never looked up from her labors.

According to Gretchen, Alaskans had taken to owning

colored hammocks. Her logic was that they saw so much white and gray in their terrain that they welcomed most any contrast in hue.

More pressing was the issue of competition. And while Gretchen threaded and weaved blue rope, I figured this was a good time for subtle investigation. "So, Gretch, there aren't any long lines of Alaskan men trying to woo you?"

"What Alaskan men?" she said and kept working. "It's just me and a few other protestors of Big Oil. I haven't been on a date since I left Lubbock."

I did not want to discuss the morality of Big Oil or her last date in Lubbock. I just hoped I'd scored points for making the journey northward. I figured this was what real men did—take the initiative—unlike the bar regulars who just wait around for a woman to wander into their territory, which I suppose is the Venus flytrap method of dating.

Gretchen continued to weave away, her hands a coordinated whir of motion. In midweave she said, "I still can't believe you're here."

I was about to utter something nonchalant like "July is hot in Lubbock," when a second young woman—tall and black-haired and of Gretchen's age—walked through the open garage doorway. She never spoke but instead went to the far right side of the building and began sorting through boxes, which were stacked upon pallets in the corner.

At first I wondered who had invaded the building and ruined my one-on-one, but then I recognized the tall woman as Gretchen's friend from Texas Tech, whom I suspected had initiated this whole clean-the-birds odyssey. "Isn't that—"

Gretchen answered in a whisper. "Yep...that's Regina. We're rooming together this summer."

"Ah, the tall and environmentally conscious roommate."

Gretchen whispered even lower. "Well, actually you'll probably think her a radical. I suppose she can be fun, sometimes. Like once in a purple moon. But she's passionate about her cause."

Wanting to know more about who was influencing the object of my affection, I said, "*Radical Regina?*"

"Shhh. She might hear you."

I lowered my voice. "Just how radical is she?"

Gretchen continued her weaving. "She was arrested once for spray painting the side of an oil tanker with bright green environmental messages."

"So, she stopped?"

Gretchen pulled blue rope through the separator board. "She stopped spray painting oil tankers, yes. But then she found out where the CEO lived and spray painted his yard, plus the side of a corporate skyscraper in Houston. She spent a few nights in jail during sophomore year."

I felt bad for my home state. "You mean Radical Regina is a *Texan?*"

"Kyle," she said with a roll of her eyes. "She's *from* California, but she headed the animal rights group at Texas Tech. She has a trust fund, and she thinks the highest use of her family's money is to protest any entity having anything to do with oil."

I had never thought of Mango Enterprises as an entity, certainly not an environmentally hazardous entity. "Any entity at all?"

Gretchen nodded. "Even 7-Elevens. Oh, and last week she even wrote a letter to the maker of Hot Wheels cars, urging them not to produce miniature tanker trucks for kids because it sends the wrong message."

I too had a message. A message from above. *Tread softly here, my son.*

My best method of soft treading was to drop the subject and observe quietly while Gretchen completed her work. I had to admit, it was a peaceful life she lived here — cleaning birds till early afternoon, hand-weaving colored hammocks till dinnertime.

I watched her attention to detail as she completed the second blue hammock and tied off its angled tips to a chrome metal ring. She inspected her work and, while doing so, pulled her cell phone from her pants pocket. Then she placed a call — to the manager of an outdoor sports store in Anchorage, she told me — and in seconds was speaking with him.

With satisfaction she folded her phone shut and made the money-rolling gesture with her fingers. "Sold!" she said to no one in particular. "Sold both of 'em."

"Do ya also make those things for volunteers to sleep in, or are they only to turn a profit?" I asked, unsure of how to congratulate a successful hammock sale.

Gretchen smiled as she rolled the first hammock into a long, skinny bundle and inserted it into a long, skinny cardboard box. "I'm no mega-capitalist, Kyle Mango. But I think I turned a nice profit. And no, we don't sleep in hammocks."

I rolled the second one for her and momentarily caught my fingers in the rope. "So you make hammocks just to help pay the rent?"

She slid the second box over the rolled hammock. "Okay, since you came all the way to Alaska to visit me, I'll give you the scoop. My rent is seventy-five bucks a week, and since the profit on those two sales just now made me forty bucks each, I just made another week's rent!"

She exuded the kind of energy that possesses people aligned

with a cause. Perhaps not an extremist's energy, but plenty enough to fuel her dual occupations. She seemed to enjoy my presence, but she also seemed quite self-sufficient. Even the way she slapped SOLD stickers on the boxes suggested a woman who commanded her world.

Across the warehouse floor she shouted to Regina. "Sold two more, roomie!"

From the far side of the building, Regina didn't reply except for a brief wave.

I lifted the first skinny box and held it under my arm. "Where's the shipping department?" I asked.

Gretchen pointed to a back wall and to a sign that read UPS Pickup. She lifted the other box, and we began toting them across the concrete floor toward a shipping counter. "So, what about your own vocation, Kyle? Is the company you work for turning a profit?"

Stride for stride with her, I avoided her gaze and a direct answer. "Um, yeah, so far so good. You'd be surprised how lean and mean the company is."

I felt bad for being elusive on the matter, but the timing for confession didn't feel right, plus I'd only been here for a couple hours and needed to gauge just how radical Gretchen had become during the course of her stay.

She bumped me in the rear with her box and said, "That's pretty good getting time off after having only been on your job for a month or so."

"An understanding boss helps a lot."

We set the boxes on the counter, and Gretchen scribbled a note for the shipping personnel. While writing she said, "Well, just as long as you don't get hired away by some oil producer like Chevron or Exxon."

Double doses of guilt pangs rocked my skull. And suddenly I couldn't speak, my mind consumed with thoughts of Uncle Benny explaining in his Texas hospital bed how he feared he'd disappointed God—and now I'd done the exact same thing in Alaska. When you fly north, guilt doesn't diminish like the temperature of the air, it stays just the same, fully adaptable to all climates. I had just processed this thought when a third and fourth guilt dagger stabbed me, informing me that I'd best forget about sins of the father as I was now infected with sins of the uncle, and surely I'd end up squandering all my money and placing bad bets on the Cowboys and paying off a bookie named Sal with my last envelope of cash. On a road to ruin because I hid the truth from Gretchen.

Not today, Kyle. The timing is still wrong.

I stuck some extra tape across the ends of the boxes and said, "Wanna grab some dinner?"

Gretchen checked my taping job and said, "Okay."

She excused herself a moment and headed for a restroom. Then I saw her roommate heading the same direction. I waited beside the weaving station and hoped Gretchen would refrain from inviting Radical Regina to dinner with us. But she did it anyway.

"I'LL HAVE THE GRILLED MANGO, PLEASE."

I didn't trust her, didn't like her, didn't want to sit at the same table with her.

Regina had spent the first fifteen minutes of dinner boasting of five years experience supporting the cause of disenfranchised wildlife. She used that exact phrase—*disenfranchised wildlife*. Even Gretchen—seated patiently to my right and picking at her salad while waiting her turn to speak—seemed surprised at the depth of Regina's radicalism.

Finally after Regina took a breath, Gretchen said, "Food prices here are higher now, Kyle, because miles of fishing waters are off-limits to boat captains."

"Tainted waters," Regina added, with extra emphasis on *tainted*. "I eat fish every night. I do it to support fishermen so profoundly affected by the mismanagement of capitalistic oil companies."

Gretchen picked a tiny tomato from her salad and held it just short of her lovely mouth. "Profoundly," she whispered to the veggie. "And capitalistic."

I did my best to engage Regina in conversation. "So, are the fishermen mad about it?"

"Not as mad as I am," Regina shot back. She did not pick

her tiny tomato from her salad; she stabbed it harshly with her fork. Juice gushed from three holes.

To keep from getting stabbed, bludgeoned, or otherwise assaulted, I spotted a waiter and immediately ordered fish. Grilled halibut.

Gretchen followed suit. "Grilled tuna, medium well," she said over her menu.

Regina, last to order, hesitated a moment. "I'll have the same," she said finally and used her menu to bolster her next point. "But inform the cook that I demand my fish be a *line-caught* fish instead of one captured in a net. Fish suffer horribly in nets."

The waiter nodded as if this wasn't the first time he'd served Regina. "Line-caught only," he said into his order pad. He jotted the instructions and made for the kitchen, at which time I noticed the long patch on his sleeve: Big Oil = Big Mess.

Gretchen saw the same thing, smiled, and said, "He's a local who helps out our cause on occasion. Likes to clean otters."

"Ah."

Regina had no more tiny tomatoes to impale on her fork, so she stabbed her pickle. "Even the locals aren't as mad as I am, Kyle. Sometimes I'd like to choke anybody who has anything at all to do with producing oil, selling oil, or refining oil."

Gretchen cocked her head in rebuttal. "What about the guy who changed your car's oil at Grease Monkey? The one you flirted with."

Regina never hesitated. "Him too."

Our threesome's appetizer discussion consisted not of food but of Regina's listing of environmental atrocities across the globe. She knew them all. I could not keep up with the various wildlife mentioned, but I noted several offending countries in her list, some of which she'd visited in the past year, including Venezuela, France, Mexico, and Indonesia. I was dining with a world class protestor. According to Gretchen—she relayed this in a whisper—Regina could protest in five languages.

Without further complication, our dinners arrived, the scent of grilled fish warming the atmosphere despite the chill brought on by Regina. But just as I tucked my napkin into place, my cell phone rang. I checked the caller ID and saw it was Chang. Being three hours ahead in Texas, Chang had nonetheless decided to call me at 11:00 p.m. Lubbock time. I figured this must be urgent and probably business-related.

I excused myself from the table and went and stood at the entrance to the men's room. From there I could talk out of range and yet still see my dinner party. "Greetings, Chang, from the Great White North."

He didn't even say hello. "Kyle, we hit a gusher! Oil is spewing all over your land in Anson!"

In rushed whispers I tried to contain my excitement. "What? When?"

"Today...this afternoon! The drilling company did just what you said. They drilled a hundred yards east but found nothing. Then a hundred yards south and found nothing. But when I walked two hundred yards west and said, 'Try here, guys'...kaboooom!"

"Kaboom?" It amused me to hear my Asian friend pronounce the word. "Really?"

"Kaboom, Kyle. Black stuff shot through the surface!" Breathless, he spoke faster than I'd ever heard him speak. "Then it shot to the sky, then it rained down in gobs and covered us all, even the guy driving the drill truck. We got nasty, but it was a blast too because it was like the sky was raining money. I'm sending you my laundry bill."

No longer able to whisper, I ducked inside the men's room. "What did the exploration guys think? Ten more barrels a week? Fifteen?"

"He estimates at least forty."

"Per *week*? That means...that—"

"It means God smiled on Mango Enterprises. And I hope it also means you'll hire me full-time—with benefits! Oh, and the guy driving the drill truck said he'll work for you too. Said he knew your Uncle Benny and would love to drill more holes in your land."

I opened the men's room door and peeked out at Gretchen and Regina, the latter doing all the talking, the former listening and nodding.

"Chang, do you have any idea how hard it is to discuss this stuff right now, knowing I have to go finish dinner with this radical?"

"Gretchen? I thought she just had a soft spot for birds."

"Not Gretchen. Her roommate, Radical Regina."

Short pause. "Just how radical is she?"

I cupped a hand over the phone to soften my voice. "She spray paints tanker ships 'cause she hates oil. And I'm afraid she's influencing Gretchen."

Longer pause. "Sounds like CEO Mango has a big problem. You better fess up, li'l doggie."

I ended the call with Chang by hinting that if what he said was true about the gusher, he'd be offered a full-time position. In fact, I would need him. Then, as I looked out across the restaurant at the back of Gretchen's head, I so wanted to share news of this good fortune. Yet with her roommate there my only choice was to walk calmly back to the table, sit between the two women, and eat my line-caught fish.

Without comment I tucked my napkin into my lap. Forks and knives tapped and scraped upon plates.

"Anything important?" Gretchen asked between sips of water.

"My coworker called to say we landed some new business," I replied. "I'll tell you more about it tomorrow. It's looking like a good year, maybe even enough to get a Christmas bonus."

Gretchen gave a thumbs-up and smiled, as if she was truly happy for me.

Guilt. Prods. Hot pokers to the skull. I wanted to tell her right then and there, tell her everything about the wells and the gusher and the fact that I didn't plan on being an oil baron; it just happened to me and I was looking out for my family. I also wanted to ask Gretchen if she ever considered using her affection for wildlife a bit closer to home—hopefully Texas critters like orphaned deer or lonely armadillos.

Regina sliced her pickle in half and said, "No Christmas bonuses for the fishermen of Alaska—they've had *their* harvest reduced by the misguided agendas of Big Oil."

Gretchen dabbed a crumb from her mouth. "Agendas sometimes get misguided, Kyle." She ate a bite of her grilled tuna and added, "But it's good that your work is going well."

Then, as if she too sensed the need to change the course of conversation, Gretchen looked across the table at Regina and said, "Regina, do you celebrate Christmas?"

Regina appeared stunned at the sudden detour. Eyes down, she mutilated the rest of her pickle before speaking. "Um, not really. Well, parts of Christmas, like the nature scenes. I like that he was born in a manger and that the wise men walked on dirt paths instead of driving gas-guzzling SUVs on modern highways paved with tar. Plus that manger in Israel was much more environmentally friendly than if he'd been born in a high-rise in Houston, where tax revenues from oil companies might have caused the baby Jesus to grow into yet another profit-hungry corporate titan, with little regard for the fragility of Planet Earth. So, yeah, I guess I celebrate parts of it."

Gretchen nodded with a kind of wide-eyed confusion; I was too baffled to respond at all.

Then, just as I figured Regina would add to her theology, she surprised me with a quick change of subject. She ate the last bite of her fish, pronounced it yummy, and asked, "What kind of car do you drive, Kyle?"

I paused for effect, even dabbed my mouth with my napkin. "I have an old Toyota Celica that gets great gas mileage. But I might be buying a new pickup truck when I get back to Texas."

"You should get a hybrid car instead."

Gretchen dabbed her mouth with a napkin. "Definitely a hybrid, Kyle."

When we all stood to leave, Gretchen asked me how long was I planning to stay, and I told her it depended on how well I fit in here, that if I could be of help and also spend time with her, I'd stay up to a week.

She smiled and said, "I like that plan."

At the cashier's desk I paid Gretchen's portion of the check, even held the door as the two women departed the restaurant. I wanted to go sit on the rocks with Gretchen, maybe watch the ocean and talk. But she said she had to help Regina write articles for their group's weekly newspaper.

According to Gretchen, their articles simply updated the local populace on the progress of restoring the environment.

According to Regina, the articles represented the unified voice of dissent, the lone voice defending innocent wildlife from profit-hungry corporate titans.

"We call our paper *The Alaskan Breeze*," Gretchen said outside the diner. The air temperature had dropped, and Texas seemed a million miles away. For a moment we all took in the stars, which were plentiful. After offering me a brief hug, a motel recommendation, and a miniwave good night, Gretchen left with Regina. I walked the opposite way, up the coastal highway a quarter mile to my rental car. Minutes later I located the cheap motel across the street and rented a room.

I lay on a hardened bed, hands behind head, and considered all the twists of the day. The most twisted image came just before slumber, as I thought about the type of articles to be published in the so-called *Alaskan Breeze*.

Gretchen's roommate was anything but a breeze; more like an aerosol can roasting in the fire of protest.

Kaboom.

"POETS, PRIESTS, AND POLITICIANS, HAVE WORDS TO THANK FOR THEIR POSITIONS" —*Sting*

The knock on my hotel door startled me into a one-eyed glance at the clock: 6:02 a.m. Her voice, muffled as it was, came seconds later.

"We're starting early today, Kyle!" Gretchen said from outside. "Regina and I will meet you down on the rocks. Lots more gulls to clean!"

"Meet you in ten minutes," I said and scrambled out of bed. I had rarely begun a workday so early; Mango Enterprises' charter held that all employees be eight-to-fivers. I feared this crew might be six-to-sixers.

"I'm leaving the new edition of *The Alaskan Breeze* on your doorstep," Gretchen called out.

"Thanks," I said to the door and simultaneously dropped my deodorant on my bare foot. I rubbed my foot and said, "Can't wait to read the gossip column."

The two of them had already disappeared up the coastline when I opened my motel door and plucked my copy of their paper from the sidewalk. The weekly contained only four pages and amounted to a journalistic defense for a very green planet. Regina held the title of editor-in-chief; she'd penned both the headline and lead article:

"Cleanup Progresses Despite Lack of Compassion from Big Oil!!"

Imagine your home as an oceanfront mansion, an abode you have worked your entire life to own, a place to raise your children. You are safe there, comfortable, at peace. Now imagine a tidal wave of black goo swamping the estate, oozing under your mahogany front door, ruining your Persian rugs, sloshing against your child's crib, and covering your plasma TV in raw icky petroleum. Such is the fate of beleaguered wildlife on the shores of Unalaska. Their nests are their mansions. The coast is their neighborhood. And today the black goo oozes ashore. Tons of it.

The article went on for ten paragraphs, detailing similar tragedies the world over, plus Regina's solution to it all, which concluded in a not-so-surprising request:

Write your Senator and your representative in Washington. Urge them to support funding for alternative energy sources. Do it before the entire planet drowns in black goo. In fact, if anyone wants a free T-shirt proclaiming "Just Say NO to black goo," I am having some printed up this week.

Regina Peters, editor

On page three I read Gretchen's piece, hoping it would not reveal her as beyond hope.

A Beachy Surprise

For the past two weeks I've written about the continuing need for volunteers here on the coast. Yesterday a most unexpected volunteer showed up. I was in the middle of my day, cleaning my umpteenth gull, and sitting on a rock in a quiet cove of Unalaska. I looked east, up the shoreline, and waved at a fellow cleaner. I thought he was a local, come down to the beach to help on a day off from work. He wore a cap low on his head, so I could not make out his features. His continued glances my way, however, had me wondering who he was. Soon curiosity led me to pick up my cage of birds and go talk to this helper with the swiveling neck.

Imagine my surprise when the volunteer turned out to be a college friend from Texas. He flew here yesterday to help our cause! And he's cool enough to stop and clean a seabird before he even spots me on the beach! For purposes of this article, I'll refer to my friend as "Kyle," even though his real name is actually Kyle. We got to know each other one night four years ago when I helped him escape Greek oppressors in Lubbock, Texas. (Don't ask.)

I mention his visit because it causes me to
wonder how many locals could lend a hand but
have not yet ventured out and taken on a job.
We need you. We need you to help us JUST SAY
NO TO BLACK GOO!

by Gretchen Trammel

Encouraged by the middle section but discouraged by the last sentence, I folded the paper, tossed it back into my room, and made my way across the street and down to the shore. This morning, out on that rock-strewn beach, a queue *had* formed. Only it wasn't a line of competing suitors but a line of dirty gulls, grungy and black and hopeless, wobbling up the coast as if waiting their turn for Gretchen and Regina to wipe them clean.

Perhaps the food the women had tossed out had something to do with their obedience, but they looked like a cafeteria line to me, never mind the whiffs of oil overwhelming the sea salt.

The three of us—loaded with towels and a spray bottle containing 1% Dawn—spread out along the beach at wide intervals, each choosing some form of boulder for a workstation. This also meant that we toiled outside of talking distance, though I didn't want to work so far away from Gretchen.

I did, however, want to impress her, perhaps even make a difference, and plenty of potential clients roamed about. Most of the birds were not covered completely in oil, most were not near death. They were, however, weighed down, unable to fly, at least not very far. And birds being birds, they lacked the brainpower to extrapolate into the future and conclude that their limited mobility would weaken their position in the food chain. Fortunately, the volunteers did possess said brainpower and were committed to restoring that chain.

Especially Regina, who seemed convinced that her measure of brainpower exceeded the cumulative total of all the capitalists on the planet. I snuck a glance at her, some distance to my right, and then a glance at Gretchen, equidistant to my left, and began a pattern: pluck a bird from the beach, sit one rock closer to Gretchen, clean the bird, find another bird, sit one rock closer to Gretchen. Lather, rinse, repeat.

Rock by rock I moved, slowly and patiently, until one young gull bolted from my grasp and into the surf, right in front of Gretchen's post.

"Kyle," she said from behind me, "you're encroaching on my area."

"Sorry, these younger birds bring out the encroacher in me."

Stooped over and reaching into the ripples, I tried to avoid getting my sneakers wet. Not a chance. With damp, cold socks and damp, cold feet, I pulled the gull from the surf, only to drop it as it pecked my hand. Its feathers stuck together, and it looked ridiculous trying to fly from the water.

Somehow the bird made it to land and hopped about as if to launch its body into the air, but the body just plopped over on the sand and rocks. Finally I caught up to the gull, grabbed it with two hands, and toted it back near Gretchen and went to work. I calmed the bird by stroking it gently, like one does with puppies.

"Read your article," I said to Gretchen. "Thanks for the mention."

"Don't mention it." She appeared distracted by her task, and

I noted how quickly the sludge had stained our shoes, jeans, and shirts.

My bird shook in my grasp, and a mix of water and oil dripped onto my feet. "Greek *oppressors?*"

Gretchen pulled some dried sludge from the tail feathers of her bird and flung it off her fingertips. "You liked that part?" She smiled.

"You left out the bad dancing."

We worked in silence and wiped the feathers of our fowl-in-progress. After we'd set two more victims inside the cage, we sat back on our rocks in a kind of coastal time-out. Regina perched at the shoreline to the west, working methodically to rid nature of the evil black goo.

Gretchen said, "I'm flattered that you came all this way to see me, Kyle. Have you ever flown before to go visit a woman?"

"To be honest, I've never had the money to do it until now."

She nodded, smiled, nodded again. "Fair enough."

It was the kind of exchange that could be taken at least two ways, one not so good, one not so bad. My plan was to work hard with her all day, show her how willing I was to support her interests and hobbies, then take her to dinner and explain my vocation and the reasons why I felt I could balance it with concern for the environment.

She beat me to the invitation.

"How about I make dinner for us tonight?" she asked. She sprayed cleaning concoction on her fingers and wiped them clean.

I kept my gaze on the sea and tried not to act like an excited schoolboy. I felt like an excited schoolboy. "Just the two of us?"

"I can arrange that, I think. And don't be too afraid of

Regina. She'll surprise you at times, make you laugh. We do laugh here, Kyle. Probably just to break the monotony."

I'd never even seen Regina *smile*, forget laughter, giggles, and guffaws.

Under cloudy skies Gretchen excused herself and made her way down the beach toward her roommate. She seemed in her element here, and her energy level confirmed that. I noted the excitement with which she and Regina conversed about their cause—and at times I felt like an outsider.

My pace of help—and willingness to help—slowed as I wandered the shore looking for another feathered victim. I wondered if the birds sensed that I was an oilman and preferred I not help at all.

A quick glance over my shoulder revealed Gretchen and Regina toting the plastic cage further up the beach. They set the cage on a level section of rock and dropped some food through a slot. From a distance I heard them talking over one another, as if they'd lit upon some topic and were outrunning each other to its conclusion.

I gathered an armful of soiled rags from the rocks and made my way down the beach toward the women. Up on the coastal highway, another news van rumbled past. This one honked, and I waved, then it honked again, and the women waved.

I did wonder, however, if Regina's and Gretchen's save-the-planet mentality bled into everything they did, such as extremist posters adorning the walls of their apartment and secret code words to which I remained clueless.

When I caught up to them, they were toting the plastic cage of birds up the sand to the highway, where I supposed the pickup truck would roll by at some point and collect the disenfranchised. I offered to help them carry the cage, but they said they could manage.

Regina turned for a moment and motioned with her head to the beach behind me. "Kyle," she said, "could you gather those other piles of dirty towels from the rocks?"

If she didn't want me around, she could just say so. I backtracked to the rocks, plucked the used towels, and looped them over my left arm, debating while I worked how I should disclose my vocational details over dinner. I had just walked farther west and stooped to gather more towels when a voice said from behind me, "Hey."

I wanted that voice to belong to Gretchen, but it was Regina. She stepped closer and stood staring at me.

"You came to help after all?" I asked, aware that I was stating the obvious but doing my best to keep all chat on the lighter side. She possessed an intimidating manner, as if she could fire off rebuttals faster than you could blink.

Regina folded her arms, and a midday breeze blew dark hair across her eyes. Beyond her in the distance, Gretchen helped the pickup truck driver load the cage into the bed.

A patronizing look came over Regina. "Kyle, I didn't ask you to help me gather towels in order to make small talk. I wanted to let you know that late last night I looked you up on the Internet."

Shakes, trembles, fear. "Unalaska has Internet?"

"I Googled you. You're the owner of Mango Enterprises, aren't you? You formed a small corporation in the state of Texas in order to sell oil from some wells you own in Anson, Texas."

Fear, trembles, shakes. "Why did you do that?"

Condemnation seeped from her eyeballs. "You also have a

partner from Korea, and thus far you haven't told Gretchen what you do for a living. Right?"

Needing a break from her judgmental gaze, I turned and faced the sea, toward the body of water that sloshed against the rocks that housed the birds that Regina valued more than life itself. "I can't believe you Googled me, Regina. Googling a person ought to be a crime, like burglary. It should at least be a misdemeanor."

She moved in front of me, blocking my view. "*Have* you told her?"

I met her gaze and stood my ground, though I felt assaulted by Regina's radical force field. "I don't have to do it on *your* schedule, if that's what you mean. You're not the arbiter of relationships here. And what do you want from me anyway? Why investigate me so thoroughly?"

She squared her shoulders to me and spoke matter-of-factly. "Half of our volunteers here have quit. Couldn't take it, or else they didn't love nature enough. I need more people to work in my crew."

She needs more people? "Are you saying that you want *me* in your crew?"

Her laserlike stare told me that manipulation had just replaced condemnation. "If you'll give me three weeks of your time, Kyle, I won't tell Gretchen what you really do for a living. Think about it—you came all this way to see her and you've already made such a good impression. Why ruin it?" She then pointed down the shore, where sad and tainted gulls waddled day and night. "And who knows, the oil on those seabirds may have come from your own wells. Tsk-tsk."

I had nothing more to say to Radical Regina. I didn't even help her gather the other pile of towels. I strode up the beach toward the highway and Gretchen, hoping the truck wouldn't pull away and take her along. Regardless, I would not be victim to Regina's agenda.

"Gretchen!" I called out across the rocks on the beach. "We need to have a talk."

She emerged from behind the pickup and said, "But I need to go with the pickup driver. Can we talk a little later?"

I strode faster until I was at the road. "Please just leave it for a few minutes, Gretch. This is more important than birds... even oil-soaked birds for that matter."

The driver looked like he didn't know what to do. But then Regina came around the hood of the truck, and she and the driver left together, Gretchen standing in the road and shrugging at Regina, Regina shrugging back through the window.

Without comment Gretchen untied a green fleece from around her waist and slipped it over her head. She pulled the fleece over her arms, and we walked down to the beach again, plenty of air between us. The smell of petroleum and seawater came and went with the breeze. "This must be important," she said.

"It is. And I should have told you earlier."

She seemed to sense the seriousness. "Go ahead, then, tell me."

We turned east at the shoreline and walked back toward our original cleaning stations. "Remember when you asked about my job?" I began, juggling in my head various ways to confess what needed confessing. "And I told you that the job involved a combination of engineering, transportation scheduling, and financial decision making?"

She paused beside the sea and nodded. "I remember."

Rather than a walking conversation, this was looking more

and more like a standstill conversation. "Do you remember the *product* my company produces?"

She thought on this for a long moment. Then she spotted a large feather on the shore, picked it up, and rubbed her thumb through the quills. "I don't think you ever mentioned the exact product."

I kneeled next to a tainted rock, swiped an index finger across its blackened surface, and held the finger up to her. "This is the basic product—West Texas crude oil. I inherited four oil wells, Gretchen. Four *productive* oil wells. From my Uncle Benny. I run a two-person small business, selling oil, drilling for more, and eventually reinvesting the proceeds." I paused for a breath and thought of one more nugget to share. "Oh, and some of the oil revenue goes to my mom because my deadbeat dad tends to waver on the alimony payments."

She looked stunned and said nothing, only blinking her shock.

"Chang is my business partner," I continued. "He's assisting an exploration company right now in drilling for more oil on the land. He was the coworker who called me last night in the restaurant."

Just as I had been unable to face Regina's blackmail, Gretchen seemed unable to face my confession. She stepped toward the water and stopped at its edge. Timid waves lapped in front of her. "You ... *and Chang too?*"

I spoke from behind her. "Yes. And that little grant you received three weeks ago from the anonymous donor, the one that allowed you to work another month here, well, that came from Mango Enterprises. You're being sponsored by oil money, Gretchen—to clean oil off oil-stricken birds."

She spun around to face me; then she flinched and shut her

eyes tight, as if the subject, like the water before her, were toxic. She appeared to want to say something, but then she turned and stared out at the sea again. The sunlight didn't reflect on the water; it made a milky cloud, the natural glow diluted by a sheen of oil.

Minutes passed. Excruciating minutes. So excruciating that I even tried to think of where I'd start looking for other prospects. Maybe I'd try Internet dating. Chang had signed up for eHarmony; maybe I should follow suit. I wasn't a bar hopper and being out of college meant more limited social opportunities.

After a couple more minutes of her silence, I couldn't take it anymore. I moved over beside her, both of us looking south, our gazes a parallel of awkwardness.

"Gretchen," I said in my best soft voice, "my oil wells don't harm—" Realizing this was wishful thinking, I halted myself in midsentence and changed course. "After the oil leaves my land I can't control what happens to it. The world needs fuel, Gretchen! And I'm not...an evil guy."

She remained silent, eyes locked on the rolling Pacific. "I just—"

"What?" I asked, desperate for a reply. "Tell me."

I knew it was coming; and it came in an animated outburst of hand gestures and accompanying body language, all of it emphasizing her point. "But Kyle, what if your oil is bought by some huge company, placed on a ship with millions of other barrels of oil, and it spills somewhere out in the Pacific and washes up on some island? Then...you know what that means? What Regina calls 'the black goo' would be *your* black goo! Then you'd be guilty, Kyle, guilty of ruining Fiji or Alaska or maybe even Maui! I can't date a guy whose black goo ruins Maui!"

"I doubt my oil ever reaches Maui, Gretchen." My tone lacked conviction, and I felt desperate to convince her that I was not some sinister oil baron.

She wasn't listening. "And what would the Hawaiian nene do if their pristine home suddenly got tainted with an oil slick? That's Hawaii's state bird, and there are less than nine hundred of them left. Where would they go?"

Her emotion swept past with all the energy of an F-16. In its backwash I paused to avoid an overreaction. Once again I summoned my soft voice. "Gretchen, I own a few small wells on the outskirts of Anson, Texas. How can you relate that to the extinction of an entire bird species on Maui?"

She folded her arms, avoided my gaze. "I extrapolate well."

"That's a huge extrapolation."

"It could happen."

I paused and thought through this with all the discernment a recent college graduate can muster. "So, if that scenario did occur, I assume that you and Radical Regina would then be found on a Hawaiian shore, cleaning the Hawaiian nene and penning articles about my evil intent in a paper called *The Hawaiian Breeze*?"

"We care about wildlife. And yes, if I could afford it, I would go help."

On that gray and barren beach, the next silence began with shared frowns and progressed to distant gazes. After several minutes of this, I faced her and said, "So, you would rather I leave?"

Gretchen folded her arms and raised her chin. Then she lowered her chin. "I'm concerned about how you'll be perceived once Regina tells all the volunteers about you. And trust me, she *will* tell them."

"So, you would rather I leave?"

She paused, her face blank. "Do you really want to be a part of this rescue operation, or are you mainly here to visit me?"

"I'm mainly here to visit you. I had hoped that you and I might, well…try again."

She didn't say anything for a while, and her body language gave few clues. "I feel called to be here, Kyle. I feel that God gave me a special affection for his creation and that I'm supposed to be making a difference here. And I suspect that you don't feel such a calling, and that—"

I nodded, and my nod cut her off. "I feel, um, called to run a small oil business in West Texas. And I happen to believe that getting to know you and running that business are not mutually exclusive pursuits."

It took her half a minute to speak again, and when she did, the words were just about what I expected. "It might be mutually exclusive for this summer."

"So, you would rather I leave?"

She could not bring herself to answer. And so our little cycle repeated: awkward silence begat awkward silence.

After returning her mediocre hug, I walked at a mediocre pace back to my mediocre motel and booked a seat on a very small plane.

I left Unalaska the next morning and connected with a Northwest 767 in Anchorage.

At twenty thousand feet and somewhere back over Washington state, I pondered my calling, asking God if owning oil wells was indeed a call on my life, or if I was simply a fortunate beneficiary, a stumbler into fortune. *An inheritor of an evil substance?* Maybe my holding on to it was the next symptom of being infected with Sins of the Uncle disease. Silently, and with my nose pressed to the window, I peppered the Almighty with direct questions.

Called to be with Gretchen?

Called to own oil wells?

Called to do both?

Neither?

One and then the other?

Surely if God was all-wise he could allow dual callings at the same time, one relational and one vocational.

Then at thirty thousand feet and somewhere back over Idaho, I took the opposing side of logic and considered, for the first time, if perhaps Gretchen was the wrong woman for me. No. I really didn't believe that. But as I would soon find out, there are varying degrees of *wrong*.

A KNOCK, A FLIRT, A JOB REQUESTED

The contrast worked in reverse too: the hot, humid mornings of Texas in July choking out the crisp, cool air of Alaska. Home again. *Gimme my Stetson, some sweet tea, and a plate of barbecue.*

Although the visit with Gretchen had not gone well, I had not given up on her. Surely there was middle ground, room for compromise. Didn't our chemistry demand it? And couldn't she realize that a man wants to make a good living and be a stable provider? My questioning conscience never let up.

Called to pursue Gretchen?

Called to own oil wells?

Like that silly melody to the "Chicken Dance," these dueling thoughts played over and over in my head. I could not rid myself of them. I showered to them, shaved to them, even poured milk over my Raisin Bran to them.

That same morning, however, I simply felt called to slip back into my jeans and boots and white button-down—my oilman clothes—and go off to work.

In downtown Lubbock I parked in the deck behind the office tower, rode the elevator alone up to the fourth floor, and found on my desk a note from Chang:

Kyle,

I'm out at the site in Anson overseeing piping installation for the new well. If you come out today, don't wear oilman clothes like jeans and boots. It hit 104 degrees here yesterday, so you'll be better off in shorts and sandals. Sorry if this doesn't fit with the dress code of Mango Enterprises, but I gotta survive, bro.

Your enthusiastic and hardworking VP,

Chang

P.S. I brought over my little dorm refrigerator and set it in the reception area. I haven't restocked it yet, but I did leave you some of my Dr Pepper.

I logged on to the Internet and checked Bloomberg for the latest oil quotes. While I'd been in Alaska the price had gyrated within a tight range as indecision grew over news out of OPEC. Those Middle Eastern sheikhs could turn off or turn on a few spigots and affect the entire worldwide industry. Such power.

I was comparing the unpredictability of the oil business to the unpredictability of pursuing Gretchen when a noise rattled me back to the present.

The knock on the door of Mango Enterprises sounded decidedly feminine. Without hesitation I hustled across the lobby and opened the door, surprised by an unknown face. Before me stood a complete stranger, not the female I wished had come calling.

She was roughly the same age as Gretchen and not unattractive with her short, straight dark hair, wide-set eyes, and friendly smile.

In the reflection of her lip gloss I searched for familiarity. Junior year? Nah. The dance at the Sigma house? Nope. Friend of Gretchen? Don't think so.

"Kyle?" she said, a trace of hope in her voice. "Kyle from Fort Worth?"

"Yes?" My brain spun into overdrive but produced no recognition. "Can I help you?"

She reached out and shook my hand with vigor. "I'm Margo, a friend of Trent's."

"Cool Trent? From high school?"

She shook my hand a few extra times, as if to ram home the point that she was here on good authority. "Well, actually I know him from college. He said to tell you hello and—"

I delayed her with a question. "How is ol' Trent?"

"Playing minor-league baseball in Florida. He said last he heard you'd started a business and that you might be hiring and that I should—"

"Hiring? You mean like offering jobs?"

She nodded with the same vigor that she shook hands.

Finally I figured Margo-who-I'd-never-met was not going to ask if I was busy, so I motioned her into the lobby and shut the door behind her. "Margo, um, I'm glad to meet a friend of Trent's, but I think you have some bad information."

She scanned the lobby as if she had ideas for redecorating, like she'd forgotten I was there. After she peeked into Chang's office, her attention orbited back to me. I stood in the hallway wondering about this woman's agenda.

"Kyle," she said, and she said it softly and moved closer. "I come from a successful family, one that helps friends of friends. And if I don't land a job soon, then I'll be the black sheep, and surely you wouldn't want a friend of your buddy Trent to—"

"A job?"

She moved toward me, looked up into my face with all the flirtarama she could muster, then reached out and traced a fingernail down the front of my shirt. "I was wondering if you might have something."

There in the lobby of my own business I wanted to take a step back but felt frozen in place, stunned at her forwardness. "*Have* something?"

A second fingernail. "A job, Kyle. I could really use a job. I mean, Trent told me about your business, that you own your own company now—Mango Dinner Spices? So I guess y'all make spices, like for casseroles and stuff?"

Why me, God?

Without reply I backed away, fearful of floozy fingers tracing on my shirt. Right now I couldn't even picture the right woman's fingers on my shirt.

Undeterred, Margo checked out my own office. Again she frowned as if the décor was too sparse for her taste. "So, can we talk about a position with Mango Dinner Spices?" she asked. "Need a VP of oregano? I could at least help you decorate."

I figured maybe she was on the rebound from a relationship, this stranger who'd interrupted my day. *Mango Dinner Spices....* I stifled a laugh and told Margo that I had no openings. "Sorry, Margo, but this is just a two-person operation. My sole partner is all I need right now."

She strolled back into the lobby, stopped beside the coffee table, and plucked a mint from the guest bowl. "No need for a receptionist?"

"No, sorry."

She popped a mint into her mouth but said nothing.

I made my way to the front door and opened it for her, hoping this Margo would get the message and depart. After three more free mints—she ate them one at a time, as if stalling—she reached into her purse.

"Well, here's my card, Kyle." She thrust the card into my hand. "Call me if you have a future opening. In fact, call me if you just want to meet for dinner sometime. Or call me for lunch. Just call me, I guess!"

After she'd left, I took a moment to fold her card into a tiny airplane. I even adjusted its little wings. On its maiden voyage—a short, domestic route with no meals or drinks or even a free pack of peanuts—that plane flew directly into a trash basket.

No survivors.

Investigators ruled out terrorism, blaming the crash instead on pilot error.

At three thirty that afternoon I arrived in Anson, Texas, having driven the one hundred fifty miles in record time, and paused on the shoulder of the highway. The dry plain seemed to welcome me as owner, and in the distance, across the baked soil and scrub brush, Chang stood beside a steel, towerlike structure. It was an oil derrick—at least forty feet tall—and housed in its center the drill pipe. I knew it was an oil derrick because I had read about them in a book about land drilling. I'd even brought that book along with me.

Page two stated, "After scientific studies indicate the possible presence of oil, an oil company selects a well site and installs a derrick—a towerlike steel structure—to support the drilling equipment. A hole is drilled deep into the earth until oil or gas is found or until the company abandons the effort."

I sat in my car for a few minutes and scanned the length and breadth of the land. I could not bring myself to see this as the breeding ground for an evil substance. It looked peaceful out here, this dry stretch of dirt. Even the two vultures on the opposite side of the highway, inspecting the carcass of some unfortunate critter, seemed at peace with the world. And I supposed, for a pair of vultures — they looked male and female — this was a romantic dinner out. I bet that Mrs. Vulture had no qualms about Mr. Vulture being in the roadkill business.

It's all a matter of perspective, Gretchen.

Through the driver's-side window I perused the property. From the other holes evidently abandoned, it appeared that four attempts had led to one success, which I knew was a phenomenal ratio. But then I thought of Gretchen's reaction if she were here, and I didn't know whether to feel lucky, blessed, or cursed.

Chang spotted me in the Toyota and waved, as did the guy operating the drill. They both looked baked and sweaty, as if they'd been out there for weeks.

They had also cut a new road — rough as it was and barely graded — from the highway. The road ran down the embankment and out across the dusty flats for several hundred yards to the drilling site. A makeshift sign greeted me. It read: CHANG AVENUE.

I made a slow left off the highway, rattled by the vibrations from this road of ruts. Not that I minded the rattles. I figured real oilmen don't walk across their land to their oil wells; they drive right up beside the wells in their pickup trucks, dust spewing from the tires. And so what if I currently drove an old Celica? Dust still spewed from the tires.

It felt good to be back in Texas.

Chang, in his shorts, Red Raider T-shirt, and white Stetson, strode through the dust and greeted me at my car door. "Welcome home, partner!" he said and half pulled me from the seat.

I shook his hand and offered a brief wave to the guy working the derrick, some twenty yards to our left. The afternoon seemed to grow hotter by the second, and when I touched the hood of my car, a sizzling sound arose.

"Great to be back, Chang," I said as I noted the progress. "Looks like you guys did good. I see that you even cut a new road to the property—Chang Avenue?"

"You like that, eh?"

"Why not Mango Avenue?"

Chang shrugged, wiped the sweat from his eyes. He tugged his white Stetson; dirty orange finger marks stained the brim. "Since your name is on the office door and our business cards, I just thought we should strive for a little balance."

"Naming a road after yourself is balance?"

Chang pointed behind him to the new well and tried to talk Texan. "See what your VP of New Oil Discovery discovered, li'l doggie?"

Hidden by the glare, the guy operating the drilling equipment laughed.

I lowered my voice. "Chang, you shouldn't call your boss man 'li'l doggie' in front of the hired help."

The drilling operator climbed down and opened the cooler he had tied over the back wheel well. I couldn't see his face as he spoke while digging through melting ice. "It's okay, Mr. Mango," he said into the cooler. "I've been trying to teach Chang how to speak Texan. Though if truth be told, I'm no true Texan myself. A New Yorker, actually."

Hands dripping with water, he popped the top of a Diet Coke

and turned to face us. Even in jeans and a New York Yankees ball cap, he had the look of a used car salesman. This time, a glimpse of recognition, an unexpected face, this one unshaven. The accent was familiar; I knew this man. I recognized this man. This man took bets.

"Sal?" I said, wondering how—and why—Chang hired this guy to handle exploratory drilling on my land. "Sal-the-bookie? What are you doing here?"

He tipped his cap and said, "Drilling is my real job, Mr. Mango. Been doing it for years."

For a moment I couldn't form words. "But you're a *bookie*. I can't have a bookie exploring for oil on my land."

Chang, propped against the side of my car and observing the interaction, appeared very confused. He asked, "Sports bookie?"

"Not always on sports," Sal explained. During the ensuing minutes he dove into a long-winded explanation about the history of betting in the United States, including the many forms that originated in Europe and were brought over with the first settlers. "I'd wager that Christopher Columbus had men on board betting that they'd never make it across the ocean."

Chang tipped up the brim of his hat. "Well, if they won that bet and never made it across, how would anyone ever collect their winnings? They'd all be dead and drowned."

Sal slowly shook a finger at Chang, as if to say, *You make a very good point, young man*. But instead Sal said, "In that case, a whole new realm of betting opens up."

I couldn't resist. "What 'whole new realm'? There can't be a new realm if Columbus and his whole crew drowned."

Sal, confident as ever, rolled his eyes, shook his finger again. "Think about it, Mr. Mango. Think about it, Chang. If Columbus and his ship goes down, what now lies at the bottom of the ocean?"

"Dead bodies?" I asked.

"Spanish treasure," Chang blurted.

Sal beamed. "Now you twos are thinking like a bookie. A bookie would then take bets—with favorable odds, of course—that shipwreck searchers would never find any of the Spanish treasure on the ocean floor. You see…a whole new realm."

Chang smiled as if he had just caught on to some mysterious riddle. But then he said, "Sal, what odds would you give that some family treasure was once buried on the very land on which you're standing and that the bullion was stolen by the owner's mother?"

"Betting on a specific name for a specific crime would require very long odds. Very little chance of that happenin'." Sal then eyed both of us as if he'd just figured out that he was talking to a pair of novices. "And you should understand that a wise bookie never speculates about a client's mother. Bad for business. Very bad. A guy could get shot."

During the ensuing minutes, as we all stood in a loose triangle of heat and sweat, the drill pipe turning behind us in slow revolutions, I questioned Sal about his oil exploration experience. He pointed to the new well and said he'd been drilling wells for nineteen years. I also questioned him about his motivation, since last time I'd seen him he was collecting the last of a bet won from my very dead and very generous uncle.

Sal put his hand over his heart, as if to show sympathy. "What can I say, Mr. Mango? I drill for oil, I take some bets. Guess I live for risk. And then, well, there's my little Tommy…"

Oh no, not the wallet-sized photo.

But here it came. The wallet. The photo. Little Tommy on a shiny tricycle—probably purchased with Uncle Benny's lost wagers.

"Ain't he the handsomest little guy?" Sal said and tapped the photo with his pinkie.

What else can you say when a parent whips out the photo? "Yeah, Sal, handsome kid."

He flashed the photo at Chang.

Chang leaned in and said, "Ah, has Daddy's mischievous grin."

To the west I took note of the new well—now the fifth one on the property—and wondered if Sal had actually done the discovering.

I pointed west. "You drilled that well?"

Sal nodded. "Did indeed." He then moved next to Chang and put his arm around my partner. "Me and Chang here did it ourselves. Today was originally going to be the last day of my four-day contract with Mango Enterprises. But now, with all this discovery going on, I'm thinking you should hire me on a longer-term basis."

Embarrassed to be clutched by a sweaty drill operator, Chang returned my glance and twitched his mouth, as if caught in a difficult spot.

I already foresaw where this was going—a threesome instead of a twosome. Kyle and Chang and Sal, rather than just Kyle and Chang. But perhaps, with much of the land still unexplored, it would be better for business to have an experienced drilling guy on board, at least temporarily. Hiring Sal certainly beat hiring Margo-the-brain-dead-floozy, who thought my business was Mango Dinner Spices.

Still suspicious of Sal, I decided to question his veracity.

"So you're tellin' me that you drive a drill truck and *take bets* in order to provide for Tommy?"

"My only son. My wife left me some years ago, for an accountant, if you can believe that. Now little Tommy is getting expensive. So, whattaya say, Kyle? Can you give a guy some work? A month of exploratory ventures on this here land of yours?"

I hesitated, did math in my head. "Same rate we're paying you now?"

"Same rate. Uh, but I don't work no Sundays. I goes to church."

Of course. The world made total sense now. Sal-the-bookie drills for oil and goes to church, my mom is Bullion Betty, and the girl I like prefers seagulls to dating.

College had not prepared me for such tangents. Not even Texas Tech, which offered seniors a course to help them transition from college life to real life.

I should have taken that course.

TWO TIRED GUYS SPRAWLED ON AN OFFICE FLOOR, TALKING ABOUT WOMEN

Wednesday afternoon I hired Sal Sabbatini on a month-to-month contract. The week had gone badly, with one burst pipe and two broken drill bits—expensive pieces of equipment that put a dent in the monthly profit. Work suddenly seemed to dominate my waking hours, though I considered myself a compartmentalized male, fully capable of balancing personal life with work life.

I was driving back from Anson again, thinking about the company expense report, when the recurring thoughts burst into my head again.

Called to own oil wells?

Called to pursue Gretchen?

Both?

Yes, both.

During the ensuing miles of flat Texas highway, those thoughts took on the form of signage. Like taunting mirages, I saw the signs hanging from the arms of cactus and trailing behind crop dusters, banners of conflict whipping in the wind.

Two hands on the steering wheel, I wondered what it would be like to be poor and struggling but to have Gretchen, and then what it would be like to be really wealthy, but to lose any chance with her. Then, somehow, I started thinking about my mom's favorite movie, *Pretty Woman*, and the comment she'd made the last time we watched it together. She'd said, "I realize that the ending is all romancy and everything for Richard Gere to come back and take Julia Roberts away from her tiny apartment and whisk her off to the easy life, but would he have been willing to leave the easy life, enter into *her* life, and live with her in the tiny apartment?"

My little sister had then interjected, "But Mom, Julia Roberts was a hooker."

Mom thought about this for all of five seconds. "Neither Richard nor Julia would need to continue with hookering, dear. They both could take normal jobs like flipping burgers. People in love and sharing life together should not mind flipping burgers together."

For a moment I grasped the parallel but lost it in the sunset as I sped west.

Chang and I arrived back at the office at 7:00 p.m., both of us wiped out from toiling in the sun all afternoon. We grabbed the last two Dr Peppers from the refrigerator and agreed to talk about the budget—and women—before breaking for the evening.

"Can we talk in the lobby?" he asked.

I said, "Sure," and watched him sprawl on the carpet, his spiky damp hair barely moving beneath the ceiling fan. On the opposing side of the lobby I sat on the floor and used the sofa as a backstop. "Chang, I'm too tired to discuss budget stuff tonight."

Laid out flat on his back, he turned his head to sip from his drink. "You like Sal okay?"

"He's all right, I guess. Kinda talkative, in a New Yorker kind of way."

Chang guzzled his drink and set the can on the carpet. "He can really operate the drilling equipment."

"Seems that way." The heat had drained my energy, and as I reclined in our air-conditioned lobby I felt compelled to change subjects. "Had any dates recently, Chang?"

"One," he said, resignation in his voice.

"eHarmony?"

"Yep."

"No chemistry?"

"Nope."

For the two of us this amounted to deep, relational conversation. "Gonna keep trying?"

"Yep."

"Good."

Chang nodded. "What about you? You still trying?"

This required some thought, this business of continuing to *try*. "If you can call Alaska a date, then yep, I've been trying. This thing with Gretchen is just so hard to figure."

For a long minute Chang said nothing. Then he placed his hands behind his head. "Women are difficult."

"Women can be headstrong too." Or perhaps it was me who was headstrong.

"Then why do you think we keep pursuing them?"

I'd pondered this often, and though the carbonation in my drink didn't spur original thinking, perhaps it did foster a certain primitive logic. "Because there aren't any alternatives. God only made male and female. Not a lot of choices there."

Chang stared up at the ceiling fan for a moment and shut his eyes. Finally he said, "I thought I smelled perfume when I walked in earlier." Twice more he sniffed the air. "Yep, still smell it. You got something to tell me, li'l doggie?"

I sniffed the air and sighed. "It was some young lady who knew a high school friend of mine. She came by to see if I would offer her a *job*."

"You offered her one?"

"We didn't need her. Plus she didn't even know what we do here."

Chang sat up and looked at me as if he had wisdom to share. "What's her name?"

"Margo."

He smiled, shook his head. "You can never get involved with any woman named Margo."

"Why's that?"

"Because if you married her, you'd have a wife named Margo Mango."

Ah.

Chang blinked at the ceiling fan. "A woman named Margo Mango sounds like a feather-haired cocktail waitress at the Copacabana."

"No, Chang, that's not the girl who worked at the Copacabana. Her name was Lola."

"Right...she was a showgirl."

The deep, relational conversation had exhausted us both. "You hungry?"

"Yeah. Pizza?"

I shook my head no and rose to leave. "Real oilmen should probably eat steak. At least once a week, anyway."

Chang did four push-ups on the lobby floor and pronounced it a workout. Then he sprang to his feet and dusted off his hands. "Let's eat steak, pardner."

A pattern began that night—Thursday night steaks and man-to-man talks about women and dating, manhood and responsibility, how to tell when a woman is truly interested, and when a relationship requires sacrifice.

On the way to my car I told Chang that the jury was still out on Gretchen; he said the jury needed to reread its instructions.

The only recent correspondence I'd received from her was a postcard of a melting glacier, her note on the back informing me that the work in Alaska was winding down and that she had no idea where she was going next. She did, however, thank me for my honesty in explaining my vocation. And though I checked both sides of the postcard, I found no drawings of dead gulls covered in oil.

A ray of hope.

I wore my oilman clothes to the restaurant, driving my business partner and admiring the fading reds of a Lone Star sky. En route Chang used his cell phone to invite our newly contracted employee to join us for steaks. While I still had suspicions about Sal, I also recognized that he had proven himself an able worker, a punctual employee, and was in the process of discovering a sixth well on the property. Or so he claimed.

In the lobby of Texas Roadhouse, we shook hands, and everyone told each other the depth of their hunger. Sal cleaned up well, though his black on black, together with two days' growth on his chin, made him look like the bad guy in a cheap Western.

"I left a ten-gallon hat full of sweat out on your land today, Mango," he said while we waited to be seated. Then he turned to Chang. "That *did* sound Texan, didn't it?"

"Sounded good to me," Chang said. The two of them, being

New Yorker and Korean, respectively, somehow knew as much Texan as I did.

A hostess seated us at a table for four, and even before the sweet tea arrived Chang solicited Sal's advice, though the advice was not intended for himself. "Ever tried to date anyone long-distance, Sal?"

Over his menu, Sal said, "Can't say that I have."

Apparently Sal had no clue as to the real intent of the question and thought Chang was only making small talk.

Chang tried again. "Well, would you try if you thought there were possibilities?"

"I might." He tapped page two of his menu. "You ordering the sirloin or the filet?"

Chang's frustration caused him to reach over and pull down the top of Sal's menu. "Sal, Kyle is pursuing a young woman who favors birds over oil, and he's having a problem convincing her to give him a chance. We thought that with you being older and all, you might have some advice."

Sal sat up straight. "Well why didn't somebody say so? I'm trying to figure out which steak I want, and you twos are talking about lovey-dovey stuff. I need straight facts, not vague girly talk."

I played with my knife and said, "She likes birds."

"Birds?" Sal repeated, with a cock of his head. "Like crows and blue jays? Or is it penguins? I do have myself a soft spot for the penguins."

"She cleans oil off birds. Seagulls mostly…in Alaska."

Sal took in this info with the blank-faced expression of one who has serious doubts. "You fell for an environmental wacko, didn't ya, Mango?"

I unwrapped my utensils from a napkin and said, "I wouldn't

call her that. Right now she's simply cleaning sludge off seagulls. And she's probably going to another disaster area after this one."

He spoke from behind his menu. "Sounds wacko to me. But hey, if she's the one for you, don't hold back. Go after her. Women like the pursuit."

Over steaks and baked sweet potatoes I told the guys that juggling international dating and our growing business could get a bit stressful, and that if Mango Enterprises was going to continue to keep all three of us on the payroll, plus send a monthly check to my mom, then we had better pursue excellence in our jobs. My goal was to be a positive and inspiring boss. "And before we know it, Sal might even bring another new well on line," I said over my steak knife.

This news was greeted by my dinner party with raised glasses and a toast to the month ahead. Vocationally it was looking like a pretty good month. Relationally it was as gray and murky as the Alaskan shoreline.

Under the scent of steaks cooked well, rare, and halfway in between, we split the check three ways and declared ourselves too full for dessert. Sal wiped his mouth and said he wanted us to know that he appreciated working with us. Then he stood, dropped his napkin on his plate, and said to no one in particular, "Yesterday I met with my pastor and repented of the bookie life."

"No kidding?" Chang said, as if encouraged to hear such news. "I've heard people repenting of drugs, alcohol, even cheating on college exams, but I've never heard of bookie repentance."

We left the table and made our way to the front, Sal explaining over his shoulder that he wasn't used to repenting of anything and that he'd been advised to "replace gambling with something positive." He pushed open the door to the restaurant and motioned us into the night. "I figure now with my oil drilling biz going well, it's time to leave gambling behind."

Out in the night air we all paused in the parking lot beside the hood of Sal's Tahoe, which was parked next to my Celica. I couldn't let his confession go without further probing. "And so you're through taking bets, for good?"

"I'm now into mission work."

"But you just signed on to work with *us* for four weeks."

Sal leaned against the front of his Tahoe. "And I fully intend to give you four weeks, Mango. But I'd like to request that I be allowed to work two, take one week without pay, then work two more."

I grudgingly agreed to his plan, given that I too had just left the business for Alaska. So I had to expect my employees to occasionally request time away. There in the parking lot Sal explained that he had sold his bookie business, had given a chunk of what he called "sin money" to his church, and then had "made plans to use my drilling skills for the common good."

Chang, illumined beneath a street light and temporarily at a loss for words, gathered himself and asked Sal for a definition of "common good."

"I'm going to help install irrigation pipes for some poor folks who need water for farming," Sal explained. He picked at a fingernail and seemed quite confident in himself.

"Poor folks?" Chang inquired. "Down in south Lubbock?"

"Nope, over in western Kenya."

Chang and I exchanged a quick glance. *Africa?*

Over the hood of the Tahoe I said, "Let me get this straight, Sal. You repent of being a bookie one day, and suddenly you feel God wants you to go dig irrigation ditches in Kenya?"

Sal nodded. "Thems the straight facts, spoken well. Thanks for summing it up for us, Mango."

On the way home I considered that maybe I needed to do some repenting myself—repent of trying too hard with Gretchen. But no, the more I thought about it, the more I became convinced that I hadn't tried hard enough.

THE UNEXPECTED INVITATION

A week later, as August unfurled yet another heat wave over Texas, I heard from Gretchen again. The note came via e-mail, and it greeted me in bold font, cyber-routed from Alaska.

Kyle,

Just thought I'd write and say hello. We're in the last week of work here, and believe it or not I already know where I'm going next.

I know this sounds crazy, but there is a small project coming together in France. I've always wanted to see France. (I won't be in Paris, but the rural part of France.) It has nothing at all to do with oil, and Regina said if you wanted to join us there you are welcome to come and that she'd not be hard on you. I really think it would be a more relaxing time for us — if you can get off work again, that is.

This project is smaller, and yet we only have two or three people so far: me, Regina, and possibly a local man who only speaks French.

Let me know! (We're arriving in France on August 30 and staying till September 7.)

Gretchen

In my apartment I tried to watch a college football game between Baylor and the Houston Cougars, though I could not get my mind off Gretchen's note. The note said the trip had nothing to do with oil—which sounded encouraging—and yet our looming obstacle had lots to do with oil—which left me flustered. Not because I absolutely had to spend the rest of my life in this business, but because I now had two employees plus my mother and siblings all benefiting from the revenue. Whenever I made any business decision, at least half a dozen people stood to gain or to lose.

Then there were Sal's words about the "common good," a phrase which now competed for thought space along with *oilman, Gretchen,* and *the "Chicken Dance" melody,* which seemed glued to the inside of my cranium. The common good felt like what I was doing already. In fact, in many ways it was uncommonly good, this stumbling into oil well ownership just by being born a Mango. *Then again, if uncommonly good job-wise makes for uncommonly bad girl-wise…*

The ball game eased into halftime, and I muted the marching band and thought of rural France. I had no idea just how to think of rural France, just that it was about to host the one person who I most wanted to be around.

By the time the second half began and Baylor fumbled the kickoff, Gretchen and I had toured France in a convertible, hiked the French Alps, kissed on a mountaintop, and shared fourteen different French desserts. All of them chocolate. Somewhere along the journey we'd even discussed ways to compromise our differences, though in the blur of my nap the details seemed as fuzzy as French fur.

No, not fur, Mango. Don't ever mention fur around Gretchen. And don't ever buy her a fur unless it's fake.

Throughout the rest of the game I came and went from France—even doing the backpack-through-Europe thing with her before settling back to Texas and domesticity.

Yep, I'd meet her there. I'd go to France. In a heartbeat.

Further boosting my confidence was the fact that I could *afford* to go, what with the new well and increasing oil revenue. Texans called it "black gold." Tonight I considered it a Petroleum VISA Card.

Chang burst into my office first thing Monday morning, sans Stetson but still in jeans and boots and button-down. "I have a big question for you, Kyle."

Across my desk I sensed enthusiasm. "You want to request that you be allowed to operate the drilling equipment? I know, I know, it's like being a kid and seeing your first bulldozer; you just want to drive the thing. I've had similar thoughts myself."

He looked excited and grabbed the edge of my desk. "No, not that, boss. I want to ask if you'd let me have some time off too—so that I can take Sal up on his offer to go with him to Kenya. He said they're taking volunteers to help build a water system for some village and that if I could get my shots we'd leave in two weeks."

Surprised to hear him so enthused about the subject, I said, "You want to volunteer too?"

Chang said, "That's right," and at the same time pointed at my chest.

I knew what he was getting at but avoided the subject. "Aren't you a little nervous about going into Africa?"

Chang stood tall, raised his chin. "Sure…but they put you up for free if you're willing to work. Sal said *all three of us* should go."

"All *three* of us?" I asked, with the expression of one picturing his leg gnawed by a hyena.

Chang suddenly possessed the demeanor of the wise scribe. "You miss the point, boss. We all three go over there and volunteer, we help the poor, we use our drilling expertise, we show ourselves to be an internationally minded corporation, and we might just qualify for a tax deduction. Charity is good for the résumé."

I did my best to be an understanding boss. "I'm glad you're wanting to help the less fortunate, Chang but, um, I can't go."

"Why not?"

"Because I leave August 31 for France.…Gretchen invited me."

Chang slowly shook his head. "Now she wants you to take her *to France*?"

"Nope. She's going with Regina. Gretchen wants me to meet them there. Says we should try again, get to know each other in a 'nonoily' environment."

Chang leaned against the wall of my office and turned up the AC. After testing the vent for a moment with the back of his hand, he said, "Can I offer you some relational advice?"

I shifted in my chair. "Sure."

"It's probably a bold move for you to go meet Gretchen in France, and it'll probably be easier on you than Alaska. But if you don't get a sense that she's willing to make sacrifices to reciprocate, you'd best reconsider the beats of your love-starved Texas heart."

Something didn't jibe in that little speech. "Chang, where do you get a phrase like 'the beats of your love-starved Texas heart?'"

He crossed his arms confidently. "Lyrics to a country song. I heard it on the radio Friday while Sal and I were drilling. The song's been in my head ever since."

"A New Yorker and a Korean listening to country together.... Now there's diversity personified."

"Country keeps us entertained. I mean, with us trying to discern the meanings and all. Seems everyone in the songs has an inordinate amount of bad stuff happen to them."

"Ya noticed that, eh?"

Chang played one bar of air guitar. "They should change the genre from Country and Western to Country and Depression."

This triggered a thought. "Ya think I'm heading for some depression by going to France?"

He shrugged. "No idea. Just realize that you two have some major talking to do, given your polar opposite passions. And you should ask yourself if she would be willing to fly across oceans to visit *you*."

I had no idea where he gathered his wisdom — if it was indeed wisdom — but it sounded good. "So you're saying that after I go to France, Gretchen needs to fly here to see me."

He counted on two fingers. "So far, this makes two trips for Kyle, zero trips for Gretchen."

True dat.

He went into his own office, and I heard him on the phone with Delta Airlines. That's when it occurred to me that if he and I flew off on overlapping trips, no one would be here to run Mango Enterprises.

Once again I scooted my desk chair so that I could see into his office across the hall. "Chang, I'm not sure I can let you go to Kenya in two weeks. I need you here to run the business."

"But I'm just twenty-two and have a chance to see Africa, Kyle. Africa! I'm getting to help people in a foreign country."

I paused to form my argument. "You came all the way from Korea to Lubbock, Texas, for cryin' out loud. That's a foreign country, isn't it?"

"I really want to go, boss."

Maybe I was being unfair. Then again, maybe not. "What if I said a flat 'no'?"

Across the hall in his chair, Chang folded his arms, pursed his lips. "What if I said a flat 'I quit'?"

I couldn't afford to lose him, though I wondered if he knew that. "You'd really quit over not getting to go to Kenya? You don't even know what to expect there."

"I'll be helping with irrigation," he said. "And possibly earning a tax deduction for Mango Enterprises . . . and helping people less fortunate than ourselves."

There it was — the compassion argument, with a dash of finance. I tried to twist his argument against him. "How fortunate do you consider *yourself*?"

His answer stunned me. "Well, my roommate in freshman year arrived after escaping the oppression of a frat house, then he inherited four oil wells from his crazy uncle and gave me a job that pays more than twice what I made last summer. Plus I get an expense account. So, I'd say I'm pretty fortunate . . . li'l doggie."

"Yes, I reckon you are."

"So, can I go to Kenya?"

I moved to the doorway of his office and pleaded my case. "But who will run the business if I'm in France and you and Sal are out on safari in Africa?"

Palms out, he could only shrug.

An hour later, in my office, I went online and checked the price of crude oil, which was up again, and this favorable news somehow tipped me over the edge into compromise.

"Chang," I said from behind my computer, "can you arrange all pickups and deliveries of our next two weeks' oil production, make sure the refineries pay us on time, call the office cleaning service and remind them to water our plants, *and* get Sal to turn in the rented drilling equipment before he leaves so that excess charges don't accrue?"

Again he shrugged. "No problem, boss. That's the stuff I do every day."

Of course he did. I knew that.

FAST MANGO
IN PARIS

On August 31, my evening began at the Lubbock airport, my destination the tiny town of Bourg d'Oisans, in the southeastern corner of France. Google Earth — and a directional e-mail from Gretchen — had revealed the town closer to Italy than to the City of Lights. Getting there required a short, direct flight from Lubbock to Dallas, followed by a long, direct flight from Dallas to Paris.

After a short layover in Dallas, I boarded a 767 and found I had a window seat, a nervous stomach, and a feeling that this trip would make or break the relationship.

Next to me sat twin teenage boys. Both held iPods in their laps, earphones inserted in their ears. After an hour I already disliked them: they were restless, they played air guitar in their seats, and they had the annoying habit of trying to unplug the other's music when they thought their twin had fallen asleep. I looked out my window at the intake of the 767's monstrous turbine engine and imagined tossing those iPods into its suction, digital splinters spewing past the tail section. I smiled, stuffed my pillow into the corner, and realized I was thinking like an old person.

Seven hours sleeping on a plane passed like, well, about like seven hours sleeping on a plane. I tried to force some kind of romantic dream about Gretchen, but an oily sheen kept dulling the vision. I didn't realize that our second long-distance meeting was imminent until wheels touched down on the runway and I heard someone in the row behind me say, "Aw, man, it's *always* cloudy in France."

I departed in a daze. Customs came and went with a grunt of hoisted luggage and a southern "*Merci.*"

Half jogging, half walking toward terminal D, I gave the French high marks for placing their train station within the airport. Americans love convenience, and I was very American.

Entering terminal C, I glanced at Gretchen's instructional e-mail and memorized step two: *You'll need to catch the bullet train in Paris. They call it the TGV, and it's about a 3-hour ride to Grenoble. Do not get off the train at Lyon. Stay put and ride another half hour to Grenoble. The two of us will meet you in the train station at 3:00 p.m. (France time, not Texas time).*

A glance at an overhead screen revealed a train schedule. Next train departure at 11:50 a.m. I already had my ticket — God bless the Internet — and when I checked my watch I saw 4:38 a.m. Still on Texas time.

Each of five bullet trains were separated from the next by a concrete loading platform. People rushed onto these platforms and inserted tickets into a machine, which stamped them with authority and regurgitated them with haste. Train doors seemed to open by osmosis.

Everyone looked as if they knew exactly what they were doing; I had little idea what I was doing. For a moment I even panicked and thought I'd misjudged the time. Limited in communication by a lifelong reliance on English, I pulled my luggage closer to the loading platforms and paused there until I overheard an elderly woman say to her friend, "Doris, I think that middle train goes to Grenoble. Let's get on that one."

I humbled myself, stamped my ticket, and followed the elderly.

Behind me I heard a buzzer buzz three times. People scurried off the platform and disappeared into train cars.

Five cars later I spotted the correct one and boarded, knowing that in my earlier haste I had outthought myself. When one is not particularly bright to begin with, outthinking oneself is rare, and, in this case, ominous.

What if I was also outthinking myself about Gretchen? What if she really did prefer helping gulls to dating me? Then again, what if I preferred owning oil wells to being with the right woman?

I sat near the back of the third car and scooted close to the window. Fellow passengers conversed in German, French, Spanish. I rested my head in the cushion and wished I'd packed a sandwich.

Fog and clouds lifted as the bullet train sped away from the city. Soon the rolling green hills hosted grazing white cattle. The scene seemed so very French—placing in fields a smattering of cows whose colors all matched. Prelude to a painting.

The bullet train sped along at something near 160 miles per hour—a pace on par with my anticipation—and central France zipped by my window in a fast-forward blur of green fields and small chateaus. In Grenoble I departed the TGV train and looked for a familiar face, preferably Gretchen's. Regina's as last resort. Foreigners of many makes and models passed in front of me, French voices blurting things I could not understand.

Then I spotted her, beneath the flashing arrival board. Gretchen waving, Regina stoic beside her.

Gretchen looked really happy to see me. She ran toward me and threw her arms around my neck. "Kyle, I can't believe you're here! France is gonna be great."

"I'm here," I said into her ear. "And I'm really gonna need help reading menus."

She hugged me a second time. That scent of honeysuckle again. The sun streaks in her hair. *Gretchen, you're squeezing all the blood into my head and here comes Regina and she's not smiling at all but then she never smiles.*

After the long international hug, Gretchen and I stepped back and Regina sauntered over, stuck out her hand, and without a hint of warmth said, "Welcome to France, Kyle."

While shaking Regina's hand I wondered if she were thinking what I was thinking: *Don't bother to hug me. It'll be awkward for both of us.*

I took note of Gretchen again, how the Alaskan summer had lent her a tan, how her daily toil on that rocky coast had toned her arms. Then I said the one thing that most dominated my thoughts. "Can I get a sandwich here? I'm starving."

Minutes later the three of us piled into Regina's rental car—a hybrid—and I sat in the back with my carry-on bag and a long sandwich that the women called an Atlantic. Inside the soft bread lay tuna and cucumber and at least six other ingredients, and it tasted Frenchly delicious.

We wound our way through mountainous turns, the view dwarfed by the snowcapped peaks of the French Alps. It was all so scenic outside the car; it was all so surreal *inside* the car, what with Gretchen turning around every so often to grin at me.

"Feel like going on a hike this afternoon?" she asked.

I lowered my window and glanced up at the height of a peak. "Steep, icy, and treacherous?"

Gretchen shook her head. "Scenic, green, and breathtaking."

The two-lane highway wound through a small town, and the town looked quite girly: quaint little shops offering handmade crafts and jewelry, others tempting you with the sweet smells of confections, most of them chocolate. Both women turned their heads in unison as we passed the confectioner, and Regina swerved the car to avoid hitting a lamp post.

"I love chocolate truffles," Gretchen offered to no one in particular. "We have some at the lodge."

Regina steered us out of the town and up a steep road. "I *do* love chocolate," she said in measured tone, "but not as much as I love protesting against oil companies."

I bit my tongue and reminded myself that it would be a crime to offer Regina a chocolate truffle with petroleum center.

We turned off the winding highway and ascended an even narrower road, this one also paved, also winding. At its end sat an old stone lodge, a two-story with long tendrils of ivy growing up the walls, an abode that blended well with the forest behind.

Regina parked with a jolt, as if she were mad at the brake pedal for being manufactured from hardened rubber, a distillate of oil.

Before we could even open the doors and admire the view and take in the scent of the surrounding flora, Regina said, "Kyle, we realize that you just arrived in France and are probably eager to see the sights, but I want you to understand our true purpose in being here—and how you fit into our plan."

Gretchen nodded.

I raised my hand. "Just what is the plan?"

Regina opened her door, as did Gretchen. They both got out of the car, so I followed suit and opened the trunk and lifted out my luggage. I turned to see Regina staring at me as if I should have asked permission before opening the trunk.

She pointed to the stone walls of the lodge, and I noted again the ivy, how old it all looked against the mountains behind.

"Kyle," Regina said in a tone reminiscent of a kindergarten teacher scolding me for marring a desk with a crayon, "that lodge is used as a bed-and-breakfast for tourists. Friends of my family own it. But people can't sleep because there are dozens of finches living in the walls."

Gretchen spoke over the roof of the car to me. "French finches are little—"

"Birds," I said knowingly. "Gotta love the alliteration."

Regina stood beside the car, arms folded, gazing across the hood at the lodge. Since she was obviously the ringleader here, Gretchen and I mimicked her posture, which created a kind of triangular across-the-car conversational atmosphere.

But then, no one was talking.

I paused near the trunk with my luggage, Gretchen at the rear passenger side, Regina still staring across the hood at her next project.

"Those finches are sorta living in the walls," Regina said and motioned toward the lodge. "They can sometimes find their way out through a crack in the chimney, but still no one can sleep at night due to all the chirping. Our job is to create new openings in the stone exterior, though we must not disturb the birds' habitat in any way, nor harm any of them when we make the openings."

I morphed into Mr. Fix-it. "Does France have a Lowe's or a Home Depot?"

Gretchen said, "Why on earth would we need one of those box stores?"

"Well, because they offer equipment rentals. So I was just thinking I'd rent a big drill with a two-inch diameter bit, drill some big holes in the stone walls, and let the birds spot the daylight and find their way out. Wouldn't take me more than half an hour, tops. Then you and I could hike the Alps for days on end."

Mr. Fix-it had arrived with a toolbox of solutions.

Regina clinched her fists in rage, even banged the left one against her thigh. For a moment I thought her head might explode. "Never!"

Silent for a moment, Gretchen eventually rolled her eyes and said, "Kyle, Regina doesn't want to risk harming or scaring any birds by using something as vicious as a *power tool*."

The way Gretchen spoke told me that even she thought Regina was nuts.

I looked at Regina and searched for some sense of reason, some subtle clue, perhaps a smile, to show a willingness to compromise. Failing in that quest, I tried the gentle but direct approach. "So, Regina, if you don't want me to rent a drill, how then do we make holes in the stone walls?"

"We make them *manually*," Regina said with authority. "We use chisels, upon which we'll tap lightly with hammers."

Stunned, I set my luggage on the ground and put one foot on the back bumper. "*Tap lightly?!*...with hammers? You make it sound like we're prisoners trying to tunnel out by scraping a few grains per night while the guards are asleep. Those stones are probably two feet thick; we don't have time to 'tap lightly.' We'll all be here till Thanksgiving."

Regina said, "I don't celebrate Thanksgiving, Kyle. At least not with a turkey."

Gretchen nodded. "Regina prefers fish instead."

"A line-caught fish, obviously," I added.

We all entered the lodge, Regina leading the way, me the caboose. The décor seemed sparse, though the place looked clean enough. Low plaster ceilings, exposed beams, and plaster walls confirmed the Frenchness of the setting. A thin staircase, very steep and sporting narrow banisters, led upstairs to the guest quarters. Gretchen excused herself and made for the restroom, while Regina simply watched me admire the house.

I heard peeps in the walls, chirps, tweets, and more peeps. The women weren't lying about the distracting noise from the finches.

I was about to ask which way to my room when Regina opened a drawer and withdrew a chisel in her left hand, a hammer in her right. She raised them both to eye level and met my curious gaze. "Kyle, when we start work tomorrow, we will tap *lightly*, and with *compassion*."

All I did was nod, just to avoid more confrontation.

Gretchen had returned to the living room almost without notice. When it was clear that Regina's orders were now complete, Gretchen quietly told me I'd be staying in the room at the top of the stairs on the right.

"No air-conditioning here, Kyle," she said as I lugged my bag upstairs to my room. "Just ceiling fans."

"I can live with that."

"How's Chang?" she asked as I reached the top of the staircase.

"Good. He's doing some traveling of his own these days."

The room — the whole house, actually — seemed an advertisement for rustic: uneven plaster walls faded off-white; exposed beams supporting a cord strung high across the room for drying clothes; a nightstand crudely built from grainy dark wood. I took a minute to unpack a few items, a second minute to look out my second-story window.

The view revealed at least two hours of daylight left. Long shadows drooped across and between the Alps. Rural France looked green and welcoming.

I opened my door and spoke loudly down the empty stair-case. "Hey, Gretchen, wanna go for that hike before it gets dark?"

After a couple seconds, her voice echoed up from below. "Yes, I would like that."

I met her at the front door and opened it wide. Our khaki shorts matched, and before we left she offered me a squirt of sunblock. I dabbed some on my arms, and she did the same with hers, then we stretched our legs and pronounced ourselves ready.

We stepped outside the lodge in the shadow of one Alp, but headed in the direction of another, a sunlit specimen whose base appeared scalable.

"Kyle, I really am glad you're here," Gretchen said. And she pointed across the gravel road to a path.

A HIKE, A CHAT, A PROBING FOR WANTS

Gretchen and I made our way up the winding trail, our breathing growing heavy as the route steepened. The hike required an abrupt right turn into a forest, then a steep, uphill climb out of the woods and between two meadows — the one on the right a carpet of yellow flowers, the one on the left narrower and less colorful but growing to the edge of a cliff. Another smell, again redolent of honeysuckle, rolled by every now and then, though the scent was not quite honeysuckle, at least not the American version. Spicier. Minty even.

"Isn't the air here crisp?" she said as we stepped over a fallen limb.

"Like Alaska," I said. "Without the oily smell."

The trail tapered even narrower as we forged ahead, and in these early minutes of our hike we walked side by side. Soon, however, I could see that the trail ahead grew so skinny — the drop-off to our left was more than four hundred feet — that we'd be forced to walk single file. A peek over the edge roiled my stomach. A fall would splatter one across merciless French boulders, all of them gray and covered in moss.

Gretchen motioned ahead at the thinning trail and insisted I go first.

"Just in case of bears," she said.

The hike grew strenuous enough to preclude long conversations. This did not, however, prevent Gretchen from getting personal.

She spoke from a few feet behind me as we ascended yet another hill. "Kyle, do you want a family someday?" she asked. "I mean, do you envision using your business to provide for them and do lots of family stuff like taking them to Disney World or maybe to the beach?"

The question both surprised me and gave me hope. Perhaps she was thinking long-term; after her lonely year of rescuing wildlife, she'd want to settle down, probably back in Texas.

I told her yes, that I did want a family someday. But that I preferred to balance my vacations—natural ones like the Grand Canyon one year, concrete and neon the next.

Since she was walking behind me on the trail, I couldn't see her reaction, but I imagined her at least smiling.

"What about you?" I asked.

We crunched our way over some fallen branches before she spoke. "I like some sense of balance too, but more tilted to outdoor settings…and I think I'd like a family someday."

We hiked down and around a bend, over a stream and across a flattened rock some twenty feet in width. The middle of the rock contained twin ruts spaced several feet apart, like from wagon wheels of long ago.

I stopped and ran my fingers through the ruts. The rock felt smooth, as if centuries of flowing water from glacial melts had honed the rut's rough edges.

Gretchen knelt beside me and touched the tip of her index

finger to the rut. "Rumor around here is that these ruts are so ancient that Caesar himself may have traveled through here on a chariot." She chuckled as if the thought was just too wild.

"Caesar? Ya think he'd use something as vicious as a power tool?"

Gretchen laughed, and I savored that laugh and projected it into old age. Then she motioned me forward on the trail and we picked up the pace.

Soon daylight and the scent of wildflowers faded in tandem, and a breeze whipped around the mountain. The subject of family, however, remained bright and flickering in Gretchen's pretty head. We stepped across a second fallen tree and ascended yet another upslope. "Think you'd enjoy playing the role of provider?" she asked.

"Sure," I said and bent a limber branch out of the way so its rebound wouldn't slap her. "Although there's some oilmen in Lubbock who think someday the government will confiscate every well in Texas due to peak oil. For me that's a scary thought."

Huffing and puffing up the hill behind me, she paused before blurting, "What'd you just say?"

"That I fear p*eak* oil. It's a catchy name for when oil supplies top out and gas goes to forty dollars per gallon, thus no one can afford to drive."

She hesitated before something clicked in her mind. "That'd be kinda nice....Less people driving would mean less oil tankers and less oil spills. Seabirds all over the world would rejoice."

"And people all over America would revolt at forty dollars per gallon."

Though she talked about family, and I had at least mentioned oil in some capacity, we were both avoiding, in these early hours of being together again, the obstacles discussed in Alaska. I figured after dinner we could stay up late and talk, so I didn't press matters here on the mountainside.

We hiked up a hill of loose rocks before Gretchen spoke again. By now she was breathing hard. "People should *walk* to work, Kyle...or ride bikes. The nation is thirty percent overweight, and I have a catchy name for that too."

"What...gluttony?"

"Peak calories. That's when calories top out in America and people get huge and no longer fit into their cars, thus no one can drive."

I laughed at her wit and told her I was glad she'd invited me to France.

"It's getting dark," she said after a glance skyward. "We'd better get back to the lodge for dinner."

Above a canyon we reversed course, and I paused to look across the chasm at a distant mountain. A long swath had been cut into the side, running from top to bottom.

I recognized it as a ski run, grown over with summer vegetation, awaiting winter and a few good snows. Or artificial snows. Although the French, being the purists that they are, would likely never stoop to manufacturing fake snow.

What caught my eye most, though, was the chasm itself. Our brief conversation still revealed such a chasm between Gretchen and me. She was still pro-wildlife, anti-oil; I was still pro-oil, no offense to the wildlife.

On the return hike I thought about reaching for Gretchen's hand, but the single-file conditions made that impossible. Plus, her "It's getting dark" reply had lent an off-kilter vibe to the journey home, as if reinforcing to me that we still had some important issues to discuss.

And we did.

Regina served tofu for dinner — on bird plates.

She claimed that her version of tofu, eaten by three people over several days, would save the lives of at least two chickens. If I'd been running that kitchen, I'd have killed, cleaned, and dressed the chickens myself, baked 'em with a side of mashed potatoes, and served hot bird to everyone in the room. With sweet tea as chaser.

Not so Regina. She spooned moderate helpings of her tofu onto three plates. Each plate contained an endangered bird centered in its porcelain. Our job was to find out which bird had joined us for dinner. After everyone was seated, I quickly ate half of my tofu and discovered the face of a spotted owl staring up at me. The owl was cool; the tofu tasted like a mix of potting soil and mulch.

Gretchen, seated across from me, chewed slowly, with an odd look on her face. She washed it all down with a swig of sparkling water. Then she wondered aloud if we should give the French finches the honor and distinction of a plate.

Regina ate a big bite of tofu and said, "There are *millions* of them in France, Gretchen. They're nowhere near extinction, unless of course some gun-toting men employed by Big Oil use their profits to buy shotguns and hunt defenseless finches for sport."

That was it for dinner conversation: Small talk versus Regina's radicalism. I called it a tie and gulped water to wash down the next mouthful of mulch.

Gretchen was first to rise from the table, and when she did she motioned for me with her index finger. "Kyle, we take turns doing dishes here. Two people per night, and tonight you and me have a turn. *Together*."

Ah.

Unsure if this was her way of letting me know she liked me, or if she only thought of me as her international travel buddy and needed help with chores, I went to the kitchen with my plate in tow. At the sink I turned the faucet toward me and ran the water till it grew warm, then hot, then finally settled in somewhere between warm and hot.

With a "howdy, dish partner" as greeting, Gretchen took up her position beside me at the sink and reached for a towel. I would wash; she would dry.

Regina grabbed a pair of pencils and a flashlight from the counter and said she was going to mark the outside walls for tomorrow's work. Over the running water I heard the birds in the walls; they sounded like a vast covey or perhaps a vast gaggle, some form of vastness in which French birds amass.

Just after I'd washed the first pair of dishes, Gretchen reached out and turned off the water.

"Listen to them, Kyle," she whispered and turned an ear to the wall. "All those trapped birdies."

"Sounds like dozens of 'em."

When it came to doing dishes, we made a respectable team—which felt good, even better when she shared her thoughts while drying the next water glass.

"Do you think everybody is looking to *belong* somewhere?" she asked as I handed her a plate.

I dropped my sponge in the water and reached in to retrieve it. "I'm not sure what you mean."

"Take Regina for instance." Gretchen paused and looked over her shoulder, as if to check if Regina were still outside. "I believe she takes all this bird stuff *way* too seriously, and by now she's so far gone that she's made up a whole new religion about it and wants us all to become charter members."

I passed her a fresh-washed plate. "You mean like First Church of the Endangered Fowl?"

"Something like that." She dried the plate and set it aside. "Regina had some radical professors in college, I know that. But if it could happen to her, it could happen to anyone. So now I'm wondering if some choices I've been making are less than wise."

I bit my lip and squirted more soap on my sponge.

She reached for the next glass and rinsed it twice. "Yep, if I kept globe-hopping with Regina long enough, I'd probably make rescuing wildlife into a replacement religion. And that would probably make God mad."

Her insight was both sudden and surprising. I remembered thinking similar thoughts myself. Funny how when a person says something you've said before—in this case making God mad—that it sorta bonds you to them. Plus, Uncle Benny had said the same thing in the hospital. Perhaps making God mad was a prerequisite to being, or becoming, a Mango. We both stood there washing and drying and not saying anything, as if we each needed to process what she'd said before offering up anything else.

Finally Gretchen wadded her towel into a ball, tossed it to the floor, and grabbed a dry one from under the sink. "Kyle, I'm not sure if my ongoing friendship with Regina is healthy. Plus, this morning she called me a *moron*!"

"No!"

"Yes. She asked me to go to the store and buy six boxes of

cereal to cover our breakfast for three days of work, and so I bought her a variety pack. You know, six little one-serving boxes wrapped in cellophane. I mean, what would you have bought if your friend told you they needed six boxes of cereal for just three days?"

I washed another plate and said, "I'd have bought the variety pack too."

"So . . . there you go."

Hands in soapy water, I had to know more. "Cheerios, Froot Loops, and Corn Flakes in that variety pack?"

"Nope," she said and re-rinsed a glass. "Froot Loops, Cap'n Crunch, and Raisin Bran."

"Good choices."

"Thank you."

Her comments about making up one's own religion caused me to wonder if I had made a religion out of my oil business. Or — and this next thought startled me good — if I had made a religion out of pursuing Gretchen all over the globe. I knew that I should pray more often, ask for guidance more often, and a friendly church home in Texas probably wouldn't hurt either. But not here in France. I heard that in France finding a friendly church home was about as difficult as finding grits and hash browns.

I yawned several times as we finished the dishes; my internal clock was 3:05 a.m., never mind the 10:05 on my watch. With little energy left, I helped Gretchen put away the dried dishes into the cabinets and wipe down the countertops. Her own yawns broadcast how tired she felt, and we agreed as the last dish was set atop its brethren that we'd talk more in-depth in the morning.

The front door opened, and Regina entered with dirty hands. She wiped them with a cloth and said, "Get to bed soon, you two. Lots of hard work tomorrow, so get your rest."

There was little rest. Those birds in the walls chirped, peeped, ruffled, and pooped all night. It was as if they were spying on me, waiting for my eyelids to grow heavy before they began their party. Twice I tried holding a pillow over my head, but then I couldn't breathe well and that kept me just as awake as if I'd been inside the walls with the birds. I even wadded up some pieces of TP and used them for earplugs, but the pieces kept falling out.

At some point after 2:00 a.m.—it gets chilly at night in the Alps—I put on my jeans and long-sleeve T-shirt and went downstairs, thinking a glass of milk and some French dessert might serve me well.

On the counter I noted that Regina had left the flashlight. Curious as to how she'd marked the outside walls, I grabbed it and made for the front door, anxious to inspect the stones.

But before I could turn the handle and sneak outside, someone coughed behind me. Gretchen emerged from the cupboard, otherwise engaged with a piece of dark chocolate, partially unwrapped.

I met her sleepy gaze and we said, "Hey," at the same time.

In long pajamas and a Texas Tech sweatshirt, she reversed course back into the cupboard and wrapped the rest of the chocolate in tinfoil. Then she tucked it behind a box of oatmeal as if to hide the treat from everyone else. "You're going outside at this hour, Kyle?"

"Couldn't sleep, so I thought I'd see where Regina marked the walls."

Gretchen came out of the cupboard and put her ear to the kitchen wall. "I still hear the birds. There must be three hundred in there now...maybe more."

Guesstimates notwithstanding, we went outside the lodge

and shone the light up the front wall. Finding nothing, we moved around to the west side, where Gretchen insisted that she should hold the flashlight, since she "arrived in France first."

About three feet up the wall we found a pair of bull's-eyes drawn on the flattest stones. The ivy had been carefully trimmed back to allow access.

Gretchen then shone the light up toward the roof and back down to eye level. "Hmmm," she muttered.

Not following her logic, I scanned the roofline for a clue. "Hmmm?"

She then jiggled the beam rapidly at my feet. "Look, Kyle, a strobe light! Just like that night at the frat house!"

The pistol of her mind had a hair trigger, and who knew what set it off. Tonight, in the wee hours on this darkened parcel of France, she'd somehow connected a flashing light beam shone on a two-hundred-year-old lodge with a frat party dancing to "Thriller."

I really, really liked this woman, and we couldn't resist ten seconds of the mummy dance before turning in for the night.

How Gretchen—who seemed so balanced and fun—could spend all this time volunteering with stone-cold Regina simply baffled me. Perhaps Gretchen had huge gobs of patience. Regardless, with each passing hour this trip was looking more and more like a good move—even after the note I found on my door the next morning.

THE NOTE I FOUND ON MY DOOR THE NEXT MORNING

Kyle —

The reason I asked earlier if you wanted a family was because I've been giving that issue a lot of thought lately. I just think that settling down and raising a family — while it is something I really do want — would be very difficult for me if my husband and I paid our bills with oil revenue. Also, I would like to continue, perhaps once a year, taking a week to go help with endangered wildlife causes. The world's environments and ecosystems need people like me. But how could I go and volunteer for other oil spill projects if I paid my plane fare with the profits from oil wells? Do you see the dilemma here?? I just thought you should know what I'm thinking. I enjoyed the hike today. And you were right — Regina's tofu does taste like potting soil.

   Looking forward to sharing tomorrow's work with you,
   Gretchen

THE NOTE I LEFT ON HER DOOR JUST TEN MINUTES AFTER I READ THE NOTE SHE LEFT ON MY DOOR

Gretchen—

Thank you for the honesty in your note. My initial thoughts are:

Can we just date for a while? Perhaps back in Texas?

I know how strongly you feel about wildlife and environmental causes. And I know you have deep reservations about my occupation. I'm willing to discuss a job change—in time. But please realize that right now I have two employees plus my mother and siblings all benefiting from the business. Can you see my dilemma here too? Maybe there is a way to bridge our dual dilemmas. I'm willing to talk more about this. Perhaps during some dinner dates back in Texas?? You are coming back to Texas, aren't you? Please don't tell me you're headed to Venezuela or Indonesia next. Ya know, if I'm going to pursue you around the globe, I'll likely need MORE oil profits, not less!

Just kidding. For today, however, let's rescue some birds and make Regina happy. She is capable of happiness, isn't she? Does she ever smile?

Ready to "tap lightly,"

—Kyle

By the time I entered the kitchen for breakfast, Gretchen

had read my note; I knew this because she was folding it and stuffing it into the back pocket of her jeans.

She wore old sneakers for the workday, plus a long-sleeve brown T-shirt with a flying seagull on the back. After we each exchanged a "good morning," she tapped her back pocket and smiled at me and mouthed a silent "thank you." I reached for a loaf of bread and said, "Thank you too," and unwrapped the tie from the bread bag.

Breakfast was help-yourself, and there wasn't much besides tofu on toast. I settled on buttered toast and OJ until Gretchen found half a tube of honey, and we reloaded a second helping. The birds in the walls chirped a French reverie and began again. And again.

I was deep into my third piece of toast when Regina came out from her room, dressed in black jeans and black sweat-shirt and black work shoes. She stopped in the doorway to the kitchen, watched us eat for a moment, and said, "Gretchen, we have to stretch our remaining food to make it last all week. My father called and said he's, um, disappointed with some things I've done with trust monies, so he's refusing to let me withdraw any more till next month."

Gretchen licked honey off her index finger. "Why would he do that?"

"He says I embarrass him…which is absurd."

No one said anything for several awkward seconds until finally I couldn't handle the silence anymore. "I'll contribute grocery money, if that'll help."

Gretchen whispered to me, "You don't have to do that; you flew all this way to help out."

Regina sat on the floor in the living room and began sharpening two chisels with a file.

"Want some bread and honey, Regina?" Gretchen asked her.

Regina drew her file across the chisel and inspected its edge. "No. I just want my father to see the world in a normal way...like I do."

The scent in the air was no longer of bread and honey. For the first time in my life I could actually smell dysfunction. And I came from a broken family at that.

The metallic screech of a file drawn across chisel almost drowned out Gretchen's next whisper. "I think she's going off the deep end, Kyle."

Ten minutes later Regina opened the front door to the lodge and insisted that we work in two teams. Gretchen and I comprised one team, and Regina and herself comprised the other. We were issued a chisel and a hammer and a pair of safety glasses as we stepped outside into a clear and cool morning.

Regina pointed toward the west side of the lodge and said, "You two start on that side."

She tromped off to work on the east side of the lodge, while Gretchen and I wandered over to our appointed station. A stone wall in front of us, a French Alp to our backs, an untold quantity of birds chirping from inside.

Centered in a flattish stone in the middle of the wall, the red bull's-eye seemed to either wink at me or taunt me; I couldn't figure which. It was drawn at waist height, some ten feet below a window. Just below the bull's-eye, Regina had written in pencil, *Careful, team! Do no harm to the precious creatures inside!*

Other than the extremism, it was a pleasant morning—*weather-wise*—in which to work outdoors. Southern France in early September felt free of humidity, stuck on fifty-odd degrees. The stone wall, however, proved much less accommodating. I held the chisel in my left hand and whopped it with a hammer — a few grains of very old stone flew at odd angles. I hit it again, this time harder.

"Ouch," Gretchen said over my shoulder. "That one hit me in the neck."

"Sorry."

I whopped the chisel ten more times before hitting on the brilliant idea of chiseling the mortar instead of the stones themselves. Two-hundred-year-old mortar, however, holds its own against stone. Progress seemed next to impossible.

Gretchen, itching to get involved, took over hammer duty and gave it a try as well, flinching with each pounding of the chisel.

"It's like trying to break rock with a Burger King straw," she said in frustration.

Soon we heard light tapping from the other side of the lodge, weak sounds confirming Regina made even slower progress than ourselves. The birds, however, sounded somewhere between happy and riotous, as if they knew we were trying to get to them but could not figure out if we would free them or cook them.

I saw one finch squeeze through a hole near the roofline, and I wondered if all the others knew the secret passageway. From their manic chirping I guessed not.

A short while later Gretchen said her wrist hurt from pounding the chisel, that this slow method of making holes in a wall was just plain stupid, and what we needed to pound with was a sledgehammer instead of a regular hammer. She noted a small storage shed at the rear of the lodge, and while I continued to lose the battle against stone, she went to the shed to have a look around. Before entering she turned to me and said, "If Regina comes to check on us, tell her I went to the ladies' room."

Regina did not come checking—at least not yet. I sensed that Gretchen was finally growing frustrated with Regina, and it felt good to have an ally in the battle for rational thought.

On my knees and pounding away on a dull chisel, I had made little progress when Gretchen peeked out from the shed and said, "Hey."

I turned to see an old black extension cord draped around her neck. Though weighed down by the cord, she was grinning with mischief. Then, from behind the shed's door, she lifted an even older piece of equipment that looked very much like a 1950s-era drill—big, bulky, and cast from iron. A three-foot cord dangled from its back end.

"I found this under a sack of birdseed," she whispered. Her expression toggled between happy discovery and guilty conscience.

I looked left and right to the ends of the lodge. No one coming.

"Does that thing work?" I asked in a hurried and whispered tone.

Gretchen dragged the drill a few feet and said, "How should I know, Kyle? I can't find a plugger-inner."

I ran over to the shed and relieved her from the drill. Its heft dwarfed anything on the market today, and its business end held a bit—though not the size we'd need. I held the bit up to the sunlight and noted the size—3/4"—marked on its shaft.

By now I didn't care how Regina might react; I was going to employ this drill, take control of this job, and, as they say in the South, "Get 'er done."

Gretchen uncoiled the extension cord next to the wall and searched behind the bushes for an outlet. A minute later she found, near the corner of the lodge, a "plugger-inner."

She ran back beside me at the bull's-eye and said, "I don't care what Regina thinks, Kyle. This is about efficiency. Birds may have bird brains, but they have enough brains to stay away from a spinning drill bit."

"Agreed."

Without hesitation I hoisted the drill, aimed the bit at the bull's-eye, and squeezed the trigger.

Whrrr, whrrr. Penetration! One hole in five seconds. I silently thanked God for electricity. Gretchen verbally thanked God for electricity.

Whrrrrrr, whrrr. A second hole overlapped the first, well over an inch of width, daylight bursting through to the birds.

Whrrr, whrrrr. The hole grew again. Then I heard a scream of anger from the opposite side of the house.

Gretchen jumped up and down and clapped, urging me to drill faster. "Quick, Kyle, drill! Just drill! She's coming to pummel you!"

Whrrrrrrrrrrrrrr. A fourth hole and a fifth, a two-inch opening now. I backed away, and in seconds the first finch peeked its little head through, saw sky and trees, and flew to freedom. A second one followed, checked us out, and it too flew away. Then a third and a fourth and a fifth—and they just kept on coming.

Then, chaos. Behind me the sound of footsteps, running footsteps, preceded the hysteria-filled face of Radical Regina.

"WHAT ARE YOU *DOING*?!?" she shouted. "YOU'LL INJURE THE BIRDS!"

She shoved me back from the stone wall. She scolded Gretchen with her glance and told her to stay back. Then she peered inside the hole I'd made, in much the same manner as a relative looks longingly into a neonatal window. Only there were no whimpers or cooing from inside that hole. Just the ump-teenth finch peeking out and launching itself to freedom — and directly into Regina's hair. She swiped at the offending fowl and fell back on her derriere as bird after bird crawled into the hole, briefly checked the surroundings, and launched itself to freedom.

Gretchen stood watching from beside me, shaking her head as if wondering how deep went Regina's rabbit hole of outrage.

For long minutes Regina remained on the ground, staring at the dirt, so angry at my method that she couldn't appreciate the result.

Amid the awkward silence I went over and disconnected the drill from the extension cord and set the drill gently beside Regina. "Power tools," I whispered to her. "What a concept."

Gretchen did her best to bundle the extension cord, and in that surreal moment she walked over to Regina and dropped the cord at her feet. "Kyle did the drilling, Regina, but *I* found the plugger-inner!"

The project over, Regina sat with her back against the lodge, avoiding eye contact and looking somewhat forlorn, as if she'd missed out on some great honor by not chiseling into the walls by hand. I actually felt sorry for her, for the religion she'd cre-ated for herself.

Gretchen picked up the extension cord and I hoisted the drill, and we toted them back to the shed. Inside, in a moment of privacy, Gretchen stood directly in front of me, took me by the hand, and said, "Kyle, I love having you here, but you might be in danger now, with what just happened."

I squeezed her hands. "Could be, and trust me when I say I don't want to be around Regina anymore. But I'm not leaving until you answer something."

"Sure, just ask."

"When you get back to Texas, can we just go on a bunch of dinner dates like normal people?"

She smiled and nodded. "Of course we can."

I went inside and up the narrow staircase to my room and packed my luggage, figuring there was no use staying in the same lodge as Regina, wondering if she might turn violent as she succumbed further to hysteria.

From outside I heard Regina scolding Gretchen for allowing me to utilize a power tool.

Ten minutes later I found Gretchen by herself in front of the lodge, sitting on a bench and looking sad. With luggage in hand, I walked up behind her, set the luggage on the ground, and said, "I'd do it, ya know."

Without turning around she said, "Follow me to Venezuela or Indonesia?"

"No, change occupations."

She reached back over her shoulder and took my hand and pulled me around in front of the bench. Then she stood, and we hugged. Then I kissed her, twice, and hugged her a second time.

We held hands for a minute or so. Then we parted hands, and she said, "I'm sorry this trip was another bad one for you. I'm looking forward to seeing you back in Texas."

"Steak, seafood, or Italian?"

"Italian. With mood lighting."

With Gretchen feeling the need to remain there another three days to help ready the lodge for fall tourism, I took a cab into Grenoble and bought a return train ticket to Paris on the TGV. After a twenty-minute wait to board the train, I sat by myself near a window in the second car and watched a sunny afternoon unfold, though the fields along the French country-side looked a duller shade of green. I missed her already, and I missed her a lot.

Three hours later the bullet train pulled into the CDG Airport. I departed with reluctant luggage and strode for the airline ticket counter. There was of course a line, and soon I felt the urge to hop out of the line and go buy a paperback in the neighboring bookstore, anything to get my mind off the fact that my time with Gretchen had been ruined once again by a seething radical.

I didn't buy a paperback, though, or even a magazine. Still in line, I nudged my luggage ahead with my foot and recalled something from the one literature course I'd taken at Texas Tech. Robert Louis Stevenson wrote, "Everyone eventually sits down to a banquet of consequences."

Happy dining, Regina.

A DETOUR OF COLOR

Inside Charles de Gaulle Airport, the customer service rep spoke English with a French accent. Contrary to the stereotype that Americans so often slap on the French, she was friendly and helpful — at least to the three people in front of me.

While I waited in line, I checked text messages on my cell phone. Three texts waited for me, all of them from Chang, and all in fractured sentences:

```
Kyle, n case things don't go well n France,
u might consider joining us in Kenya. People
here so happy to see us Sal says u can sleep
on the cot in our hut. When u arrive, call
the # I gave u.

P.S.

It's hot here.
```

By the time I'd finished reading, the people in front of me had departed, and I stepped to the counter.

"Where would you like to go, sir?" said the rep. I read the text again before answering.

"Next flight to Dallas, Texas," I said to the service rep. "Then a connector to Lubbock."

I had a business to run. Chang and Sal could show me pictures of Africa when they returned home.

I stared at the flight board but saw nothing but the eight hundred acres in Anson, my wells pumping steadily, going about their daily routine with no comprehension that they were a deterrent to my romantic quest. Then, without warning, images of my acreage morphed into the Serengeti, with lions and cheetahs stalking unsuspecting wildebeests, a muddy river in the distance hosting a pair of rhinoceros. But even this vision didn't last, replaced by the realization that Chang and Sal helped suffering *humans*, not birds or beasts. And people had souls; I had no idea if animals and birds had souls, though I kinda doubted it.

Had Kyle Mango done anything to benefit a fellow human being since graduating college? Or had life consisted only of benefiting myself, plus the occasional helping hand to wildlife while I pursued Gretchen?

At first the vision felt like a vague prompting—one I dismissed as just a childhood dream unfulfilled—but then it felt like a tap on the shoulder from God's Spirit of Invisible Tappings, perhaps the angel in charge of international detours.

The service rep said something about Dallas, but I was at that moment digging wells with Chang and Sal. For a minute I couldn't speak. Geographic tangents held me like magnets.

Would the Lord frown if I returned immediately to Texas? On the other hand, would he smile if I took a risk without having a female attached to that risk?

"Sir," she said across the counter in a tone that let me know other people waited in line behind me, "the next flight to Dallas is booked solid. Can I interest you instead in a flight to Denver that would connect into—"

"Kenya," I blurted.

"Sir, Denver does not connect to *Kenya*. Not directly anyway. I'm not even sure it connects indirectly. Plus I thought you said your final destination was Texas."

I plucked my passport and my driver's license from my pocket and set them on the counter for ID. "I just changed my mind. I want to go from Paris to Nairobi, Kenya. And I don't care what it costs."

The rep looked at me as if I were just another confused American. "One moment, sir."

The ticket rep had just placed my ticket in the envelope when I heard my name spoken in the terminal. For a moment I dismissed it, knowing that many Kyles occupied the planet and that no one knew my exact whereabouts. But then the voice called out again, this time accompanied by rapid footsteps, and adding for clarity my last name: "Kyle! Kyle Mango!"

I stood on my toes and peered over the line of people behind me. "Gretchen?"

She rushed around the line and to the front, disheveled and toting a duffel bag that weighed down her right arm and shoulder. "I can't stand another day with Regina," Gretchen called out in full trot. "I'm just not a purebred environmental wacko, and I can't keep worshipping at the Church of Endangered Fowl. . . . I'm Methodist."

Stunned to see her, I watched her rush past the people in line and run right to me and throw her arms around my neck. Over a black velvet barrier rope we hugged for all of two seconds. "So you left the lodge right behind me?" I asked.

Breathless, she stood next to the counter and gushed over her luggage. "I caught the next train after you left. I almost missed it, those trains are so confusing. Don't the French have customer service? I mean, Target and Wal-Mart have customer service, so why not the French?!"

A sigh and a snicker arose from the line.

In a whisper I informed Gretchen that although I was excited to see her here, she was breaking in line and that perhaps we shouldn't bank on the kindness of strangers.

But she looked pitiful, what with her luggage half open and a worn Alaska sweatshirt hanging out the side pocket, her hair unkempt, a splash of mud on her sneakers. Perhaps the people in line saw the same and had sympathy; regardless, no one raised an objection.

I felt the ticket rep staring at us.

"Gretchen, dear," I said, "have you already booked your ticket back to Texas?"

She shook her head. "No, not yet."

"Would you consider a detour—to help *people,* in *Kenya*—if the detour ticket was paid for with oil profits?"

She looked around at the strangers staring at us from the line. She mouthed "I'm sorry" to the lot of them.

I begged her for an answer. "Gretchen, I'm meeting Chang and our new employee, Sal, in Kenya to do some kind of water project for a village full of kids." Behind us the people grew impatient. "We have to hurry, Gretchen. People are waiting."

"Yes," a Russian accent called out from the rear. "People *are* waiting, people who were here well before you Americans showed up and ruined our day."

By now the woman working the ticket counter looked as if she wanted to put us on the fast train to Guantanamo. Gretchen looked past her at the flight board, and I saw the battle forming in her head. "If I go with you to Kenya and let you pay for it with oil profits, will you sell the oil wells when we get back to Texas? So that we can date in peace and harmony?"

A British voice in line called out, "This line was peace and harmony before you arrived on the scene, miss."

The line clapped their approval.

The ticket rep tapped her fingernails on the counter, waiting for us to reach a decision. I told Gretchen that I would act as soon as I could, given that I had employees and family somewhat dependent on me.

When she nodded I turned to the ticket rep and spoke quickly. "Add one more ticket to Kenya, please."

While the transaction processed, I turned to see Gretchen messing with her watch.

"Watcha doing, Gretch?"

She spoke to her wrist. "I'm calculating the travel time."

The British voice in back said, "Care to calculate how many weeks we've all been here?"

Now even the ticket rep held a hand over her mouth.

People snorted behind us.

I told Gretchen Kenya could be dangerous.

She said she didn't care.

She got seat 22A.

I got 23A.

The plane to Nairobi, filled nearly to capacity, held the most diverse assortment of human beings I had ever witnessed.

Upon takeoff Gretchen turned and blew me a kiss.

"You're sweet," she said.

I pointed to the little screen on the seat in front of her. "Wanna play world trivia?"

"Sure," she said. "Wildlife for eight hundred, Alex."

ANOINTED WITH OIL

When the plane descended through white clouds, I spotted across the runway shirtless boys with dark skin playing soccer on a dirt field. Slender and fast, they paused for one brief moment to wave up at the jet. Their backs glistened with sweat, and in an instant they'd resumed their game.

The past days of travel had worn on me, and I struggled to compare and contrast the scene below with anything familiar, be it rural France or Lubbock. My experience must have been shared by Gretchen, as she peered out of the window in the row ahead but said nothing.

As tires skidded then rolled briskly along the tarmac, she still said nothing. Even a talker like Gretchen seemed bridled by where she found herself. I felt the same way; in America, watching infomercials about starving kids, we're all grounded on familiar soil, we talk freely. But once you're on the ground here for the first time, the feeling is overwhelming, silencing even. *You are in Africa.* You are a blind, privileged, and pampered American — and none of it matters.

Gretchen appeared nervous as she pulled her carry-on bag from the overhead, and I suppose I bore a similar countenance. Neither of us spoke until we'd departed the plane — no tunnel—just down the staircase and across the hot tarmac to customs.

We passed customs without incident, save for the looks we received for being midsize Americans—which was by comparison *big* by local standards—and of course for the lightness of our skin. There were other Caucasians around, sure, but we were in the minority, and that alone proved a new experience.

Inside the terminal I stopped and used a pay phone to call the number Chang had given me. A man with a very African accent answered the phone and informed me that he ran a taxi service. I told him where we needed to go, and he told me to walk to transportation and wait on a dark blue car with double white stripes running across the hood and trunk. He said it was a Chevy Caprice and that it had large chrome rims and rode high, a "cockroach on roller skates."

I motioned for Gretchen to follow me to transportation, but she'd stopped to retie her sneakers. "Do you really need to do that," I asked, "or are you just stalling?"

"I'm not scared, Kyle, if that's what you're asking."

"I was hoping you'd admit to being a little bit scared."

She finished tying, stood erect, and grabbed her luggage handle. "Do you say that because *you're* scared?"

"Maybe a tiny bit. I'll feel better if our ride is waiting for us when we get to the pickup area."

Gretchen turned around and stared behind us. "I just saw a guard in black fatigues, and he carried a *machine gun*."

I pulled my luggage along and motioned for her to do likewise. "That surprises you?"

"No, I guess not."

It felt good to have her as a traveling companion, in these parts especially. And I was proud of her for having the gumption to part ways with her radical friend and go off to help people for a change.

We pushed through revolving doors and stepped to the curb to await our ride. Buses in bright colors came and went, as did the taxicabs. Ten minutes later, tires screeched in the distance. The dark blue car with the twin white stripes across the hood rambled up to the curb, chrome rims shiny in African sunlight. The passenger window was already down, so I leaned in to speak to the driver, a dark man with very large hands and very white teeth.

"You know where Chang and Sal are?" I asked. "You'll take us there?"

He grinned and pointed north. "Yes, yes... in a distant village." Then he made a shoveling motion. "You work hard, very hard. But if you do not like big bugs—ha-ha!"

I thanked him just as he pressed a button and popped the trunk. I tossed my bag in the rear, and Gretchen did the same with her own.

The driver honked his horn, and through the back glass I saw him waving at me. I hurried over to the passenger window. "Yes?"

"The young man, Chang, said only one person—you. Who is this woman on the curb with you?"

I tried to imagine Gretchen explaining her arrival here, but I figured I should do it myself. Plus the driver appeared in a great hurry, though not hurried enough to help us with the luggage. I pointed to Gretchen standing at the second door. "She's a relief volunteer, sir. Another worker for Africa." I made the shoveling motion back at him.

Gretchen whispered from behind me. "Tell him I'm good with kids too."

"She's good with kids, sir."

After a moment of hesitation, the driver waved us both into the backseat. "Ten dollars more," he said. "In, get in! Hurry before sunset."

I peered across the roof of the car, noted the sun still high in the sky, and wondered how far of a drive he had in mind.

Gretchen and I scrambled into the backseat. Since the driver was a tall man, the seat back didn't contain as much room behind him. So Gretchen, being shorter than me by a couple inches, slid over behind the driver side.

"How far to Chang and Sal?" I asked over the seat back.

Our driver sped us away and nudged a pair of mirrored sunglasses atop his nose. "Not far. Less than half a day."

We rolled out of Nairobi on a highway that began smooth enough but quickly thinned of both width and tar. To not know where I was going felt unsettling; to trust this driver felt worse; but to not know where I was going *and* have to trust the driver, well, that made me almost dizzy with anxiety. I reached for Gretchen's hand at the same time she reached for mine.

Soon my mouth felt dry. We'd not thought to purchase bottled waters for the trip, though Gretchen did offer me a tic tac, which I accepted without comment.

Eyes wide and observant, Gretchen lowered her window and stared out, and I did likewise with my own. Locals sold fruit and grains in open air markets; an old man held up a whole fish as we sped past. I offered the meekest of waves. *I'm in Africa.*

"Kyle?" Gretchen said my name like it held comforting powers.

"Yep?" I replied without turning my head from the view.

"Regina went nuts after you left. She even dug a hole and buried that power drill in the ground."

Our driver tilted his head to us, an obvious eavesdrop. He allowed a truck to pass us, and boils of dust rolled along the shoulder of the road. We raised our windows. A minute later we lowered them again.

"Still scared?" I whispered to Gretchen.

"Some…but not as much."

Our driver held the wheel with one of his enormous hands and craned his neck. "Ha ha ha," he said in a mocking tone. "Your friend Chang told me you'd be scared."

"I'm not scared."

"Me either," Gretchen whispered.

Our driver sped up and passed the truck that had just passed us minutes earlier. "Yeah…you're a little scared."

Two hours passed in a blur of roadside beggars, beverage billboards writ in English, and a pair of baboons sitting on their haunches as if they'd been put in charge of greeting tourists. The air inside the car grew warm. The driver apologized for the broken air-conditioning.

"Must get it fixed next week," he mumbled under his breath. I figured he said that to every passenger he plucked from the airport curb.

He sped us across the Kenyan countryside, between plains of grass and limited flora, past Masai tribesmen commanding their herds. Traffic thinned along the two-lane highway, then it disappeared altogether. Chang had said nothing of the remoteness of his location.

I watched the driver reach under his seat. At first I feared the worst, but then he produced two small bottles of water and held them up near his rearview mirror. "Thirsty, you two?"

"Very," I said with relief.

Gretchen nodded to me, wide-eyed as if she didn't know

what to think of this place. The water bottles were not cold at all. Lukewarm, if that. But we considered ourselves fortunate and drank without comment.

Soon the sun drooped behind odd-shaped trees, and in the dull orange glow of sunset Gretchen remained unusually silent, just sipping her lukewarm water and staring out her window.

I knew the reason for her quiet demeanor, and it was a shared realization: while France had offered similar standards to America — minus the language difference, of course — here the entire atmosphere yanked us from our comfort zones. We passed shacks instead of suburbs; bicycles instead of BMWs; wooden-wheeled carts of fruit instead of stucco-covered malls of fashion. Even the smells seemed off, if not off-putting.

I spotted a pile of trash on the roadside and wondered if they had sanitation standards. I saw ant mounds that stood as high as children and wondered if the stores sold Raid. All my thoughts were Americanized, and I knew this put me at a disadvantage. It wasn't that I was a white American; it was that I was such a white, *middle-class* American.

It was dark when the road turned from asphalt to dry dirt, perhaps another hour after that when the driver flashed his headlights and braked hard. A pair of yellow eyes shone in the road, and our driver stuck an arm out the window and waved a lumbering wildebeest across our path.

I leaned forward for a better view. "That happen a lot here?"

"No, just him," the driver said. He pulled around the animal and glanced back in the mirror. "He's the dumbest animal in all of Africa. Ha-ha!"

Gretchen nudged me across the seat and whispered, "I'm glad the driver has a sense of humor."

In minutes the headlights shone through an open gate,

across a dirt playground, and into an open-air hut, what looked like a dining area. Three people wiped off tables, and I recognized one of the three as Sal. The other two were dark-skinned and wore bright red shirts, women that Gretchen quickly identified as friendly Kenyans. "Well," she said to the window, "at least they look friendly."

I didn't see Chang anywhere, though the wooden buildings past the dining area, some of them with lights on, gave me hope.

Our driver parked facing the dining hut, and suddenly he became Mr. Nice. He opened the door for Gretchen and helped her out of the car, then he rushed around to the other side and did the same for me.

He even opened the trunk and lifted out our luggage.

"Thanks, Mister...," I said and received my bag from him. "I didn't get your name."

"Jo Jo," he said through his big white teeth. "Everyone calls me Jo Jo."

I asked about payment for the ride, and he shrugged as if he had no idea how to calculate an exact total.

Finally he said, "I think eighty US dollars."

I gave him ninety, Gretchen chipped in five euros, and Jo Jo left with a smile, a handshake, and a warning. "Don't heckle any animals, Mr. Mango," he said across his roof. "Especially the lions and hyenas. Ha ha ha!"

His car departed in a whirl of dust, and as I turned to watch him go, Sal called out, "Hey, it's about time you got here, boss!"

I left my luggage on the ground and hurried over to greet Sal, a half moon providing just enough light to see that he still rarely shaved. "I feel like I just flew around the planet," I said. "With a stop for fuel in France."

Gretchen had followed me—she still seemed in shock over where she'd arrived—to the dining hut, and between two picnic tables I introduced her to Sal. They shook hands, and Gretchen blurted, "Pleased to meet you, sir, and I'm sorry but can you point me to the ladies' room?"

Sal pointed her to one of the lit buildings, one with plywood sides and a shingled roof.

"Oh, it has *walls*!" Gretchen gushed as she hurried off in the dark. "Praise God."

Sal showed me to a round hut in which he and Chang and two other men were staying. One plain lightbulb hung from the middle of the ceiling, its yellow glow fading at the room's perimeter. Simple cots, arranged symmetrically around the room, made do as beds. Two of the seven looked empty, so I claimed one and tested its bounce.

"What's it like here so far?" I asked.

Sal sat on one of the other cots. "Hard work, friendly natives, hot days, cool nights."

The straight facts. Of course.

"And Chang?"

"Has kitchen duty tonight. He'll be along shortly."

The last time I'd shared a room with so many guys was summer camp, when I was twelve. "So how are you two getting along with the other workers?"

"Oh, I think we get along just fine. Everybody gets dirty together, everybody eats together, we sleep hard. Irrigation work is tough, but it'll make you appreciate hot and cold running water."

Sal said he had to finish wiping down the tables from the evening meal, that I looked tired and should ready my cot for sleep, and that he'd bring me and Gretchen leftover ham sandwiches if we were hungry.

"We eat meat every other day," he said on his way out.

Ah.

"And that's a luxury."

I retrieved my luggage and noted the smallish pillow occupying my cot.

The cot to my right held Chang's luggage — I recognized it simply because his white Stetson rested on top. At the edge of his cot lay a folder labeled IRRIGATION PROJECT.

Curious as to what I'd gotten into here, I opened the folder and read the first page of type:

```
Our goal is to install a new irrigation sys-
tem in a drought-stricken village south of
Narok, Kenya, We selected this location due
to the concentration of people in the region
and because parts of Eastern Africa have
suffered greatly (one of the worst droughts
in years).

The main goal is to work with villagers to
install a windmill (or two) to pump water
from the well and to add long irrigation
lines into the fields. Also important is
instructing the villagers in how to maintain
a water pump and windmill, and also how to
expand an irrigation line.

The use of drip-line irrigation—basically
a network of plastic pipes which transport
water under low pressure—will enable watering
of up to fifteen acres of land. With proper
maintenance of the system, eight different
```

crops can be harvested—enough to feed about
thirty people per acre of crop (about 120
families).

Notes: Drip irrigation stretches the Kenyan
water supply, which is hugely important during drought. Development of irrigation systems here is still low, thus education is
crucial in order to increase agricultural
production.

I heard Chang outside, asking someone where I was, and
rushed out to greet him. When I reached to shake his hand,
he slapped it away and gave me a bear hug, though that ended
quickly when Gretchen walked out from the restroom and saw
us hugging in the dark.

She giggled and said, "Am I interrupting something?"

Chang and I took two steps back from each other as Gretchen
hurried over and gave Chang a hug. "Good to see you, ol' buddy."

Then she yawned twice, bid us good night, and disappeared
into the women's tent. An armylike tent had been set up for
the women, larger than our hut and covered with mosquito
netting.

Chang turned around, glanced at the tent, and whispered,
"Kyle, you brought Gretchen!"

"I know that."

"You meet her in rural France, then woo her to Paris and fly
her *here*? You Casanova, you!"

I shook my head. "She and I both fled France before we
got bludgeoned by Radical Regina. Regina's off the deep
end…probably heading for the abyss."

He appeared stunned at the news. "You had to flee? Really?"

"All because I used a power drill to help some stupid birds."

He ran a hand through his spiky hair. "In Kenya a person would give a month's wages to own a power tool."

I looked around at the humble nature of the village. "Funny how circumstances dictate agendas." I didn't want to talk anymore about France, so I abruptly changed the subject. "How 'bout you, Chang? Any single women volunteering here?"

Only slightly embarrassed, Chang said, "Yeah, the one who organizes this whole project, her name is Cindy. She may be the smartest woman I've ever met. Probably out of my league."

I gave him a thumbs-up but yawned out of sheer exhaustion and motioned toward the hut. Across the village Sal came out of the men's shower—a wooden structure with walls that began at knee-level—complaining of blisters on his hands.

"You'll have 'em too by tomorrow night, Mango," he said and pulled a towel from around his neck. "Lots of digging left."

We all collapsed onto our cots. And by the time three more volunteers had made their beds for the night and Chang had switched off our lone lightbulb, stories began to flow around the room. They told of oppression and hunger, of slaughter and AIDS, of a people still hopeful despite malnourishment, of people crossing the Somalian border at night to escape to safer territory in Kenya, and of corrupt officials not allowing relief supplies to get to those in need, crates of food rotting on a tarmac.

I felt unqualified to participate in the storytelling. I simply listened and remembered, *I'm in Africa.*

Wiped out from the day's travel, I shut my eyes and wondered why any place on earth—especially *this* place—would allow a crate of food to just rot out in the sun. And then, seconds later, a privileged and pampered American fell fast asleep.

FROM MY WELLS TO YOUR WELLS

By noon the next day I stood knee-deep in a ditch, one of fourteen diggers bent on moving enough dirt to support a drip-line irrigation system. Kenyan natives, Americans, two Canadians, an Australian, a few women, and at least ten men toiled in the ditch. Small Kenyan children stood watching from a distance, half of them with no shirt or shoes. Gretchen, strong from her toils in Alaska, dug near the front of the line, while I ended up twelfth of the fourteen. Soon our wrists and arms ached, as did our backs, and we all welcomed a lunch break. We ate stewed potatoes with bits of leftover ham mixed in, along with some fruit and lots of water to drink. Thirty minutes later we climbed into the ditch again and took up our shovels.

Sal, being the resident digging expert due to his years of experience, led our work team in what he called coordinated home-team shoveling. This involved everyone plunging their shovels into the dirt and shouting, "Dallas," then heaving dirt in unison to the refrain, "Cowboys!"

"All together now, team," Sal said and raised his handle.

Shovels plunged into soil. "Dallas!"

"Cowboys!"

After ten minutes of this, one of the American men complained that our method was insensitive to New England Patriot fans.

Sal said, "Won't work."

And he was right.

"New England!" and "Patriots!" just didn't have the same rhythm. This work required two-syllable football names only. So we all went back to using Dallas and heaving with monotony until we saw the navy blue car with the white stripes pull onto the grounds.

Jo Jo leaped out and opened the door for his passenger, a statuesque blonde in jeans, slate-blue blouse, and black sneakers. She paid him in cash, and after he'd pocketed the dough he turned to observe us in our ditch. He called out, "Fought off any lions yet, Mr. Mango?! Ha ha ha!"

Before I could think up a reply, he'd jumped back into his car and sped away in a cloud of dust.

"Who *is* that guy?" I asked the portly man shoveling in front of me.

"Jo Jo? He's just an ex–rebel fighter from Sudan. Claims he found God and that God told him to be a cabdriver."

Though I should have expected it, people were different here. His comment, however, kept me preoccupied while digging dirt. I felt strongly that God wanted me to help here in Africa, very strongly that he wanted me to pursue Gretchen, but not so strongly that he wanted me to remain in the oil biz.

Every few minutes Gretchen turned from her position near the front of the line and grinned at me. She had twin dirt streaks on her forehead, and it made it even funnier when I realized she was oblivious to it.

"Why are you laughing?" she said over the backs of fellow diggers.

"Tell ya later," I said and plunged my shovel in the soil. "Just keep digging."

Sal urged the team to take a break, and I looked up from the ditch to see the blonde in jeans striding toward us.

"That's *her*," Chang said from behind me. "Cindy." Chang was covered in dirt and sweat, and despite these shortcomings he never took his eyes off her.

Cindy walked over to our work site, folder in hand.

Chang greeted her with a wave. "How went the meeting with the officials?"

"They didn't approve funding for the second windmill," she said and smiled at Chang in the manner Gretchen had smiled at me in the Paris airport. "We'll just have to get by with one unit."

Like Chang, Cindy proved ultrasmart. When someone in back of the line asked why we were using a drip-line irrigation system instead of common sprinklers, she didn't say, "Because it works better." She said, "Applying water to roots in a low-volume manner enables plants to thrive as soil achieves a healthy air-water balance."

And all who stood in the ditch simply nodded like they agreed in full.

Then, to my surprise, Cindy grabbed a spare shovel, climbed down into our ditch at the back of the line, and joined our line of diggers. "'Dallas' and 'Cowboys' again?" she asked us.

We all nodded. And fifteen shovels plunged into the earth.

Several times Chang and I accidentally clanged our shovels as we tossed dirt, and after the third incident I paused to wipe sweat from my forehead and ask him a question. "Do you feel like the oil business is something you just have to be involved in?"

Chang said, "I'm not wedded to it for life, if that's what you mean."

I leaned on my shovel. "I mean, would it bother you if at some point I decided to sell the business?"

He used his shirtsleeve to wipe his face, then shook his head. "Nope. It's your business."

"I'd pay a good severance."

Chang kept on digging, until a few shovelfuls later he muttered, "Love you, man."

As part of a team and toiling toward a common goal, I found myself no longer thinking about what I could add to my life, but found myself pondering how, at age twenty-two, I had become so wrapped up in trying to maximize my ability to acquire money, not to mention the niceties that such money could provide. Perhaps I was copying all of Uncle Benny's bad traits—at least I hadn't buried money in the ground yet, though my money did come *from* the ground—while not paying enough attention to Uncle Benny's good traits—his teeming generosity.

I kept glancing across the field to those shirtless children, all of them blank-faced and observing our progress, perhaps wondering if this digging would really translate into bigger and better meals. With my foot I pressed my shovel into the dirt and joined the chorus anew, realizing as I did that all my life I'd taken food for granted; Texas never ran out of food, be it steak, chicken, potatoes, or greens.

Some minutes later, as my back ached and the ditch grew longer, I said in midshovel, "Looks like you've met an impressive woman, Chang."

He tossed dirt upon the bank and said, "Just hope I can catch her eye."

Months earlier Chang had told me that he had no issues with dating a non-Korean. This fact and a future "what if" occupied my mind for a moment, until two shovelfuls later I thought of an important question. "Does she abhor oil or have an unusual affinity for birds?"

Chang grinned the dirty grin of a ditchdigger. "Nah, neither. In fact, back in Virginia she goes quail hunting with her grandfather."

Man.

By Friday our team had taken delivery of a windmill, erected it on a parcel of land that Sal had named "The Ditches at Kenyan Pass," and hooked it up to pump water into the pipes. My skin had tanned steadily, and I could not even remember when I was supposed to return to Texas. Time seemed liquid here, one day spilling into the next or draining off into yesterday.

Also helping my perspective were the nightly prayer sessions around the picnic tables. Sal led these little events — volunteers praying if they wanted to, most centering on the needs of Africa and for good attitudes for a tired work crew. After a few days of listening to the others, I managed to join in and briefly thank God for the community I'd found here — the first time I'd prayed in public since I was fifteen, when my father took us once a month to the Baptist church in Fort Worth.

I was also glad to see that Chang had found a new female friend, though things were very new between them. I reminded Chang that Cindy seemed even more of a globe-trotter than Gretchen and that "you'd better save up your frequent flyer miles."

The next afternoon, after the crew took a half day off, the four of us went on a double-date photo safari. Jo Jo the cab-driver took our foursome some twenty miles north and let us off at a fence that looked like it might stretch all the way to Egypt. We set out walking with a guide, and over the course of the afternoon Gretchen got photos of a rhino rolling in a mud puddle, as well as me and Chang pointing at a distant lion. Cindy—who'd apparently been all over Africa during her short career—pointed past the lions and asked us if we knew how to tell the difference between a male hyena and a female hyena.

"Same as with dogs?" I asked.

"Hardly," she said, laughing and walking ahead with Gretchen. "The females are bigger and stronger."

Pity those male hyenas.

The two women walked along together for a while, Cindy saying, "So you really went to Alaska to clean gulls?" Then Gretchen nodding and asking, "So you really installed irrigation systems in *Zimbabwe*?" I supposed the two both possessed deep wells of compassion; they just channeled it differently.

Until, of course, we were all back in a ditch and digging—which we were on Monday morning.

To conserve energy and promote morale, we split up into two groups, alternating the day between working on the irrigation system and getting to know the children, who wore perpetual smiles, if not much else.

That afternoon I spotted across the fields Gretchen with eight kids in tow, all of them walking beside a huge camel, a two-humped one with a box hanging off each side of its saddle. The boxes were tethered to one another with rope, and the camel walked obediently behind a young Kenyan man.

During dinner with all the gang—a nonmeat day, with soup and crackers and lots of fruit—I discovered that what I had seen was not merely a camel and its owner; I'd bore witness to a mobile library. The young man collected donated books—many of them curriculum studies—and transported them across his corner of Kenya via camel. He'd leave two or three books per child, accept any donations offered, and move on to his next stop, sometimes staying the night for a meal, which he did with us.

Gretchen, perhaps in an attempt to make up for the fact that she had yet to care for any wildlife in Africa, took this mobile library and its loping expansion as her pet project. She brushed the camel, watered the camel, even asked the camel if it had a girlfriend in some neighboring village.

At the picnic tables, while I took my turn cleaning up, she then drafted a letter to the president of Barnes & Noble.

Before we all collapsed again on our cots that night, Gretchen called me aside in the dining area and showed me her letter.

"I hope it's not too blunt, Kyle," she said and sat down with me at a table.

"I'm sure it's just fine," I replied, and in dim light I read her writing:

Dear Sir,

    I understand that your company throws out, sends back, or otherwise destroys thousands of books every month. I'll be blunt: we NEED lots of these free books here in Kenya as part of our Camel-to-Kids Literacy Program.

    No, sir, this does not mean we are teaching camels to read. The camels are the transportation, *much like a Mercedes or other fine car that you probably drive is your own transportation, though I don't think camels smell as nice as a new Mercedes with fine Corinthian leather. But back to the point.*

    My point is that we could really, really, REALLY use some free books for the kids here in Kenya. Mostly we'd want hardbacks, since the books get banged around a good bit inside the wooden boxes we strap onto the camels. Did I mention that camels smell? Well, I hope you can help us out here. I will include the address on the enclosed card.

Thank you for helping us, sir! Since I know you will give generously, I hope your company stock goes up in price and that you will reconsider owning your big, gas-guzzling Mercedes that I hope someday will run on electricity instead of gas. Oh, and I promise to shop at B & N this Christmas! (Especially if y'all are serving that ginger-spice latte in the café.)

Sincerely,

Gretchen Trammel

From a poor village in Kenya

"Think it'll work, Kyle?" she asked before heading off to the women's tent.

I handed her back the letter and said, "He'll be blown away."

We all stayed on an extra week in order to see the project through to completion.

The work was hard, but the fellowship was outstanding. Camel Guy returned and even gave us rides on his camel, and Gretchen donated an Annie Dillard book to the mobile library. Over the course of the week, Sal became something of a grandfather figure to the kids. So many were orphaned — and so many never got to meet older adults due to the lower life expectancy here — that a big energetic guy like Sal became the kind of lumbering teddy bear that kids the world over love to climb upon and wrestle. He even sat under a shade tree and read to them.

Gretchen said that watching an ex-bookie read *Clifford the Big Red Dog* to Kenyan children was positive proof that there is a God who changes lives. Her comment stewed in my head the following workday, until at night we sat by ourselves at the last of five picnic tables and I pressed the issue. "Gretchen, how do you think God is working on you?"

"I was going to ask you that same question."

"You first."

"No, *you* first." With thumb and forefinger she formed a pistol and shot me with it. "You brought me here, Kyle Mango. Take the lead."

After three deep breaths and a man sigh, I led. "Okay, seeing people here so excited to have running water…it just makes me realize how good I've had it all my life."

She nodded as if she felt the same. "Anything else?"

I knew what she wanted to hear, and I obliged. "The answer is 'yes, I'll sell the oil wells'…but only if you come back to Texas for a while and go on some steak-and-potato dates, not tofu-that-tastes-like-mulch dates or —"

"Smelly camel dates?"

"Those too."

Gretchen sat with her hands in her lap, occasionally pulling at strands of hair displaced by a dry Kenyan breeze. "I suppose you now want to hear what I feel God is saying to me."

"I do."

One deep breath and a girl sigh. "Okay, perhaps I need to balance compassion for people with compassion for wildlife."

I held her hand and nodded. "Anything else?"

"And maybe I should pick my friends a little more carefully."

"You mean Regina?"

In this moment of honesty and blank faces, she broke

into a grin that was a mixture of wonder and astonishment. "You shoulda seen her burying that power drill, Kyle. She even stomped it with her foot!" Gretchen did her best to demonstrate extremist stomping, and we both laughed at the impersonation.

The African night, however, was much too inviting and romantic to waste it with words about Regina.

So I pulled Gretchen to her feet, thanked her for being her, led her in a slow dance, and kissed her good night.

Twice.

At breakfast the next day—our last before heading back to the States—I met privately with Cindy and two other leaders of her organization, asking them how much funding they were short after the Kenyan government turned down their request to sponsor a second windmill.

Over cornflakes and orange juice Cindy opened her folder, scanned some numbers, and said, "Fifteen hundred dollars a month, for fourteen months. That's the best financing deal the manufacturer of the windmill could offer us. But we just can't afford a second one."

She didn't have to say anything else.

On the long flight back to Texas, seated next to a sound-asleep Gretchen, I felt strongly what was required of me—I just had to figure it out as I flew.

THE PART THAT COMES AFTER THE MAIN STORY

I figured it out. Or perhaps I simply became more attuned to God's voice, especially after Gretchen and I joined a contemporary church in Lubbock and learned to tone down our natural independence. I was also learning the importance of balance. To toggle between roles as Gretchen's fiancé, my new job as a water resources engineer for the city of Lubbock, and supporter of shirtless Kenyan kids seemed about as good a use of a Mango life as I could imagine.

In the two years since our initial journey to Kenya, we'd been back three times: twice during our "year of dating internationally," as Gretchen called it, once as an engaged couple. The engagement took place on a summer night at Texas Tech, when most of the students were away. With an assist from a sophomore who was the "Big House keeper" for the summer—and had no idea I was a former pledge—I snuck Gretchen onto the roof of Sigma house, where we munched on grapes and cheese, our picnic awash in moonlight until I finally summoned the nerve to propose.

After she shouted "yes!"—and hugged and kissed me umpteen times—she made me do the mummy dance with her. It felt goofy and silly and undeniably right. Down on the street, someone in a car even honked at us.

Then Gretchen turned to me in the dark and said, "Kyle, are we gonna have to jump down onto a bush again?"

Hand in hand, I led her across the roof. "No, I rented a ladder. It's on the other side of the house."

In addition to embracing Gretchen, I also embraced charity. A month after the initial trip to Kenya, I had sold the oil wells along with the Anson acreage. The buyer was none other than Sal Sabbatini, who formed a partnership with some banker friends and offered me the healthy sum of $275,000 for the whole shebang, this just before he added a sixth, seventh, and eighth well on the property.

Sal had the exploratory golden touch and gave himself the title of President. He hired Chang as VP of Operations and Philanthropy. The three of us still met every Thursday night at a barbecue joint, mostly to talk about work, relationships, mission opportunities, and of course, the Dallas Cowboys.

While Gretchen did occasionally chide them for remaining in the oil biz, she was okay with things as long as I had no part in the industry. "I don't mind you being friends with oilmen," she confirmed over steaks one night.

"That's good because oilmen will be two of my groomsmen!"

The oil issue pretty much disappeared in the fury of wedding plans. Even after I bought her a newer used Honda—the driver door fell off her old Civic on the day she was going to get fitted for her dress—she never asked if the money came from the sale of oil wells. And I never brought it up.

I did my best to be responsible with the proceeds of the sale.

Eighty thousand dollars of the money went to my mother; twenty thousand went to Kenya to buy the second windmill; and Chang got ten thousand as a "we're still pardners, li'l doggie" bonus. The bulk of my share went into savings.

My mother, wanting to move out of a house that still fostered bad memories, promptly sold the place, and together with my brother and sister came up with a plan that surprised me. Over the summer all three of them had become hooked on water skiing. "Let's live near water!" they said. And now with the monies from the sale of the home combining with the oil monies, they went house-hunting north of Fort Worth, around Lake Texoma. Oddly, the house they fell for—one of only a few they could afford—sat on the Oklahoma side of the lake.

On the phone I teased them about being "Okies," at which point my eavesdropping fiancée snuggled beside me on the sofa and whispered that I was now the last Mango in Texas.

"But only up until the wedding," Gretchen assured me. "And in a few years we might even add some little—"

"Mango-ettes."

Sal and Chang came along each time Gretchen and I returned to Kenya. The territory south of Narok continued to be gripped by drought, and more people than ever remained in need of irrigation systems. We all did what we could, though we felt like such a small answer to a humongous need.

Chang and Cindy, after two more "just happened to run into each other" rendezvous in Kenya, entered into a long-distance relationship that was also very *mobile*. They used their combined talents and work ethic to install irrigation systems in various needy corners of the globe. Chang called it "damp dating." He'd fly off to Haiti one weekend and come home dirty.

Then three months later he'd meet her somewhere in Africa again—and come home with clothes soiled in mud. How two ultraintelligent people stayed so dirty was beyond me.

Gretchen by now was eighteen months into leading a non-profit group she'd begun in order to channel books and school supplies into remote areas of Africa. And in the backyard of the townhouse we'd purchased—she was living in it until we were married—no less than nine bird feeders hung from the trees.

In return for our Kenyan efforts, Gretchen and I received monthly postcards of camels toting boxes of books. Sometimes we got hand-drawn camels from the kids. One even wrote my name on the camel. I shed a tear at that one, as embarrassed as a former oilman is to admit it.

Last we heard of Regina, she had ventured off to South America with a fresh band of protestors. From the coast of Brazil she penned an op-ed piece for an animal rights Web site. The piece ended with a line that compared the oil industry to the very worst of humanity, and her words confirmed just how far she'd fallen: *Sadly we watch the Nazi-like march of Big Oil, a regime of greed goose-stepping through virgin forests.*

Mercy.

The following May, just four months after our wedding, Gretchen and I organized a fifth trip to the village—with Sal, Chang, and a few other volunteers. Sal for months had sent checks to support the people, increasing the amount as his oil revenue rose. With the inflow of funds and the hard work of the natives, the village had grown in size as well as production. The well-watered crops produced a harvest larger than the people could store, and on this trip we spent half our time teaching them how to market and sell bulk grains and vegetables.

They were now net exporters of food. And I suppose that we, the little team from Texas, were in some respect net exporters of grace.

As newlyweds, Gretchen and I had hoped to be able to room together in Kenya, but some things had not changed. One hut for women volunteers, one for men.

The second night I lay in my cot, wishing I had skipped the caffeinated coffee after dinner.

"Chang?"

No answer. He snored with a quiet tenacity.

"Sal?"

Best he could do was roll over and pull a pillow over his head.

All I wanted to ask them was if they wanted scrambled eggs or omelets in the morning. Tomorrow was a meat day, it was my turn to help make breakfast, and I had to be up at quarter to six.

I guessed omelets, then rolled over and looked out the open-air window. A half moon illuminated the plains. Lubbock—and Texas—seemed a million miles away.

Uncle Benny, however, seemed closer than ever. Each time I traveled to Kenya, I wished he were there to see it, how his land, though owned by someone else, still pumped life into another corner of the planet.

At 5:45 a.m. I woke and left the hut and went into the village kitchen to make breakfast. I was not alone there, however; we cooked in teams of two. Standing over the stove, already mixing batter, she looked more alive than I'd seen her in years. Our newest volunteer.

"Mornin', Kyle," she said and handed me an apron.

"Mornin', Mom."

Bullion Betty had made it to Kenya, and her gift was silver dollar pancakes.

AUTHOR NOTE

Though I did not attend Texas Tech, I've always loved to watch them play football—the Red Raiders's high-scoring offense keeps games exciting. And from what I've observed, their students and alumni comprise one of the more close-knit college communities in the nation. My apologies for portraying their Greek system in a less than balanced manner. My own "minor Greek tragedy" occurred elsewhere, at the-school-that-must-not-be-named. The eighties music, however, is both fact and fiction.

READING GROUP GUIDE

1. Kyle escaped his Greek oppressors while the song "Thriller" played in the frat house. If you were planning an escape (from wherever), what song would you want for your background music?

2. Would you agree that anyone who chooses Hanson's "MMMBop" or Barry Manilow's "Mandy" or anything by Air Supply as their escape song deserves to get caught during said escape?

3. Gretchen had a heart for wildlife and was willing to make personal sacrifices to make a difference. Have you ever given to environmental causes?

4. Have you ever met anyone like Regina? If so, how long did it take for that person to drive you nuts?

5. Would you consider carpooling in order to reduce the demand for oil? If you would not choose to carpool, is it because you don't consider it important or because you have annoying neighbors and can't stand to ride in a car with them?

6. If your neighbor was an environmental wacko and roller-skated to work rather than driving a car, and this same neighbor ridiculed you for owning a gas-gulping

Corvette, would you (A) cave and trade the Corvette for a hybrid car, (B) keep the Corvette and ignore your neighbor, or (C) attach a ski rope to the back of your Corvette and offer to pull your neighbor whenever he needed to get somewhere fast?

7. If you inherited oil wells and had a huge increase in income, what would you do with the excess monies? Travel? Give to the poor? Support mission projects in underdeveloped nations? Buy up all the Hanson, Barry Manilow, and Air Supply albums you could find? All of the above?

8. What person in your life most resembles Uncle Benny? How?

9. God's Word says that "every good and perfect gift is from above." What does that say about oil (since oil is "from below")? Does that make the gift of oil wells a bad gift? Discuss at length.

10. What can you do this week to use your own gift(s) to benefit others?

11. When was the last time you made silver dollar pancakes for your friends or family?

12. *That* long?

13. Then go buy some pancake mix, serve a yummy breakfast to your friends and family, and afterward urge them to go buy the latest Ray Blackston novel. Thank you!

CREDITS

Some of my Alaska research came from four fishing buddies—Tony, Sandy, Alan, and Patrick—who shared stories of their journey as well as many photos. Thanks also to Bob, Jane, Stan, Connie, and Kathy, who urged me to sign up for a construction mission trip to France and introduced me to the best chocolate croissants on the planet.

My uncle Luther "Buddy" Smoak gave me my first silver coin when I was seven years old. I still have it. To my knowledge, however, neither Uncle Buddy nor I have ever buried coins in the desert. (Why travel that far when you can just bury them in the backyard?!)

ABOUT THE AUTHOR

RAY BLACKSTON lives and writes in South Carolina. He left the corporate world in 2000 to focus on creative writing. In 2003, his first novel, *Flabbergasted*, was one of three finalists for the Christy Award for best first novel, and was chosen as Inspirational Novel of the Year by the *Dallas Morning News*. More of Ray's background is available at his Web site, www.ray blackston.com.

If you enjoyed *Last Mango in Texas*,
you'll love

A PAGAN'S
NIGHTMARE

A tongue-in-cheek look at contemporary culture through the eyes of a screenwriter who pens a hit about the last nonbeliever on earth navigating through a Christian world.

An unwary "pagan" finds himself one of the last remaining unbelievers in a world populated by Christians. Or so imagines Larry Hutch, a copywriter with hopes of writing a hit screenplay. While struggling in his faith and dealing with personal crises, he conceives of a strange new world where radio stations alter song lyrics to conform to "Christian" standards (the Beatles belt out "I Wanna Hold Your Tithe") and French fries, newly labeled "McScriptures," are tools for evangelism.

Larry's screenplay is a big hit with his agent, Ned. But Ned's wife—a committed Southern Baptist—is less than amused. Both men's futures will be on the line when the world witnesses A PAGAN'S NIGHTMARE.

Available now at a bookstore near you!

And be sure to check out

$\mathscr{P}$ar for the $\mathscr{C}$ourse

Golf, politics, and romance collide as golf-range owner Chris Hackett meets an attractive political correspondent who turns his world upside down.

Chris Hackett owns and operates Hack's Golf Learning Center, an eccentric golf range in Charleston, South Carolina. Chris jumps at the chance to step up his game when an attractive new student and political correspondent, Molly Cusack, suggests that Chris capitalize on the highly polarized presidential election. His pitting of Right versus Left means even more income, plus a sharp new girlfriend, and soon Chris, his sidekick Cack, and their unique golf range are the talk of the town…until someone takes the political insults too seriously.

The question is, will Molly stick around long enough for Chris to learn the true meaning of "playing politics"? Or is she just another "moving target"?

Available now at a bookstore near you!